Praise *for* Rexanne Becnel's NEXT novels

"Humor, smart women, adventure, and danger all add up to a book you can't put down.... Constant surprises and characters that will win your heart."
—*Romantic Times BOOKclub* on *The Payback Club*

"Becnel deftly captures the way actual women think …Brisk and entertaining, with a welcome focus on middle-aged sexuality, this tidy tale proves that Becnel is just as much at home writing high-quality contemporary fiction as penning the historical fiction for which she's known."
—*Publishers Weekly* on *Old Boyfriends*

"Rexanne Becnel skillfully weaves multiple storylines with lively characters and unexpected plot twists in an emotionally satisfying book."
—*Romantic Times BOOKclub* on *Old Boyfriends*

And other praise for Rexanne Becnel

"Ms. Becnel creates the most intriguing characters."
—*Literary Times* on *The Bride of Rosecliffe*

"Becnel skillfully blends romance and adventure with a deft hand."
—*Publishers Weekly* on *When Lightning Strikes*

"Rexanne's stories stay with the reader long after the final page is turned."
—*Literary Times* on *Heart of the Storm*

Rexanne Becnel

Rexanne Becnel, the author of twenty-one novels and two novellas, swears she could not be a writer if it weren't for New Orleans's many coffeehouses. She does all her work longhand, with a mug of coffee at her side. She is a charter member of the Southern Louisiana Chapter of Romance Writers of America, and founded the New Orleans Popular Fiction Conference.

Rexanne's novels regularly appear on bestseller lists such as those of *USA TODAY*, *Amazon.com*, Waldenbooks, Ingram and Barnes & Noble. She has been nominated for and received awards from *Romantic Times BOOKclub*, Waldenbooks, The Holt Committee, the *Atlanta Journal/Atlanta Constitution* and the National Readers Choice Awards.

Rexanne Becnel

LEAVING L.A.

LEAVING L.A.

Copyright © 2006 by Rexanne Becnel

isbn-13: 978-0-373-88107-9

isbn-10:   0-373-88107-X

This edition published by arrangement with Harlequin Books S.A.

® and TM are trademarks of the publisher. Trademarks indicated with
® are registered in the United States Patent and Trademark Office, the
Canadian Trade Marks Office and in other countries.

TheNextNovel.com

PRINTED IN U.S.A.

Dear Reader,

I enjoyed writing *Leaving L.A.* more than any book I've ever done before. I think it was that I loved my heroine so much. She was fun and sassy, and troubled, too. But she was working hard to improve her life.

As in my previous titles, *Leaving L.A.* is set in southern Louisiana. I was almost finished with the book when Katrina hit New Orleans, where I live. My family and I spent a week in our house surrounded by water, then another two weeks away, before returning to start rebuilding our lives. It has been, shall we say, "interesting." We lost a lot, but we know so many people who lost everything, including loved ones, that I actually feel blessed.

Leaving L.A. is set in a Louisiana pre-Katrina. My current work-in-progress deals with Katrina, both during and after. It's been an emotional roller coaster, but it has also been cathartic.

Many thanks to all of you who have worried about us, volunteered to help us, or donated money to the many charities set up to aid us. A special thanks to the first responders, who worked so hard and often put their lives on the line. There will never be enough thanks.

I hope you enjoy my latest efforts,

Rexanne

For the Pizzolato family
of Baton Rouge, who provided
us safe harbor after Hurricane Katrina,
and to Joanna Wurtele who
got us there.

Also to David, Rosemary,
Brian, Valerie, Chuck and Karen,
who weathered the storm with me,
and to Katya and Mike, who
kept it together across town.

CHAPTER I

I come from a long line of motherless daughters. I used to think of us as fatherless: my mother, my older half sister, me. But the truth is that the worst damage to us came from being essentially motherless.

That's the conclusion I reached after six days, thirty cups of pure caffeine and two thousand miles of driving back home. Of course all that philosophical crap leached out of my head the minute I crossed the Louisiana state line. That's when I started obsessing about what I would wear to my big reunion with my sister. I'm not proud to admit that I changed clothes three times in the last one hundred miles of my trek. The first time in a Burger King in Port Allen; the second time in a Shell station just east of Baton Rouge; and the third time on a dirt road beside a cow pasture just off Highway 1082.

Okay, I was nervous. How *do* you dress when you're coming home for the first time in twenty-three years and you're pretty sure your only sister is going to slam the door in your face—assuming she even recognizes you? ˋ

I settled on a pair of skin-tight leopard-print capris, a black Thomasina spaghetti-strap top with a built-in push-up bra, a pair of Rainbow stilettos and a black dog-collar choker with pyramid studs all around. My own personal power look: heavy metal, hot mama who'll kick your ass if you get in my way.

But as soon as I turned into the driveway that led up to the farmhouse my grandfather had built over eighty years ago, I knew it was all wrong. I should have stuck with the jeans and the lime-green tank top.

I screeched to a halt and reached into the back seat where my rejected outfits were flung over my four suitcases, five boxes of books and records, and three giant plastic containers of photos, notebooks and dog food.

"This is the last change," I muttered to Tripod, who just stared at me like I was a lunatic—which maybe I am. But who wants a dog passing judgment on you?

I glowered at him as I shimmied out of the spandex capris. They were getting kind of tight. Surely I wasn't already gaining weight?

I was standing barefoot beside my open car door with my jeans almost zipped when my cranky three-legged mutt decided he'd had enough. Up to now I'd had to lift him into and out of the high seat of my ancient Jeep. That missing foreleg makes it hard for him to leap up and down. But apparently he'd been playing the sympathy card the whole two thousand miles of I-10 east because, as soon as I turned my back, he jumped down through the driver's door and took off up the rutted shell driveway, baying like he was a Catahoula hound who'd just treed his first raccoon.

"Idiot dog," I muttered as I snapped the fly of my jeans.

The day I adopted him he'd just lost his leg in a fight with a Hummer on an up ramp to I-405 in Los Angeles. Not a genius among canines, and an urban mutt, to boot. The only wildlife he'd ever seen were the squirrels that raided the bird feeder I'd hung in the courtyard of my ex-boyfriend G.G.'s Palm Springs villa.

But here he was, lumbering down a rural Louisiana lane, for all intents and purposes pounding his hairy doggy chest and declaring this as *his* territory.

I paused and stared after him. Maybe he was on to something. Straightening up, I took a few experimental thumps on my own chest. "Watch out, world—especially you, Alice. Zoe Vidrine is back in town, and this time I'm not leaving with just a backpack and three changes of clothes. This time I'm not going until I get what's rightfully mine."

Then before I could change my mind about my clothes one more time, I slid into the driver's seat, shoved Jenny into first gear, and tore down the Vidrine driveway, under the Vidrine Farm sign, and on to the Vidrine family homestead.

It was the same house. That's what I told myself when I steered past a large curve of azaleas in full bloom. In a kind of fog I pressed the brake and eased to a stop at the front edge of the sunny lawn. It was the same house with the same deep porch and the same elaborate double chimney. My great-grandfather had been a mason before he turned to farming, and the chimney he'd built on his house would have fit on a New Orleans mansion.

I was in the right yard and this was the right house. But nothing else about it looked the same. Instead of peeling white paint interrupted with gashes of DayGlo-red peace signs and vivid green zodiac emblems spray painted in odd, impulsive places, the walls were a soft, serene yellow. The trim was a crisp white, and shiny, dark green shutters accented the windows on both floors. A pair of lush, trailing ferns flanked the wide front steps, moving languidly in the gentle spring breeze.

The day I'd finally fled my miserable childhood, there had been no steps at all, only a rickety pile of concrete blocks.

Now a white wicker porch swing hung on the left side of the porch, and three white, wooden rockers sat to the right.

It was the home of my childhood dreams, of all my desperate, adolescent yearnings. Nothing like the place I'd actually grown-up in.

I shuddered as my long-repressed anger and hurt boiled to the surface. How dare Alice try to gloss over the ugliness of our childhoods! How dare she slap paint down and throw a few plants into the ground and pretend everything was just fine and dandy in the Vidrine household!

Then again, my Goody Two-shoes sister had always looked the other way when things got ugly, pretending there was nothing wrong in our chaotic house, that we were a normal, happy family. Judging from the *House Beautiful* photo-op she'd created here, she hadn't changed a bit.

If I'd had any remaining doubts about claiming my legal share of this…this "all-American dream house," they evaporated in the heat of my rage. She might believe her own crap, but I sure didn't.

I shoved the gearshift into Park and turned off the motor. That's when I heard the barking—Tripod and some other yappy creature. From under the porch a little white streak burst through a bed of white impatiens and tore up the front steps, followed closely by my lumbering, brindle mutt. Up the steps Tripod started, then paused, his one forefoot on the top step, daring the little dog to try and escape him now.

Tripod hadn't treed a raccoon. He'd porched a poodle. He'd made his intent to dominate known in the only way the other dog would understand. That's what I had to do with Alice.

I jumped down from the Jeep and marched up the neatly edged gravel walkway, feeling my heels sink between the pebbles with every step. Damn, I should have changed shoes, too.

Just as I reached Tripod and the base of the steps, the front door opened. Only it wasn't Alice. A lanky kid in a faded Rolling Stones T-shirt burst through the screen door. First he scooped up the fluff-ball of a dog. Then he crossed barefoot to the edge of the porch. "Hey," he said. "You looking for my mom?"

His mom. So Alice had kids.

"Hush up, Tripod," I muttered, catching hold of the dog's collar. "Yeah. I am—if your mom is Alice Blalock." Blalock was Alice's father's name. Since Mom hadn't been sure *who* my father was, I'd remained a Vidrine, like her.

"Alice Blalock *Collins*. I'm her son, Daniel." He gestured to Tripod. "What happened to his leg?"

"A big car. Where's your mom?"

"She's up at the church. Who are you?"

I planted one fist on my hip and shrugged my hair over my shoulder. "I'm your aunt Zoe." *I'm your bad-seed relative your mother probably never told you about.* "I'm your mom's baby sister. So. When will she be home?"

I could see I'd shocked the kid—my nephew, Daniel. While he went inside and called Alice, Tripod made a methodical circuit of the yard, marking every fence post, tree trunk and brick foundation pillar. He hadn't done this at any of the rest stops we'd slept at or the Motel 6's I'd snuck him into. But somehow he seemed to know we'd reached our destination and that this place belonged to him.

At least half of it did.

As for me, I sat down on the porch swing and tried to get my rampaging emotions under control. I was here. It wasn't what I'd expected. Then again, I don't know exactly what I did expect. Mom had been dead twenty years, and I'd been gone even longer. It made sense that Alice would have changed things. Of course her life would have gone on. Mine had. She wasn't a nervous twenty-year-old anymore. Just like I wasn't a scared seventeen-year-old.

But today, back here in this place, I felt like one all over again. And I didn't like the feeling.

"Come here, Tripod," I called. "Good boy." I fondled his ragged ears until his crooked tail beat a happy tattoo. "Good boy. You showed that snooty little cotton ball who's boss, didn't you? Come on. Get up here with me."

I hefted his fifty-five-pound bulk up onto the swing beside me, somehow reassured by his presence. We were a team, me and Tripod. A banged-up pair of survivors who weren't taking anybody's crap. Not anymore.

From my perch on the swing I peered through the window into the living room. I saw an upright piano and two wing chairs with doilies on the headrests. Beyond them I saw Daniel pacing back and forth in the dining room, talking on the phone. I stilled the swing and strained to hear his end of the conversation.

"…yeah, Zoe. And she's definitely not dead."

She'd thought I was dead?

"But if she's my aunt, how come you never—"

He broke off, but I filled in the empty spaces. How come she'd never mentioned me to him? No wonder he'd looked shocked. The kid, if he'd even known of my existence, thought I was dead.

Now that made me mad. It was one thing for Alice to wonder if I was dead. After all, I hadn't talked to her since right after Mom died. And if she didn't follow the music industry and see my occasional photo in an appearance with one of my several rocker boyfriends through the years, she might be excused for speculating that I was dead. But to not even tell her son that she'd ever had a sister?

I snorted in disgust. Obviously nothing had really changed around here except for a fresh coat of paint. Underneath, our family was as ugly and rotten as ever. Alice might want to pretend I didn't exist, and she definitely wouldn't want me in her house.

Problem was, it wasn't *her* house. It was *our* house.

One thing I was certain of: my mother wasn't the type to have written a will. Too conventional for her. Too establishment. That meant, according to Louisiana laws, which I'd checked into just last week, since Alice and I were my mother's only children, we were her only heirs. And we shared equally in her estate.

Daniel edged out through the front door and stared uneasily at me. I raised my eyebrows expectantly.

"She'll be here in just a minute."

I smiled and with my toe started the swing moving. I needed to go to the bathroom in the worst way. But I wasn't going to put this kid on the spot by asking to use the bathroom. I had to keep in mind that he wasn't a part of my issues with Alice and this place. I remembered what it was like to be caught in the middle of warring adults, and I didn't want to put him in that position.

"How come you're not in school?" I asked, trying to be conversational.

"I'm homeschooled."

"Homeschooled?" Oh, my God. Hadn't Alice learned anything from our experience with Mom? I managed a smile. "So. What grade are you in?"

"Tenth. Sort of. Eleventh grade for English and history. Ninth for math and science. It averages out to tenth."

"Yeah. I see. You have any brothers or sisters?"

"No." He shook his head. "Just me."

I nodded. "So… You like the Stones?"

He looked down at the logo on his T-shirt, a classic

Steel Wheels Tour-shirt from the early nineties. It was probably older than he was. "Yeah," he said. "They're like real cool for such old guys."

Okay, Aunt Zoe, here's your chance to impress your nephew, who's obviously never even heard of you. "You know, I've met Mick Jagger a couple of times. Partied with him and the rest of the Stones."

His eyes got big. "You have?"

"Uh-huh. Keith Richards, too."

His eyebrows lowered over his bright blue eyes. Alice's eyes. Mom's eyes. "My mother says Keith Richards is depraved."

"Depraved?" I would like to have argued the fact. Anything to contradict Alice. But what was the point? So I settled for a vague response. "You know, not everyone who lives a life different from our own is depraved."

"I didn't say they were." He looked at me, this earnest kid of Alice's, and I suddenly saw him as girls his age must see him. Tall, cute, maybe a little mysterious since he didn't go to regular high school.

Or maybe weird and nerdy, an oddball since he didn't go to regular high school.

Damn, but I'd hated my brief fling with the local high school.

No. What I'd hated was being the girl who lived in the hippie commune. The girl whose mother never wore a bra. The girl who didn't have a clue who her father was. At least Alice had her father's last name. But I was just a Vidrine, like my mother, and other kids were merciless about it.

Love Child, they'd called me, and sung the Diana Ross song whenever I walked by.

Tripod put his head on my knee and whined. That's when I realized I was trembling, vibrating the swing like a lawn-mower engine. Even my dog could tell I was wound just a little too tightly.

I looked away from Daniel, wondering when Alice would get here, then wondering how I was supposed to make this plan of mine work if just talking to this kid got me so upset.

"Did it hurt?" he asked. "You know, when the car hit your dog?"

A new subject, thank God. "I guess it did. The first time I ever laid eyes on Tripod he was flying off the front fender of this giant black Hummer." *Which Dirk, my ex-ex-boyfriend had been driving.* "I stopped and so did this other car." *Dirk drove off and left me on the highway.* "Anyway, we got him to a vet, who said his leg was shattered and did we want to put him to sleep or amputate."

"Wow. You saved his life and adopted him?"

I shrugged. It sounded so altruistic the way he said it. The truth was, I'd charged the vet bill to Dirk's credit card, then kept the dog to remind me how glad I was to be rid of that SOB. Never date drummers, I'd vowed after that six-year fiasco had ended.

But at least I had Tripod. We'd been together for almost four years now. I rubbed his left ear, the one that had a ragged edge from some incident that predated the Hummer. "He may be an ugly mutt, but he's my ugly mutt." *And the only semitrustworthy male I'd ever known.*

We both looked up when a Chevy van pulled into the driveway, swung past my Jeep and pulled around the side of the house toward the garage.

For someone who hadn't seen her only sister in over twenty years, Alice sure took her sweet time. She came in through the back door. I caught a glimpse of her in the house—much slimmer than I remembered but still pleasantly plump. She paused at a mirror and fiddled with her hair. Even then it took her another full minute to join us on the porch. I guess she had to brace herself. After all, she obviously felt like I'd risen from the dead.

As kids she and I hadn't exactly been close. You'd think we would have clung to each other in the midst of all the chaos thrown at us. Instead we'd become each other's primary targets, both of us competing for the meager fragments of Mom's love and attention.

Later, when I'd begged her to leave with me, I couldn't believe she meant to stay. As furious at her as I was at our mother, I'd left without her, scared to death but determined to go.

I'd had my revenge two years later, though, when she called me about Mom being sick. I told her point-blank that I didn't give a damn about Mom and what she needed. Four months later Alice had tracked me down again to say Mom had died, and what did I think we should do about a funeral?

Though now I know it was illogical, my response at the time had been utter rage: at Mom for dying and at Alice for crying to me about it. And maybe at myself for feeling anything at all for either of them.

"Don't you get it?" I said to her in this cold, unfeeling voice. "I don't care what you do with her or anything else in that hellhole of a house. I left Louisiana a long time ago, Alice. Get over it."

And that had been that. Our last conversation.

But even though that had been twenty years ago I could feel the old animosity rise, like a fever that the antibiotic of time had only held at bay. We were still competing for Mom's scraps. Only in this case it would be our inheritance.

"Hello, big sister," I said with a wide, for-the-camera smile.

Alice's wasn't quite so eager. "Zoe. Well, hello." She stood there, just staring at me as if she hadn't believed Daniel, as if she wasn't sure she even believed her own eyes. She glanced at Daniel, then away, clearing her throat. "I see you've met my son."

With my left foot I set the swing into motion. "Yes. He seems like a great kid, though I could swear he's never heard of his aunt Zoe."

If it was possible her pinched expression grew even tighter. "Go inside, Daniel."

When he didn't jump right up, she turned a stern look on him. "I said go. Finish the history chapter—"

"I already did."

"Then start the next one. And take off that awful T-shirt!"

He muttered something under his breath, but he did as she said. When he opened the door, however, the poodle slipped out. One yip and Tripod sprung off the swing, nearly knocking Alice over when she snatched her obnoxious pet up from the jaws of death.

"Make him stop!" she yelled at me while Tripod bayed at the fur ruff she held up over her head.

It would have made a hilarious photo, my ugly, three-legged hound up on his hind legs trying to reach her sweetly groomed little dog while she screamed bloody murder. A great album cover for a band like Devil Dogs.

Slowly I unfolded myself from the swing. "That's enough, Tripod. Come on, now." He could probably tell I didn't really mean it. That's why I had to haul him back by the collar while Alice put "Angel" back in the house.

Then still not sitting down, she said, "So what brings you back to Louisiana?"

I perched on the porch rail like I used to when I was a kid, before it was torn off in a drunken rage by one or another of Mom's so-called boyfriends. "This is home, isn't it? I've come home."

She got this wary look on her face. "What do you mean? You've been gone over twenty years, and all of a sudden, out of the blue, you decide it's time for a visit?"

"Something like that. Only this isn't a visit, Alice. I'm back to stay."

That's when she sat down. I guess the shock made her knees weak. "You mean you're moving back to Louisiana? But…you said you hated this place. You called it a hell-hole."

In my opinion it still was. But I only shrugged. "Things change. Not only am I moving back to good old Oracle…" I said, watching her wariness turn to horror. "I'm moving back here," I added, sweeping my hand to include the house and its forty-plus acres. "In case you've forgotten, it *is* half mine."

Just like her son, Alice's first reaction to the little bomb I'd laid on her was to run inside and get on the phone. I suppose she was calling her hubby so he could hurry home and somehow make me leave. Like that would work. It might have been an angry impulse when I ditched Palm Springs and my sunbaked, half-baked existence there. But I'd had six long days of driving with only a nauseated dog and a string of country and western stations to keep me company. Lots of time to think. And now I was committed to my plan. I wanted my half of our inheritance, and I wasn't leaving here without it. Keeping this farm was the only thing my mother ever did right. With my share I could start a new life, someplace where neither G. G. Givens nor my mother's ghost could find me.

So Alice could call her husband and all his kin, too. But she wasn't getting rid of me until I had my money.

I heard voices from inside the house. Daniel was yelling at his mother and she was yelling back. But I couldn't see them through the window. Well, it was my house, too, wasn't it? So I got up and walked inside.

"...it's still a lie," Daniel shouted down at his mother from halfway up the stairs. "A lie of omission. Just like you said I did when I told you I was going to New Orleans with Josh and his big brother but didn't tell you we were going to the Voodoo Fest."

"That's different," Alice retorted. "You *knew* if you asked me to go to that Voodoo thing that I would say no. That's why you didn't tell me, and that's why it was still a lie."

"And you thought I would *approve* of you pretending you didn't have a sister?"

Good point, kid. I crossed my arms, waiting for Alice's reply. But when Daniel's eyes shot to me, she turned around, too. She was shaking. I could see it on her pale face. It should have made me happy, seeing my Goody Two-shoes sister caught in a lie. Instead it made me vaguely uncomfortable. I didn't care if she felt bad. But some small part of me didn't want to make her look bad in front of her son. I remembered how awful it used to feel when my mom pulled some monumental screwup, some embarrassing public incident that I couldn't overlook even with my hands over my eyes and my thumbs in my ears.

"She thought I was dead," I blurted out. "Okay? I've never been very good about keeping in touch, so…" I shoved my hands into the back pockets of my jeans and shrugged. "You might say we've never really been close. But now I'm back," I added, switching my gaze to Alice. "So where should I put my stuff?"

When she just stared at me with big, round—scared—eyes, Daniel answered for her. "There's plenty of room upstairs. Two guest rooms plus mine and a study."

"Daniel—" Alice raised a hand to him, then let it fall in the face of his anger and hurt. His mother had lied to him. I guess that hadn't happened before. Lucky boy.

"Fine," I said into the tense standoff between them. "It won't take me long to unpack. Then maybe you and I can have a nice long talk, Alice, and catch up on the past—" *twenty-three* "—few years."

I was just lugging my second-to-last load up the front steps—why had I brought so many records and books?—when a third car turned into the yard. A burgundy Oldsmobile. An old man's car, and given that the guy who got out had a full head of white hair it seemed like I'd guessed right.

I ignored him and let the screen door slam as I went inside. Once I got everything in my room, I planned on taking a bath. Then I was getting the hell out of this house for a while, because already it was giving me the creeps. It would take more than a few coats of Sunny Yellow and Apple Green latex to paint out the stains of my miserable childhood.

Outside I heard Tripod barking, then a man's voice yelling, "Shoo. Get away!" Then, "Alice. Alice!"

Upstairs I looked at Daniel's closed bedroom door. He'd been in there ever since his fight with his mother. Downstairs I heard Alice fussing at Tripod. I guess the man of the house got inside unscathed. I dug around for a dog biscuit before heading downstairs for the last box. Tripod deserved a reward for sticking up for me.

In the front parlor Alice sat hunched over on an elaborate settee, her husband next to her with an arm around her bowed shoulders. When he heard me on the stairs, he looked up and glowered at me. "Is this any way to treat your only sister?"

I planted one fist on my hip. "I've ignored her for twenty-three years and she's done the same to me. How does that make me the villain and her the victim?" Then I strode forward and stuck out my hand. "Hi, I'm Zoe. And you must be…"

By now Alice had bucked up enough to speak for herself. "This is Carl Witter, a...a friend of mine."

A friend? He looked a bit possessive of her to merely be a friend. And he ignored my hand. "Oh," I said, pulling it back. "A friend. Where's your husband?"

If possible, Carl's pale eyes turned even colder. "Reverend Collins died thirteen months ago," he bit out. "Which you would have known—"

"If she had told me," I threw back at him. *Alice had been married to a minister?* I pushed that question aside. "I guess that makes you the new boyfriend."

"I'm her friend," he bit out. "And I'm not about to let you take advantage of her sweet nature, especially with an impressionable young man in the house."

"An impressionable young man who didn't know till now that he had an aunt." The more I thought about that fact, the madder I got.

He leaped to his feet. "Given the aimless, Godless life you've led!"

"Stop it, Carl," Alice begged, tugging on his arm.

"You don't have to let her stay here," he told her. "This is your home."

"Which happens to be half mine," I said.

That stopped him cold.

"Look," I said before he could start up again. "Why don't you and Alice go back to whatever you were doing. I can finish moving in without any help." Then flashing them a smug smile, I flounced out of the house.

From behind a closed door—what used to be the "Meditation Room" when we were kids but what had actually been the "High Way Room" for getting loaded—I heard Angel yapping. From his spot on the porch, surveying his new domain, Tripod let out a warning bark.

"Good boy," I told him, rubbing his ears the way he liked. "I think we've each won the first skirmish." It was mighty interesting that, considering she thought I was dead, Alice and her creaky boyfriend sure seemed to know all about my "aimless, godless life."

I straightened up and looked around me. The porch, the house, even the grounds looked nothing like how I remembered. But the ghosts of my childhood were still there, waiting to jump out at me. God, I hoped it didn't take long for Alice to give me what was my due. I didn't think I could last very long in this haunted house of ours.

CHAPTER 2

I hung up my clothes, put the folded things into the pretty oak dresser, lined up my shoes in the bottom of the closet and stacked the boxes of records and books in the corner behind the bed.

"Now what?" I said to the world at large. I'd accomplished the first part of my plan. That had turned out to be the easy part. Now I needed a plan for Part Two.

My stomach gurgled and I rubbed one hand over it. "You stay here," I told Tripod, who'd already stretched out on the faintly dusty pine floor. "Guard my stuff while I…"

Go somewhere. Do something. I wasn't sure what.

All I knew was that I wasn't sitting up here in the room my mother had called the Venus Trap. I'd once seen three women and two men doing stuff to each other here that no eleven-year-old should ever be exposed to. The room was painted pale blue now, with eyelet curtains framing the two windows and an old-fashioned chenille bedspread covering the pretty iron bed. But I could see the black and hot-pink walls beneath this pretty facade as clearly as if the paint was bleeding through.

"Ugh." I shuddered and closed the door behind me.

Directly across the hall Daniel's solid door seemed to beckon me. I knocked, a short lilting rhythm. After a minute he cracked the door.

"Hey. Listen, I'm going out. You know, to drive around and check out the changes in town." I made that decision barely a split second before the words spilled out of my mouth. "You need anything? A ride anywhere?"

He shook his head, not meeting my eyes. But he didn't close the door in my face either.

"Look, Daniel. I didn't come here to make trouble between you and your mother. She and I...well, let's just say we weren't raised in a real close family. I'm sure she has her reasons for not telling you about me." *Lousy reasons but reasons all the same.*

"But she *lied* to me." He lifted his eyes—Mom's eyes—to me.

"Look, kid. Everybody lies. All the time."

"That's not true." When I only shrugged, he said, "Well, they're not *supposed* to."

"But they do. The trick is to figure out their motive. Are they trying to hurt you with the lie or just trying to help themselves out of a bad situation?" Then for some stupid, maudlin reason I added, "Or maybe they're lying because they think it will somehow help you."

"Well, it didn't help me." He gave me this long, steady look. "Why'd you decide to come home now?"

I didn't want to say. It was one thing to demand what I was owed from Alice. It was another thing to discuss it with her kid. "I figured twenty-four years away would have been too long. So," I went on. "Do you need anything while I'm out?"

He hesitated only for a second. "Maybe I will take a ride with you. To my friend's house."

"Okay. Let's go."

Tripod started to howl. How he knew I was leaving the premises was beyond me. Daniel gave me a questioning look. Normally I'd take the dog, too. But I didn't trust Carl Witter not to take my stuff and throw it outside. I knew Tripod wouldn't let him get past the door.

We didn't see anyone in the living room. "I'm going to Josh's," Daniel called toward the kitchen.

No answer.

"She's not going to be happy when she finds out I drove you," I pointed out as we climbed into Jenny.

"I'm fourteen, not four," he muttered. "Almost fifteen. I can take care of myself."

"Okay then." I started up Jenny's cranky engine. "Which way?"

Driving down the old roads of my childhood was like negotiating a foreign country. Like a *Twilight Zone* episode where everything was so strange and yet somehow familiar. The town square and St. Brunhilde's church, and the Landry mansion were familiar. The P.J.'s Coffeehouse in the old Union Bank building, the Wendy's on the corner of Barcelona Avenue and the Walgreens opposite it were all new. The park that meandered along the river was the same. Bigger trees and bigger parking lot but otherwise the same. That's where that stupid Toups kid and his friends had chased me once, wanting to know if it was true that hippie kids didn't wear underwear. I'd jumped into the river to escape them and nearly drowned.

Mother had laughed when I'd finally got home, shivering in my wet clothes. I'd shown them, she'd chortled.

Her boyfriend at the time, Snakie somebody or other, had stared at my fourteen-year-old breasts beneath my clinging knit top and promised to get even for me. And he had. The old sugar-in-the-gas-tank trick. I heard Bonehead Toups had to go back to his bicycle. Sweet justice, literally.

But of course, it had a downside. Snakie had wanted a sweet little reward for being so heroic. A reward from me, not my mom.

Unfortunately for him, after the river incident I'd checked out a library book on self-defense for women. That knee-to-the-groin business really works. He moved out the next week.

"Turn left up there, by the gas station," Daniel said, bringing me back to the present. We went down an old blacktop to just past where it turned to gravel. "There." He pointed to a pair of shotgun houses with a rusty trailer parked farther behind them.

"Do you need me to pick you up later?" I might as well ingratiate myself with him before his mother turned him completely against me.

"No. Josh'll give me a ride home."

"This Josh is old enough to drive?"

He grinned. "He has a four-wheeler. We'll take the back route through the woods."

I grinned back. "Sounds like fun."

"Yeah. But don't tell my mom that part." His grin faded. "She says it's too dangerous."

"It *is* too dangerous. But that's what makes it so fun."

"Yeah." He slammed the door, then gave me a head bobble that I guessed passed for "thanks." "See ya."

Then it was just me and Jenny Jeep and my old hometown.

On the surface, Oracle, Louisiana, is just like every other small town I've ever been in: an Andy of Mayberry downtown, a big, brick elementary school, a couple of churches. It had more trees than most. And more humidity. I'd been in a lot of little towns, especially when I toured with Dirk and his Dirt Bag Band. I'd done everything on those tours: arranged the shows, driven the bus, collected the money. Collected the band too when they were too stoned to find their way back to the bus.

I hadn't collected very much money for myself, though. I was Dirk's girlfriend. What did I need with money?

His words, not mine.

That's when I'd started my T-shirt and jewelry sideline. Small-town wannabe rockers and wannabe groupies had snapped them up. Too bad I hadn't saved more of that money. But Dirk had thought what was mine was his, and he would have blown my profits on booze and drugs and music equipment. So instead I blew them on becoming the best-dressed rock band manager you ever saw.

Anyway, you see one small town, you've seen them all. I turned onto Main Street. Creative street name isn't it?

That's when I saw the library. Except for the white crepe myrtles flanking the front doors, it hadn't changed a bit. There weren't many places in this town I had good associations with; the library was one of them.

I parked in front of the newspaper office next door to the library. Through the paper's front window I saw an old woman staring at a computer screen. So the *Northshore News* had gone high tech. With only a few keystrokes they could more easily report on this weekend's softball tournament or the Jones's fiftieth anniversary celebration. Woo hoo. Big news.

At least there weren't any parking meters to feed. I jumped down from Jenny, locked the door and slammed it.

"You must be from out of town."

Startled, I looked up. "Why do you say that?" I replied to this guy who had stopped in front of the newspaper office, his hand on the doorknob.

"You locked your car. People around here don't do that."

His comment shouldn't have made me feel so defensive, but I guess I was feeling extra touchy today. Added to that I wasn't in the mood to be hit on, especially by a guy who had to know how good-looking he was. "They don't? Well, I've been mugged in a small town like this." *A drunk coming out of one of the Dirt Bags' concerts, who got frustrated when I wouldn't go home with him.* "And had my car broken into." *Amps stolen out of the band's bus.*

I hiked my purse onto my shoulder and tossed my hair back. "So you see, I've learned not to be too trusting. Even in a nice little town like this."

He tilted his head to one side. "Sorry to hear that." He stared at me. At me, not my chest, for one long, steady moment, the kind of look that forced me to really look at him in return. If I were looking for a guy, he would have fit the bill just fine. *If* I were looking. Several inches taller than me, even in my heels. Wide shoulders, trim build. Not cocaine skinny like too many of the men I've known. Not self-indulgent fat like too many others. Which left the equally unappealing other third of men: probably a narcissistic health nut trying to stave off middle age.

"I'm Joe Reeves." He stuck out his hand.

I didn't want to know his name or to know him. But I had no real reason to blow him off. So I took his hand—big, strong and warm—and shook it. "Zoe Vidrine."

"You visiting here, Zoe? A tourist?" he asked, once I'd pulled my hand free of his.

"Oracle gets tourists?"

"You'd be surprised. Oak trees dripping with Spanish moss. Natural spring waters. We have our own winery now and a railroad museum. Not to mention all the water sports on Lake Pontchartrain."

"That cesspool?"

"It's clean now. Regularly passes all state requirements for swimming."

"Gee, it all sounds so exciting." But I softened my sarcasm by laughing.

He grinned. "That's the point. It's quiet and relaxing here. The perfect escape from the rat race."

"Yeah? Well, we'll see."

"So you're not a tourist. That means you're visiting someone."

I glanced away from his lean, smiling face. He was too smooth, too easy to talk to. Then I realized he'd been going into the newspaper office, and all my senses went into red alert mode. "You work here?" I gestured to the office.

"Sure do. Editor-in-chief."

Editor-in-chief? Shit!

"Plus beat reporter, features reporter, obituary writer and head of advertising. We're a small outfit, Wednesday and Sunday editions only."

"Cool," I said. But I meant just the opposite. The last thing I needed was for some local-yokel reporter to figure out that Zoe Vidrine was actually G. G. Givens's ex-girlfriend Red Vidrine and try to make a big deal about it.

I shifted my purse to my other shoulder. As I did so, his gaze fell to my body. Just one swift, all-encompassing glance. But it was enough to remind me that he was a man like every other man in the world. To them I was just a hot babe who looked as if all she wanted was his leering, drooling attention. "Well. See you around," I said. Then I turned and made for the library, my sanctuary when I was a kid, and hopefully my sanctuary now. I willed myself not to look back at him, but I knew he was watching. I felt it.

Inside, the library was cool and dim and so much like when I was a kid that a wave of relief shuddered through me. Same big wide desk; same art deco hanging lamps; same oriel window where I used to sit for hours reading everything from *Seventeen Magazine* to Alexandre Dumas to Shere Hite. I learned a lot about sex from Shere Hite. Too bad more men hadn't read her.

Anyway, my oriel was just like I remembered except for new, dark green upholstery on the cushions.

I looked around. Mr. Pinchon couldn't still be the head librarian. I approached the woman at the front desk.

"Can I help you?" She smiled like she really meant it.

"I was wondering, does Mr. Pinchon still work here? When I was a kid he used to suggest a lot of books for me to read."

"Mr. Pinchon? I don't know him. Oh, wait. He retired a couple of years ago before I started working here."

"Oh." I looked away. I shouldn't feel disappointed, but I did. The one person who'd understood me, who'd cared enough to make sure I read across the spectrum. He'd made me a lifelong reader—and a sometimes writer. But of course he was gone. He was old back then. By now he was probably dead.

"Can I help you with anything else?" the librarian asked. "Do you have a current library card?"

"No."

"Well, we can easily remedy that." She handed me a pen and a registration form, and I started to fill it out. Until I caught myself. I didn't need to advertise that I was in town. I'd planned all along to keep a low profile, to just swoop down, collect my inheritance and split.

Then why'd you tell that newspaper guy your name?

I slid the pen and paper back across the desk. "I'm just

in town for a week or two. Um…could you direct me to the microfilm records, the ones for the *Northshore News?*"

"Sure. You know, their office is right next door if you need to talk to Joe or Myra. She's worked there forever."

"Thanks." I gave her a bland smile. "How long has he been there?"

"Joe? Let's see now. I think three—no, four years. He used to be a big-time reporter in New Orleans. For the *Times-Picayune.* But when he and his son moved here, he decided celebrity news wasn't as exciting as it used to be."

I stiffened in alarm. *Celebrity news? That's what he'd written about? Great.*

"Well, I can see why he left it behind," I said. "Most of it's a lot of PR hype. But what I'm looking for…" I went on, wanting to change the subject "…is local news from the mid-eighties on." I'd left town in 1983, Mom had died in 1986 and Alice had obviously married sometime after that. I wanted to see what had been said about the Vidrine hippie commune, how it had petered out and how Alice had changed everything. Because like it or not—like *her* or not—I had to admit she'd done an amazing transformation of the place.

Some time later the librarian—Kenyatta was her name—startled me as I hunched over a microfilm screen. "Sorry to disturb you," she said. "But the library closes in fifteen minutes."

"What time is it?"

"Quarter to six."

I'd been here three and a half hours?

"Okay. Thanks. I'll finish up here in a minute. What time do you open tomorrow?"

Right after she left I went back to the article I'd been reading about the christening of Daniel Lester Collins at the Simmons Creek Victory Church. The picture was grainy, but it was obviously Alice holding her newborn son. Next to her stood a gaunt, older man. Surely that wasn't her husband?

But it was. The Reverend Lester Collins had presided over the christening of his firstborn child. He had a huge grin on his face.

And why shouldn't he? He had a young, pretty wife who—knowing Alice—had probably done his every bidding. And she'd given him a son. For him, life must have been pretty damn good.

Had it been good for my sister?

As I left the library and headed up Highway 1082 to the farm, everything I'd read rolled around in my head. Mom had died of AIDS.

About three months before her death, her illness became public knowledge. In 1986 rural Louisiana that had been a horror too huge to ignore, and all sorts of hell had broken loose. There had been letters to the editor. Demands that the farm be quarantined, that the house be burned down to kill the germs. The American Civil Liberties Union in New Orleans had actually become involved.

By the time Mom died, only she and Alice were left on the farm. All Mom's freeloading friends had split. There was no official obituary notice, but afterward there had been a slew of articles and more letters to the editor about the wages of sin and the plague festering at Vidrine Farms.

I frowned and turned down the azalea-lined driveway. How had Alice stood it? Why on earth had she stayed? And why, when she called, hadn't she told me it was AIDS?

Then again, that wouldn't have changed my reaction.

I sighed. Despite my carefully cultivated disdain for my spineless, mealymouthed sister, I had to give it to her. She'd showed them all in her own, do-gooder way. I would probably have sponsored a rock festival on the farm and invited the most offensive acts I could find. Then I would have ended it by making a giant bonfire out of that house.

I pulled to a stop and stared at the house now, so pretty and neat and innocuous-looking. I would have lit the fire gladly but not for the reason ranted about in that stupid newspaper. I would have burned it down for my own satisfaction, to obliterate once and for all the miserable childhood I'd lived in it.

The sun was sinking behind the house, casting it in soothing shadows, a photo-op for *This Old House*. I closed my eyes and rested my forehead on the steering wheel. Burning it down wouldn't have helped. I would have loved doing it, watching the destruction, feeling the heat, smelling that scorched wood stench. But it wouldn't have changed anything. I was the product of my rotten childhood, pure and simple. And nothing symbolic would change that.

But collecting my half of its value in cold, hard cash would go a long way toward easing my pain.

I slammed out of the car, resolved in my goal to just collect my due and get started on a new, normal life. From upstairs I heard Tripod's mournful howl, and I spied his ugly snout pressed against the window glass. He probably needed to visit the nearest tree.

I trotted up the steps, crossed the porch and walked into the house—only to be confronted by Carl.

"The least you could do is knock."

I ignored him. "We need to talk," I said to Alice, who stood farther down the hall, in the doorway to the kitchen. "By the way, better collect your toy dog. I'm about to let Tripod out."

"And that's another thing," Carl hollered up after me. "That dog is too big to be allowed indoors—"

He broke off when Tripod charged down the stairs in one big hurry. The dog leaped up, planting his one front paw on the front door, barking his impatience.

"What's the matter?" I cooed to him once I reached the door. "You're acting like an old man with prostate trouble." I turned pointedly to Carl and smiled. He looked a good fifteen years older than Alice and not particularly well preserved.

I opened the door, Tripod ran out, then I turned to Alice. "Where do you want to go to talk?"

"Can it please wait?" she asked, her voice soft, her hands a nervous knot at her waist.

My sister is really pretty. She takes after my mother with her sunny hair and vivid blue eyes. She was over forty now and still heavier than was considered healthy. But she was a lot thinner than I'd ever seen her. She looked good. Sweet and soft. Put her in a blue bonnet, and she'd be my image of Little Bo Peep.

I, meanwhile, apparently took after my unknown father. Red hair, pale skin. Thank God not too many freckles. I was taller than Alice and Mom, with bigger boobs—which I sometimes loved and sometimes hated. Let's just say they have their uses and have got me past a lot of locked doors a lesser endowed woman couldn't have entered.

But that was neither here nor there. "Wait for what?"

"Daniel's missing."

"Missing? No, he's not. He's at his friend's house. He asked me for a ride."

"Without telling me?" All of sudden Alice's soft side turned fierce.

"He told you he was going. I heard him."

"Well, I didn't. What friend?"

"Some kid. I don't know. Josh," I said as the name came back to me. "Yeah, Josh." *Of Voodoo Fest and four-wheeler fame.*

Alice and Carl shared a look. "I'll go get him," Carl told her. "If you'll be all right," he added, shooting me an aggrieved look.

"I'll be fine," she said, patting his arm.

I slapped my hands, rubbed them together, and grinned. "Well, good. That's settled. So, big sister. Shall we have that talk?"

I walked past them and into the kitchen. My stomach

had started growling the moment I drove up. Since the house was half mine, I decided that everything in it was, too.

I stood in the open refrigerator checking out the healthy selection of white bread, bologna and processed cheese. Yuck. I strained to hear the muffled conversation in the hall. Though I couldn't make out most of the words, I didn't have to be clairvoyant to know Carl was royally pissed.

Poor Daniel. I didn't envy him the ride home.

Bending back to the refrigerator, I noticed some bacon and took it out, then found eggs. "Do you have any grits?" I asked when Alice came in. "I haven't had any decent grits since—" *since G.G.'s last Southern tour* "—since forever."

She handed me a Martha White bag and a pot, then sat down while I started the grits, put the bacon in the microwave and slapped a thin pat of butter into a cast-iron skillet. I was seriously hungry. "Want any?" I added as an afterthought.

"No."

I worked in silence as the grits bubbled and thickened. Once I turned them off, I broke three eggs in the skillet. "So here's the deal," I began as I scrambled them. "Mom was Granddad's and Nana's only heir, and we're her only heirs." I turned off the skillet and scraped the eggs onto a plate. "This place is half yours and half mine. And I want my half."

She frowned. "You want me to split the farm in half?"

"I don't want any part of this godforsaken place," I said. "What I want is half the value of the property. And I want it as fast as I can get it."

I sat down at the kitchen table and started to eat, as if I was totally nonchalant and this conversation was not absolutely critical to my escape from my past—my pasts in both Louisiana and California.

She shook her head. "But I don't have any money, Zoe. I can't afford to buy you out. And this place is hardly godforsaken. It might once have been but not anymore. Lester and I made it into a good home. A God-fearing home."

"Well, good for you. But that doesn't change anything. It's still half mine and I'm willing to sell you my share. Surely your wonderful husband had life insurance."

She stiffened. "He only had a burial policy."

"You've got to be kidding! With a family and all—"

"He had health problems. A bad heart. Life insurance was too expensive, okay?"

I wanted to ask how old he'd been when they got married, fifty? Sixty? But I didn't. "So he left you in the lurch. Isn't that just like a man." I fixed her with a sharp eye. "Is that why you're hooking up with good ol' Carl? Need another sugar daddy?"

Finally I got a real rise out of her. "Just because you've lived a debauched life doesn't mean the rest of us have!"

I gave a sarcastic snort. "I was here for seventeen years, Alice. I know exactly what sort of debauched life *we* lived."

"I was raised in it, yes. Just like you. But I never lived my own life that way."

"What makes you think I did?"

Her eyes narrowed. "Come on. I saw that music video, Zoe."

"Really? Which one?"

"There was more than one?" Her face was a study in horror.

I just smiled, folded my hands on the table and nodded. But inside I was raging. How dare she judge me?

"The one I saw was about ten years ago. You were dancing in this low-cut dress, rubbing up against some guitar while this man watched you." She shuddered.

I, too, shuddered in disgust when I thought of Dirk and the Dirt Bags, but for an entirely different reason, though that wasn't her business. "How did *you* ever come to see that video?"

"Sue Ellen Jenkins. She saw it and she thought it might be you. So she recorded it and showed it to me."

"So, what did *she* think?"

Her chin started to tremble and it took me aback. Why was she getting so upset? "I told Sue Ellen it wasn't you," she said in a shaky voice. "I told her you'd died in a car wreck in Texas."

CHAPTER 3

"You told everyone that I was dead?"

It didn't matter that Alice looked contrite. It didn't matter that she ducked her head in shame. She'd told the whole world that I was dead even when she knew for a fact I wasn't. Except for her son, I was her last living relative if you didn't count her father, who'd disappeared long before I was born.

For her I was it. Yet she'd rather I be dead.

You abandoned her first.

I didn't want to think about that, but it was an inescapable fact. When she wouldn't run away with me, I'd run away without her and had never looked back. But that hadn't been about her. It had been about this place. I'd had to get away; she'd been content to stay. That's why now I ignored any excuses she had for her lie about my early demise. "You told Sue Ellen Jenkins that I was dead? Why? Were you afraid it would dirty your standing in the narrow, self-righteous church community you married into?"

I shoved my plate across the table, crossed my arms and glared at the top of her bowed head. Tears were dripping from the end of her nose. Phony, crocodile tears. "Tomorrow I'm getting a lawyer, settling the estate and putting this place up for sale."

Her head jerked up. "You can't do that!"

"Wanna bet? You can hire a lawyer to fight me, Alice. But that's going to cost a lot of money, and in the end I'll still get my inheritance. You can't stop me." I paused a beat. "So why not just strike an agreement with me now?"

She stared at me though teary eyes. "You don't understand. I can't. This is my home, mine and Daniel's."

"Oh, come on! There's plenty enough land to go around. Just get the property appraised, split it into two parcels of equal value, and if you don't want to buy my portion, then I'll sell it to someone else."

She shook her head. "It's not that simple."

"Well, that's just too damned bad, isn't it? You can't poor-mouth your way out of this. You've lived here over twenty years, Alice. That's a lot of free rent."

"That's not fair. Yes, I lived rent-free. But I've worked like a dog on this place. I've cleaned and scraped and sanded and painted. I've planted every single tree and shrub—"

"And it looks great. So what? Consider that sweat-equity your rent. I don't care. It doesn't change anything. This place is half mine, and I need my share!"

I hadn't intended to get mad. I had meant to stay cool, to sit back and let her flail around on the hook of what's-fair-is-fair. But just being in this house made me crazy. Decadent or painted up like an Easter egg, it didn't matter.

This place was a hellhole and I hated it. I wanted my money and I wanted out of here. The sooner Alice realized I was serious, the better.

So I leaned back in the chair and tried to calm my galloping pulse. "If you want the house, fine. I'll take the back acreage and sell it."

"But you can't," she muttered, head down again.

"Why the hell not?"

"Because… Because Lester and I…we built our church on it."

I couldn't help it. I started to laugh. "You built a church on it? On this foul piece of ground you built a church? *That's* the church Daniel was talking about?"

"I'm not surprised that you'd laugh at a church." Alice threw the words at me, rising from shame back into her comfort zone of righteous indignation.

"Oh, relax, will you? I'm not laughing at your precious church. Church or house, I don't care, Zoe. All I want is what's legally mine."

"You don't understand," she said in a lower voice. "You can't take the church because…"

I waited expectantly for whatever justification she would come up with.

"Because we sold the land it's on to the church board. It belongs to them now."

I wasn't sure I heard her right. "You sold it? How could you have sold something that wasn't yours to sell?"

"Everyone thought you were dead!"

"Everyone except you! You knew I was alive. You'd seen

that video." My rage boiled over, bone-deep and fire-hot. "You lied to get your hands on my inheritance. That's illegal. That's fraud. I could have you arrested."

I pushed out of the chair and stormed to the back door. Then I whirled around and stared at her. She was scared. Good. She'd better be scared. "What did you do with the money? My money?"

She pressed her lips together. "Most of it went to fix up the house. And to build the church."

"Okay. Fine. I'll take the house then."

"No, Zoe." She stood up and reached a hand to me. "Please. This is my home. Daniel's home."

"No, it's my home now—"

I broke off when the front door banged open. Someone stormed up the stairs. Daniel. Then Carl strode into the kitchen.

His frown turned into a scowl when he saw Alice and me facing off. "What's going on?" He crossed to Alice. "You all right?"

Of course she immediately burst into tears.

I rolled my eyes. Alice didn't like the way I used my sexuality to get what I wanted. But how were her phony tears and feminine helplessness any different? Naturally Carl leaped to her defense in the same way a hundred men had leaped to mine in the past. Rockers or preachers, they were all the same. They flexed their muscles, pounded their chests, leaped to the little lady's defense and hoped like hell that would get them a free ticket into her pants.

I'd become very adept at using men yet keeping them

out of my pants. I wondered if Alice was as adept at it. Or was she already sleeping with good ol' Carl?

"What did you do to her?" he shouted at me.

"Caught her in a crime that could land her in jail," I said. Then with a glib wave of my fingers, I waltzed out the back door. I didn't slam it. That would only signal that I'd lost control, and I wasn't about to let Alice and that creep ever think that. But boy, I wanted to slam it.

Instead I stood on the bottom step and made myself take deep, calming breaths. I stared at the sky. The sun had set and a half moon rose, skimming the tops of the pines. Down by the creek the frogs were calling back and forth, tempting any lady frogs within distance with their macho bluster. Were there no worthwhile males anywhere in the animal kingdom? Or were they all just swagger and smoke?

From upstairs I heard the sudden thump of hard-driving music. Nothing I recognized. I stepped into the yard and looked up at Daniel's window, its drapes drawn tight against the night. How long till he, too, became an absolute asshole?

Then Tripod came galloping toward me, tongue lolling and tail whacking from side to side. "At least you love me," I said, squatting down to rub his ears. "And I love you, you ugly, old thing. Looks like you're the only one around here having a good time."

He rewarded me with a slap of his tongue that my face only partially avoided. "Okay, okay." Then he was off again, happy as I hadn't ever seen him. I started after him, I guess because I didn't really feel like being alone. He might be at home in the country, but I wasn't. A condo in Miami was more my speed. Or Austin, Texas. Some place with a good music scene. But not L.A. or New York.

New Orleans would be perfect.

I shook my head against the thought. Too close to this place. Besides, what did I want with a good music scene? Certainly not a musician for a boyfriend. I was giving up the Red Vidrine lifestyle for a quieter, calmer one. Zoe Vidrine, soccer mom.

I stopped at the outer edges of the mowed yard and stared into the wild thicket that carpeted the woodlot, on down to the creek. Where I moved to would depend on how much money I could get from selling this place. All I needed was a nice little condo—two bedrooms—in a neighborhood with a good school.

With my left hand I made a slow circle over my deceptively flat stomach. "I'm doing this for you," I whispered into the night. "So I can stay at home a couple of years and devote myself to you. We come from a long line of motherless women, but that's going to change with you." All I needed was a small home, a few writing gigs a month—music reviews, band interviews—and the two of us could get by.

The three of us, I amended when Tripod came crashing through the undergrowth, wet this time. "The three of us," I said, fondling his ugly mug. "Come on, let's go inside and get you your dinner, unless you've already eaten Angel."

Though I didn't want to deal with Alice and her other lapdog, Carl, no way was I letting them think they could intimidate me. Alice had cheated me out of a lot of money.

She knew it and I wasn't going to let her forget it. So I strode into the kitchen—only to find it empty.

Just as well.

I fed Tripod, all the while conscious of the heavy rhythm of Daniel's music shuddering through the ceiling. I was up on all kinds of music, from hardcore punk to ambient noise, to hip hop, to grind core. But I didn't recognize this band. As I started up the stairs, though, I got a brilliant idea. Daniel was fourteen or so, just coming into his own when it came to musical preferences. If I chatted him up about his music, it would probably piss the hell out of Alice. But it could also be the start of a great article: Tomorrow's Music Connoisseurs—What They're Listening To Today. Plus, I needed to learn how to relate to kids.

I knocked twice before Daniel cracked the door. He looked like a younger version of G.G. when he was in a foul mood. Lowered brow, downturned mouth.

"What?" he asked. I couldn't hear the actual word due to the volume of his music, but I could read his lips.

I smiled. "I was wondering who that was. I don't recognize the band."

"What?"

"The band!" I shouted. "Who is it?"

"Oh." He opened the door to let me in. Then he lowered the volume and handed me the CD cover. *Power of Odd*.

"Never heard of them. Are they local?"

"Sort of. One of them went to Covington High School and they've played at a couple of youth revivals."

"Youth revivals? You mean they're Christian rock?"

"Yeah." He gestured me to sit on his bed, then picked up a handful of CDs for me to look though. As I checked them out I listened to Power of Odd. No reference to Jesus in the lyrics, at least not directly. No wonder I hadn't pegged it. With the pounding drums—it sounded like a double set—and the howl of angst delivering the lyrics, it had more in common with Metallica or White Snake than what I thought of as saccharine church music. Debbie Boone it was not.

"These guys aren't as fierce," he said, as he reloaded the CD player with a different group. "More lyrical. Good for relaxing."

"While Power of Odd is better for raging?"

He ducked his head and shrugged. "It's been a weird day, you know?"

"Tell me about it."

We listened to the beginning of the first song, about temptation and love and getting your strength from above.

"Why'd you come back here?" he asked me.

I straightened up. No way was I discussing this house and my half of Mom's inheritance. "Doesn't it make more sense to ask why I left?" Another bad subject but not quite so dangerous.

"Okay. Why'd you leave? How old were you, anyway?"

"Seventeen. And this place was nothing like it is now." What a monumental understatement.

"You ran away?"

"Yep."

"How come?"

I laughed. "My mother, of course. She was crazy. And cruel. And selfish."

"Just like mine," he muttered.

"Oh, no, buddy boy. No way. Your mother is *nothing* like our mom."

"Oh, yeah? Well you never had to live with a religious fanatic who thinks you're five years old!"

"That's true," I admitted. "But at least you know she loves you. Cares about you. My mother treated us like we were adults. We had to feed ourselves, clean ourselves, take care of the house and pets—and her while she was loaded, which was most of the time. It was up to us to keep this place functioning while a bunch of pothead dopers crashed here whenever they wanted to."

He stared at me in shock. "Grandma was a drug user?"

He didn't know? If Alice hadn't told him that, it stood to reason that she would be furious when she found out I had. Digging up all our buried family secrets and baring them to the light.

But too bad. It was *his* family history, too.

I slid onto the floor, sat cross-legged on the rug and leaned toward him. "My mother—your grandmother—lost her father when she was five. He died in Korea. Her mom promptly had a nervous breakdown. That's what they called it in those days. Anyway, my mother was raised here on the farm, for the most part by her grandparents, who were already old and devastated by the death of their only son. From the stories she used to tell, it seems like nobody really took control of her, and she grew up pretty wild. By the time your mother was born, both of the old folks had died. So it was just Mom and Alice out here on the farm and, later on, me."

He was listening intently, chewing on one side of his lower lip. "Even though Mom's last name was Blalock, Grandma never married my mom's father, did she?"

"No."

He nodded. "That's what I figured. But Mom won't ever talk about it."

"It wasn't easy for us, growing up around here." Another understatement. "Back then Vidrine Farm was known as Hippie Heaven. You know, a commune."

I could tell by his blank look that he didn't know what I was talking about. I rolled my eyes. "Go to the library and check the local newspaper during the seventies and eighties. There are lots of articles about Caro Vidrine and the Vidrine Farm."

"Maybe I will," he said, frowning. "Once I'm not grounded anymore."

"You're grounded? Why?"

"They said I split for four hours without telling them where I was going. But I did tell them!"

"Yeah, I heard you."

"And anyway, it's not Carl's place to ground me."

"Carl grounded you?"

Daniel flung himself on his bed. "He thinks he's my dad or something. But he's not."

I considered a long moment, then decided, so what if I

was pumping the kid for information? "Are your mom and Carl, you know, a couple?"

He shot me an aggrieved look. "If you mean, like, are they getting married——" The rest was muffled when he slapped a pillow over his face and screamed into it.

I stared at him in shock. He was a strange mixture of polite kid and raging teenager. Homeschooled and protected but part of a sick family history of neglect and depravity. Self-control versus self-indulgence, that sure described me and my poor, uptight sister. And now Daniel was trapped in a new version of the same hellhole. Mom the drug addict; Alice the religion addict; and me the——

What?

What was my addiction? What made me feel safe and in control? Shopping? That was temporary. Adulation? Unfortunately that too was temporary, especially since I didn't have enough talent as a model, actress or singer to make the big time.

So where did I turn for comfort? Certainly not to men. Men have their uses. But after my first disastrous love affair, I've never had any delusions about them.

My hand moved once more to my stomach, and that's when it dawned on me. This child. I was banking on her— or him—to be my happiness.

I'd never wanted children. Certainly I'd been very careful to always use birth control. *Always.* But somehow I'd managed to conceive this child. And once I'd figured out why my breasts were so sore and my period was late, I'd become fixated on her.

Me, a mother.

I was determined to do it right, to do it as close to perfect as I could. That's why I needed to get settled down in the right place and the sooner the better. My child would have the safest house and the best mother any child ever had. At least I hoped so.

Daniel sat up abruptly, startling me back to the moment. "How long are you staying here with us?"

"I'm not sure. Why?"

"What do you think of Carl?"

Now that was an interesting question. I decided to be honest. "He seems too old for Alice. And too rigid. And mean."

He snorted. "Nice description of the man who's trying to be the next pastor at our church."

"You're saying he wants to run the church *and* marry the former minister's widow?"

"You got it."

I tried to picture Carl married to my sister, to picture her crawling into bed with him, and felt a shudder rip right through me. "Do you think she loves him?"

He gave a hopeless shrug. "I don't know. All I know is I don't like him, and he'll never be my dad." He looked up at me. "Did you ever meet my dad?"

"No." I shook my head. "Sorry."

Again he shrugged. "So how come you were gone so long? Mom says it's like, twenty-five years."

"Twenty-three. And I left because I hated this house and everybody in it."

He picked up his remote control, pointed it at the stereo and lowered the volume. Then he stared intently at me. "You hated my mom, too?"

I let out a long, slow breath. "When I left here…yeah. I hated her, too. I begged her to leave with me. I'd been begging her to leave ever since she turned eighteen. But she wouldn't go." *Chicken-shit bitch.* I managed a careless smile. "So one day I just took off on my own. But don't you be getting any big ideas like that," I added. "You're only fourteen. And from what I can see, you're not exactly in any danger here."

"You were in danger? In your own house?"

I straightened up, stretched my legs out and flexed my ankles. "I thought I was. The kind of men who hung around here weren't above hitting on a teenaged girl."

He digested that a moment, then in a low voice asked, "What about my mom?"

"You mean, did they hit on her?" I thought back to those days, to how fat Alice was then, how frumpy and maternal. Meanwhile I'd been the leggy daughter, willowy and tall for her age, with an untamed head of fiery red hair— and a fiery temperament to match. To a certain sort of self-indulgent man, that's like a signal light flashing "come and get it."

"Alice had a way of discouraging dirty old men. Look," I went on, needing to change the subject. "I doubt your mom wants you knowing all this sh—all this stuff. The reason I knocked on your door was to try out an idea on you."

"An idea? On me? What do you mean?"

"I write articles for magazines, newspapers. Usually they're interviews with musicians or music reviews. Stuff like that. Anyway, I was thinking about an article on kids your age—what they're listening to, what they might be listening to in the future. Sort of a check-in with the young teen music-lover. And I thought I'd start off with you."

He'd become somber during my description of the old days in this house. But the thought of being featured in a music article brought an eager smile back to his face. He swiped one hand through his sandy hair, leaving part of it sticking up straight. "Yeah. Sure. And I can hook you up with some of my friends, too."

"Great. Do you know any online chat rooms with mostly young teenagers talking about music? I thought I could— What?"

His face had grown dour again. "I'm not allowed to go online for anything except school stuff. Especially not to chat rooms."

"Okay. That's okay," I said, wondering how long Alice could choke him before he burst free. "I'll figure that part out myself."

"There's one more thing," he said, when I stood up.

Another question about his mom in this house, I figured as I braced myself. "Okay, what?"

"If I'm gonna help you with this article, well, I thought maybe you could help me with something in return."

"If you mean putting in a good word for you with your mother, sorry, Daniel. I'm not exactly her most favorite person. If I asked her to go easy on you with this being grounded, it's more likely she'd double your punishment."

"No." He shook his head and shoved his hands into the pockets of his jeans. "It's not that."

"Then what?"

His eyes narrowed. "I don't want my mom to marry Carl."

Uh-oh. Tricky territory. I shook my head. "There's nothing I can do about that either."

"I know you and Mom aren't too cool with each other right now. But eventually you'll straighten things out. I mean, you're sisters. You can't be mad at each other forever."

Ah, the innocence of youth. "Maybe. Maybe not. But I know one thing, she won't be asking me for any advice about men."

He frowned. "All I'm asking is that you discourage her from marrying him. Is that so hard?"

"No. On the surface it's not hard at all. But there's so much going on beneath the surface here, Daniel, that I'm just afraid anything I try might backfire on you."

"Well." He plopped down on a blanket chest beneath the window. "Be subtle then."

Subtle. Never my strong suit. But what could I say? Besides Alice, Daniel was my only living relative. "I'll tell you what." I stood up and sidled toward the door. "Let me think about it, okay?"

He hesitated, then nodded. "Okay."

I would think about it, but in the end I was pretty sure the answer would be the same. No. And yet as I stared at him I felt the weirdest sensation, the strangest sort of affection for this kid that I'd only met today.

Not a rush of love or anything sickly sweet like that. Not a rush. But maybe…a trickle.

CHAPTER 4

I slept like G.G. used to when he was mixing drugs and alcohol: comatose for twelve hours straight, and I felt groggy
when I woke up. A little clock ticked on the small, round
table next to me, but I felt like it was shaking the whole
bed. Then I realized that it was Tripod's whiplike tail
whacking the mattress in rhythm with the clock.

"Okay, okay," I mumbled, squinting at the brightly lit
window. Nearly eleven? No wonder Tripod was getting antsy.
I rolled out of bed, found my same jeans and
T-shirt—I really needed to unpack—then on bare feet headed
downstairs. The house was quiet, and I could tell I was alone.

I saw a sticky note on the office door: "Leave Angel inside." Sure enough, fluff-ball's shrill yapping started up.
Tripod's ears perked up. Once he sniffed and snorted at her,
however, only silence came from the other side of the door.

"What the hell," I muttered, and opened the door.

I'll give Angel credit; she was fast. Through the door,
across the foyer and halfway up the stairs before Tripod
could even turn around. There she stood her ground,
ceding the first floor to Tripod but daring him to try for the
second.

Tripod, of course, leaped joyously into the dare. But I caught him by the collar and dragged him to a standstill. "Cool it, mutt. Let's go outside."

Once we were on the porch, Angel ventured down, resuming her yapping at the front door. I figured the two of them would eventually sort things out. The real question was how I was going to sort things out with Alice.

One hour, one shower and one cup of coffee later I was on my way. There were a couple of lawyers in the several towns around here, but I worried that some of them might know Alice and her recently deceased minister husband. So I picked the sleaziest, most likely to be godless one I could. According to his yellow pages ad, Dick Manglin was just what I needed. Personal injury, criminal defense, DWIs and bail bond reductions. Someone whose only goal was to win, win, win.

I didn't call for an appointment. I figured my snug-fitting dress, stiletto sandals, red toenails and redder lipstick would get me in.

Sure enough, by the time I left Dick's office he was dictating a demand letter for my sister that would give her one week to produce my portion of the property sale to the church, as well as one-half the value for the remaining acreage and house. It would be hand-delivered tomorrow. Otherwise, the letter concluded, we would take legal action to challenge the sale as fraudulent and to force the sale of the house. Copies to be sent to the Simmons Creek Victory Church.

Alice was going to shit a brick.

Oops. Alice was going to freak out, I amended. I'd given

up cursing in deference to the baby, who all the books said would be able to hear long before she was born.

Anyway, Alice was going to freak out, which was the whole point. As for Daniel, I'd better interview him soon, before Alice turned him entirely against me. But he hadn't been home when I left, and I didn't want to go back there anyway.

I climbed into my Jeep. The whole day stretched ahead of me, but I wasn't sure where to go or what to do.

As if in answer, my stomach growled.

"Food," I muttered to Jenny Jeep. "Find me a restaurant, baby. Preferably one with oyster po' boys and fried onion rings." My ob-gyn in Los Angeles had given me permission to eat whatever I wanted to. No dieting at all, at least for the first few months. She probably hadn't had fried onion rings in mind, but it wasn't like I ate them everyday. Besides, most days I couldn't eat much breakfast. It made sense, then, that I make up for it at lunch.

I found a place—Sara Mae's—that looked like it had been serving lunch specials for the past fifty years. It was well past the lunch hour, but there were still enough cars there to reassure me that the food was good.

I slipped in without fanfare—I thought. Of course, every head in the place swiveled my way.

This is a small town, idiot. And you're a stranger. The outfit didn't help either. As I slid into the first empty booth, I reminded myself that from now on it would be jeans and T-shirt for me. Nothing flashy. And I needed to keep my always-rioting hair in a ponytail or bun.

I gave the waitress my order, then took out my cell phone. Three more messages from G.G. I slapped it closed. The hell with him. He probably just wanted to know where the file for the next tour was. And if I *was* really leaving him, could I please return all the jewelry he'd bought me?

Fat chance. I'd already sold most of it. I had a little nest egg started. Barely five figures, but if I was frugal, it would keep me going a few months until I received my inheritance. Then I'd settle in, just me, Tripod and my sweet baby.

The waitress returned with my lemonade and onion rings just as the door opened.

"Hey, Joe," she called out. "You're late today."

"You got any pork chops left?" the man called to her. *That* man. *That* Joe.

Like radar, his eyes seemed to find me.

Shit. I mean, shoot.

He greeted a couple of old guys at the bar. The regulars. It reminded me of *Cheers*, a place where everyone knows your name, so it was no biggie to figure out who would be the big topic of conversation once I left the joint.

"Hey," he said, stopping at my booth.

I'd done the mental calculations in the short time it had taken him to reach me. Six feet tall, maybe six-one. One-eighty or so. G.G.'s height but a good thirty pounds heavier. Probably never been strung out. A big plus in his favor. Too bad he was a reporter.

"Hello," I responded, not smiling.

"You're eating alone."

"I am. Unless, pushy reporter that you are, you intend to invite yourself to join me."

He grinned. Damn, he had a great smile. I meant darn. "You don't like reporters. Now why is that?"

"I don't like lawyers either," I said. "Or dog catchers, or tax collectors."

His eyes glinted with humor. "Surely the fact that I'm not a lawyer, love dogs and *pay* taxes instead of collecting them should offset the fact that I'm a reporter."

I've always been a sucker for charming men. Charming, smart or talented, preferably all three. G.G. had once been charming and talented. They hadn't dubbed him "Guitar God" Givens for nothing. But fame and cocaine had eventually ruined him for anything but staring in the mirror.

This man, Joe Reeves, was charming and probably a talented writer—and smart, too. Unfortunately he could also be a threat to my need to lie low. But there were ways to deal with a man like him.

So I perched my chin on my hand, smiled up at him. "At least you like dogs." I gestured to the bench seat opposite me. "Go ahead then, and sit. Have an onion ring."

The waitress appeared with his iced tea and a house salad. "Thanks, Marie," he said. "Have you met Zoe?"

We exchanged pleasantries as she sized me up. Thank God he hadn't mentioned my last name. With all the old-timers in this place, someone was sure to remember me.

"Find what you needed at the library?" he asked.

"I was just browsing. How's the newspaper business?" *We're not talking about me, buddy, so just forget that you're a reporter.* I leaned forward and smiled. "How did you get into writing for a living?"

"I don't know. I was an oddball kid. Part nerd, part jock. I worked on my high school newspaper and yearbook staffs, and played baseball and basketball."

"And had all the girls crazy about you, no doubt."

He chuckled. "Not as many as I would have liked. And probably not as many as you had guys chasing after you."

I wasn't going to bite. But it was hard. He had this very observant way of looking at you, like whatever you said was really, really important to him. A good trait for a reporter, I reminded myself.

Marie showed up with my po' boy and his pork chop and white beans.

"You eat here often?" I asked as we dug in.

"Couple of times a week. Mel advertises in the paper. I come in to keep them honest in the taste department."

"Mel?" Inside I began to shake, but on the outside I kept it cool. "As in Melody or Melvin?"

"Melvin Toups. He owns this place."

Melvin Toups. Oh, my God! That creep Melvin Toups who'd chased me into the river? I kept my breathing even. In through the nose, out through the mouth. "Why do they call it Sara Mae's?" I asked, just to fill in the awful silence.

"This was his mother-in-law's place before Mel took over."

That meant he had a wife? Poor woman. When Melvin and his thug friends had chased me to the river to escape them, I'd been so scared. Four teenaged boys; one teenaged girl. I'd been petrified that they'd meant to rape me.

I suppressed a shudder and bit into my po' boy. I love oyster po' boys, and no place makes them like the small mom-and-pop joints spread around southern Louisiana. But this one could have been cardboard for all I could taste. Melvin Toups had made this sandwich and these onion rings.

I felt the rise of bile in my throat. *You will not be sick. You will not be sick.* I chanted the words, breathing slowly, deeply, knowing I had to get out of here. I dropped the remains of the po' boy on the plate and pushed it away. I wanted to throw it across the room.

"You okay?" Joe asked.

I shook my head. "Too much mayonnaise." I snagged my purse, dug out my wallet and pulled out a twenty. "See you around." Then I pushed out of the booth, shoved the money in Marie's hand and fled. The last thing I heard was someone chortling. "Hey, Joe. What in the hell did you say to the little lady?"

I didn't know where to go, what to do. I hated the farmhouse. I would have gone to the library, but it was right next to Joe Reeves's office and I sure didn't want to run into him again. If I could have, I would have loaded up Tripod and all my gear and just left, heading to Florida or the Carolina coast, anywhere warm and near the water. But I needed my money. My inheritance. Without it I would have to put my baby in a day-care center while I worked, and I was determined not to do that. Bad enough she wouldn't have a father. The least I could do was give her a stay-at-home mother until she started school.

So I jumped in Jenny Jeep and just drove. Down two-lane blacktops, turning onto gravel roads, veering onto rutted, overgrown dirt trails. I had to switch into four-wheel drive as I careened down one muddy lane. It ended at a river, coffee-colored and moving fast. The water was high, but then that was typical in the spring. By August this same river would be way down, warm and moving slowly.

I turned off the car and got out, but open-toed sandals aren't any good for tramping through underbrush. Between snakes, poison ivy and blackberry canes, I was bound to lose the fight.

But instead of frustrating me, that actually helped to calm me down. Some things were beyond my control: the woods, the river. My past. The cruel people in the world.

I climbed onto the roof of my Jeep and sat there cross-legged, staring through the pines and sweet gum and oaks toward the river. It wasn't my fault Mel Toups had been a mean kid. Maybe he was nicer now, but I doubted it. The point was, he couldn't hurt me anymore. I wasn't the scared little girl I used to be. I had power of my own. More important, I knew how to marshal other people's power. In fact, I bet Mr. Joe Newspaper would just love a juicy story about how Mel and his buddies tried to grab a girl in the woods way back when. Joe might not want to write bad news about his neighbors, but he was a true newshound, and he wouldn't be able to resist. I could see the headline: Former Oracle Resident Returns To Confront Attempted Rapist.

I smiled grimly at the relentless flow of the river. I might not be able to prove the allegations, but it would sure upset

Mel's wife. Maybe she'd be so repulsed that she'd divorce him. Then he'd lose his job at his mother-in-law's diner, I speculated. He'd turn into a homeless bum, eating out of the Dumpster behind the place he used to run.

By the time the first drops of rain started to fall I was feeling much better. Nothing had changed and I wasn't about to fill Joe Reeves in on the ugliness of my childhood. But the mental exercise of getting revenge on Mel Toups had helped.

It had begun to pour by the time I backed Jenny around and picked my way out of the maze of narrow lanes and back roads. Where in the hell was I anyway? It took an old man sitting on his porch with two ancient hound dogs beside him to steer me correctly.

"Thanks!" I waved to him and in ten minutes was back at the farm. Except that I really didn't want to be in that house, especially not alone. So I ran in, changed into long jeans and tennis shoes and, with Tripod next to me, set off for a walk.

The rain had barely touched the farm, only dampened the fields a little and left the woods drippy. Tripod was in his glory. I couldn't say the same about myself, but at least I hadn't thrown up. Up to now morning sickness hadn't been a serious problem. Instead I was periodically surprised by a sudden wave of nausea. Midday, midnight and anytime in-between.

I rubbed the rounded little mound beneath my belly button. "Temperamental and unpredictable. Is that what I should expect from you?" Given her mother's temperament—and her father's—what else could she be?

I followed a path I hadn't thought about in years. It had hardly changed. A narrow woodland track that wound through the thickest part of our woodlot, down an incline, skirting a lush stand of wood ferns already thigh-high. Must have been a mild winter.

The ground grew soggy, but once past the Black Bog, as Alice and I had dubbed it, the ground rose again. But something was different. It was too bright up ahead.

Then I saw the short, square steeple, and I realized where I was. Alice's church. The back acreage on the far side of the Black Bog. This was the land she'd sold without my consent.

I stopped at the edge of the trees and stared. The church wasn't all that much to look at, a metal warehouse-type building with an awkward front tower and a plain cross above it. A clearing had been carved out of the woods in one big square. Trees rimmed the square, the ugly church squatted in the middle and a partially paved parking lot circled the whole thing.

A smaller building stood off to one side, probably some sort of activities center. Several cars were parked nose-in next to it, including Alice's. I suppose traipsing through the woods was too messy for her little neat-freak, do-gooder soul. She had to get into her eight-cylinder gas-guzzler and drive the half mile around to the road that fronted the church.

I turned away, furious at the ugly blight she'd inflicted on my land. The least they could have done was build a handsome church, something inspiring and comforting.

I turned back for the house, whistling for Tripod, then

abruptly took another trail, the one that circled the northern edge of our land. Tripod followed behind me, nose down, pretending he was a hunting dog. He didn't let me get too far ahead, though. Nervous, I guess.

But I wasn't. I was remembering so much. Like the half-hearted tree house Alice and I had discovered in a big oak tree. Some other long-ago kids must have started it, but we had finished it, making it our own, dragging up wood, rope and pieces of tin, fixing it up, thinking we could make it impregnable, our own little respite from the madness back at home.

It had been our secret, hers and mine, until Mother had followed us one day. She and her man-of-the-moment had laughed with glee when they'd discovered our hideaway. Then they'd climbed up there and christened it—her term for screwing in a new place. Or in an old place with a new man.

Whatever. The magic had been ruined.

But I'd got even. I'd broken a dozen glass bottles on the tree house floor, and when that hadn't stopped her from going back, I'd set it on fire.

I don't know why the whole woods didn't go up in flames that day. Maybe because it had been raining so much that summer. But the floor of the tree house had burned away, and so had the rope ladder. Most important, Mother never went up in our tree house again. I ruined it for her, just like she'd ruined it for Alice and me.

Is it any wonder I equate sex with power? Every bit of my mother's power came from sex, but she'd used it indiscriminately. In the end it had ruined her life and probably that of several men. Certainly it had ruined my life and Alice's.

But I learned from her mistakes. She who commands men with her sex rules the world—if she can keep her cool about her. Cleopatra. Helen of Troy. Queen Eleanor of Aquitaine. Elizabeth I.

One thing I certainly didn't associate sex with was making love. And I don't much equate it with pleasure either. I've had one or two considerate lovers. But the other boyfriends have always been about *them*selves and *their* pleasure.

Not that I really cared. I've always thought sex was highly overrated.

Tripod started barking, drawing me back from my sour thoughts. Sex had given me this baby, and that's all that mattered anymore. So I changed directions to where Tripod stood barking for all he was worth at a big, curled-up water moccasin.

I grabbed my idiot dog by the collar. "I suggest you stick to poodles, if you want to stay alive," I muttered. For once he listened and followed me down another path that took us to the edge of our property.

Beyond the woods I saw an old white house, plain and ordinary except for the incredible display of flowers that surrounded it. Wow! When I was really young, an old man had lived here. Then he'd done what seemed like the oddest thing. As old as he was, he'd married this really nice, really old woman.

At that precise moment my eyes picked her out. It was her, sitting under a sweet gum tree on a wide, wooden bench painted cardinal-red. Twenty years ago her hair had been turning gray. Now it was completely white.

She was the one who'd taught me how to jitterbug and how to waltz. She'd showed me the samba and the rumba. And the tango.

I started forward with the first genuine smile on my face since I'd arrived in Oracle. She didn't notice me right away, not until a huge yellow cat spied Tripod and leaped up onto her lap.

I don't know much about Tripod's early years, but I know he's as terrified of cats as he is of big trucks and SUVs. No doubt he'd come up on the short end of a confrontation with a cat or two. At least he hadn't lost a leg to a cat. But that didn't change anything. He saw the cat, stopped dead in his tracks, and started to bark furiously—from a safe distance of at least a hundred feet or so.

"Will you please shut up?" I muttered to him. To the old woman—Harriet was her name—I waved. "Hello there."

"Why, hello." She smiled and gestured me over.

I went. Tripod remained behind, howling like I'd abandoned him on the side of the road. As if.

"You're Harriet, aren't you?" I began. "I don't know if you'll remember me but—"

"Zoe." Her eyes lit with recognition, and the loveliest smile brightened her sweet, old face. "Zoe Vidrine. I'd recognize that flame-red hair anywhere." She reached out a hand to me and squeezed tightly. "Even prettier than I remembered. But I could swear someone told me you were…" She trailed off, too polite to finish the thought.

"Dead?" I grimaced. "That seems to be the story Alice spread around. But it's not true."

"But why did she think you were dead?"

Because she's a lying thief, I wanted to say. But I didn't. "We lost touch for a while. But now I'm back."

"Well, I'm as pleased as punch," she said, beaming at me. "After you ran off I worried about you for the longest time."

It was a very simple statement: she'd worried about me. But something about it—her inflection, the kindness in her expression, the sincerity in her eyes—got to me big-time. No one had ever worried about me. I was tough. I could handle anything. But she said she'd worried about me, and I believed her. My eyes began to sting as if I was actually going to cry.

So much for being tough. One kind word from Harriet LeBlanc and I turned into a hopeless mush-ball.

I turned away, faking a sneeze. "Allergies," I mumbled, wiping my eyes, probably smearing my mascara.

"Yes. There's a lot blooming right now," she said, stroking her big yellow cat. "If you like, we can go inside."

"No, no. I like it out here. Your garden is wonderful."

"Thank you. Every since Hank died I've put all my energy into my flowers. But come, sit down right here beside me and tell me what you've been doing all these years."

I told her. And the more I told, the more I felt compelled to tell. Like a Catholic in confession or a recovering alcoholic doing his fourth and fifth steps, I just spilled it all. From the time I took the Greyhound to California, to my days as a Shoney's waitress, then a cocktail waitress. How I'd met my first rocker boyfriend while I worked at a daiquiri bar. How I met my last one while working at The House of Blues. About managing a band and their road tours, and about my couple of acting gigs. She loved that part, having been a USO performer during World War II and the Korean War.

I told her everything except about the baby. Nobody knew about that but Tripod and me, and he wasn't talking any more than I was.

"And now you've come home," she said, once I'd run out of words.

"I wouldn't go so far as to call it home. You know I hate that place. I always have."

"Yes. I remember." We sat there a long moment in silence, warmed by the sun, serenaded by a mocking bird and a bevy of honeybees busy in her flowers. Then she gently lifted her old cat from her lap to the ground. "Give me your arm, would you? My knees aren't what they used to be."

That's when I noticed the cane leaning against the side of the bench. "So no more dancing?" I asked.

She laughed. "'Fraid not. But I can't complain. I've spent more hours on the dance floor than just about anyone I know. Do you still remember the dances I taught you? The waltz. The tango. The—"

"The jitterbug," we said together, then laughed. "Oh, yes. I remembered them all. You made me a lifelong dancer, you know. I continued my lessons in L.A. and for a while I danced professionally, too. Though I never did earn enough to live on."

She chuckled. "Few dancers do."

"For a while I taught dance." I laughed. "Mostly to men dragged in by their fiancées so they wouldn't make fools of themselves at their wedding receptions."

"Good for you."

We'd reached her front porch and she leaned on me as she struggled up the three steps. "How about some tea? Or would you like lemonade? I grow my own lemons."

"Lemonade sounds wonderful."

Why couldn't she have been my mother?

That's what I used to wish when old Mr. LeBlanc had first married her. I used to show up at their house at all sorts of odd times of the day and night. I would have come more often except that I was terrified of wearing out my welcome. I might have been only a kid, but I understood that even though they were old, they were still newlyweds and needed their alone time.

Now, twenty-three years later, my first reaction after seeing her again was the same. Why couldn't she have been my mother? Harriet, who'd had no children of her own, would have made the best mother in the world. Meanwhile my mother, who'd never thought one minute past what she wanted that very instant, had borne two children. She'd aborted several others. I figured that out from things she'd said now and then. No telling why she'd decided to keep Alice and me.

But that was the past and I needed to forget it. The future was my big concern, as was the present. I gazed around Harriet's cozy, comforting kitchen with its enamel-top table, pressed-back chairs, and oak pie safe standing against the far wall. There was a 1940s feel to the place, like what she would have had as a young wife. This was what I wanted for my baby. For me. I wanted to be a good mother and raise a happy child. I wanted to be like Harriet.

And maybe when I was fifty or sixty, I'd be lucky enough like her to finally meet a man worth keeping.

I helped her make the lemonade, slicing the lemons, juicing them on an old glass juicer. I picked three stalks of mint from a pot near the back steps and crushed them in the sugar, then stirred the sugar, lemon and water together.

It smelled wonderful, and I felt amazingly domestic as I filled two tall glasses with ice and poured lemonade into them.

Nothing to it. Just find a place to live, move slowly and with real purpose and be nice to everyone I meet.

Yeah, right.

I must have been frowning because Harriet said, "Okay, Zoe. You've given me the short, sweet version of the last twenty years. Are you ready to tell me why you really came back to the place you ran away from? The place you hate? The place that, like it or not, is still your home?"

So I told her. About G.G. and the baby and my inheritance. I didn't hold back anything this time—except for my fear that she would think I was a totally despicable human being.

I should have known better.

She listened and poured me a second glass of lemonade and didn't give me one disapproving look.

"The maternal urge is incredibly powerful," she said when I was finished.

"I guess." I'd slumped back in my chair, exhausted by my revelations like a medieval patient at the end of a blood-letting, weak but still hopeful.

"Of course it's powerful. Look at you, not three months pregnant and already determined to change the direction of your life. And why? Your baby."

"But what if I'm a terrible mother?" I mumbled. My biggest fear; my greatest nightmare.

"Why should you be?"

"Come on, Harriet. I've lived a crazy life, made bad choices, especially about men. I don't know anything about kids or mothering. God knows my own mother was the world's worst role model."

"So you'll learn. You *want* to be a good mother, that's the main thing. The rest you'll learn as you go."

"I hope you're right. You know," I said, deciding to finish my confession once and for all. "When I was a kid I used to wish that you were my mother."

She smiled. "I guessed as much. You were such a lonely child. And so sweet."

"Lonely, yes. But sweet? Hah. I was wild. Insane."

"No, you were just needy. You needed love and its sta-bility. That's why you came over here so much."

I nodded. "Yeah." I bit the side of my mouth, then sat

up straighter. "Listen. Would you consider being my baby's grandmother? I mean, she's not going to have any grandparents or sisters or brothers. Or a father."

She smiled at me, so sweetly that it made me want to cry. I knew she'd say yes. But hearing it was like a balm to my soul. "Of course I'll be your baby's grandmother. But you know, Zoe, your baby already has an aunt and a cousin. I hope you don't forget the importance of that."

I frowned down at my hands. Even though I was beginning to like the idea of being an aunt to Daniel, I hadn't actually thought of Alice as my baby's aunt. It was disconcerting, to say the least.

"I haven't told her about my pregnancy," I said. "Considering how she tried to steal my inheritance from me, I don't think she deserves to know."

Harriet sighed. "I can hardly believe that Alice sold that property without consulting you. Are you sure she didn't think you *were* dead?"

I shook my head. "She admitted to me that she saw me in a music video ten years ago. How long ago was the church built?"

Harriet made a face. "About six years or so." Then she chuckled. "I suppose I should be glad Alice isn't as perfect as she always seems to be."

"Yeah. Perfect daughter. Perfect wife. Perfect mother. But not such a perfect sister."

But the truth was, neither of us had been a good sister to the other. She'd abandoned me when I had needed her, and I guess, in a way, I'd abandoned her when I hadn't helped her with Mom. Or at least come home for the funeral.

But that was then. This was now. She'd had the luxury of raising her child in a picture-perfect world. Now it was my turn. And my baby's.

CHAPTER 5

That evening I mainly watched and listened. It was Wednesday, apparently a big night at the church. I was alone with the dogs. Tripod and Angel were forging an odd sort of truce. Tripod seemed to have claimed all the floors. Angel got the furniture. As long as Angel was on the couch or on a chair, Tripod stayed calm. The minute she jumped down, he leaped up, barking like he'd tear her apart.

It was just a matter of time before she realized he was bluffing.

I was in the kitchen, fixing myself another plate of bacon, eggs and grits and making a mental list of groceries I needed to buy when the phone rang. It wasn't for me, so I let it ring. But when Alice's answering machine kicked in, it turned out I was wrong.

"This is Joe Reeves calling for Zoe Vidrine. I'm assuming she's staying with you, Alice. Could you have her give me a call—?"

"Hello?" My heart was pumping like a bellows. I did *not* want to talk to this man. This reporter. But I needed to know why he was calling.

"Alice?"

"No. Zoe."

"Zoe. Great. I was hoping you were there. You know, you and Alice sound a lot alike on the phone."

"Do we?" I let the silence stretch out. After all, he'd called me.

He cleared his throat. "I was concerned when you ran out of Sara Mae's today. Were you sick? Are you okay?"

"I'm fine."

"Good. Then I guess it must have been something I said. Whatever it was, I apologize."

I didn't know how to respond to that. *It wasn't about you; it was about Mel Toups?* No way was I going there. "I'm fine, Joe. A spot of indigestion. It comes and goes."

"I see."

Another silence, but I waited him out.

"I'm getting the distinct feeling that if I tell you why I called, you're going to shoot me down."

What did that mean? He couldn't be calling me for a…a date? My heart began to race.

Or maybe it was for an interview. After all, he knew my name and had somehow figured out how to find me. What else might he have found out?

I licked my dry lips. "Why don't you just tell me why you called and we'll see what happens?" *That's right, play coy. String him along.*

He chuckled. "You're not making this easy, are you? Okay. Since you're new in town—or newly returned—I thought you might have a little time on your hands and want to go to the Strawberry Festival with me this Saturday."

Well, blow me down, as Popeye used to say.

"My son will be with us," he went on. "But I'm sure he'll wander off with one of his friends."

"That's okay. I like kids," I said. At least I was beginning to.

"Is that a yes?"

I pressed a hand to my forehead and studied Tripod and Angel, who were staring each other down from the floor and footstool, respectively. How was I supposed to say no to such a deep, sexy voice? Besides, Saturday was three days away. Plenty of time for me to create a fictional past that even Alice would approve of.

"Sure. It sounds like fun."

"Great. I'll pick you up at Alice's about eleven, okay?"

"Fine." Only it wasn't Alice's house anymore. It was mine. But he didn't need to know about that.

After we hung up I sat there a long time, my bare feet on the polished longleaf pine floors, just me alone in my old home. My new home. Finally I jumped up, too antsy to sit still. It creeped me out, being here alone. If I could afford it, I'd stay in the local Holiday Inn. But possession was nine-tenths of the law—or so I'd heard. My new lawyer had told me to settle in, to not budge an inch, and that's what I meant to do.

But damn, it was hard.

So what was I going to do with myself? Maybe unpack just to impress Alice that I was serious about claiming this place as mine. So I trudged up the stairs, checked out the other empty bedroom and decided to claim it as mine. It had a daybed, a dresser and a chair. Sparse but usable as my sitting room. And the study, which had a wall of mostly empty shelves, a big office desk and a pair of mismatched chairs, would become my office.

I moved my books and records into the study, rearranged my sitting room, put a tapestry throw over the daybed and went outside to cut a spray of flowers and greenery for my side table.

My apartment, I thought with a little spurt of pride and a bigger spurt of self-righteous glee. Alice wouldn't like it but too bad. She had the downstairs; I'd take the upstairs— except for Daniel's room. I wasn't going to put my nephew out. I liked the kid. And anyway, none of this was his fault. He'd get to keep his room upstairs in exchange for my use of the kitchen downstairs.

I took a shower, washed my hair, put on my favorite shorty pajamas—with a robe for Daniel's sake—and still nobody had returned home. It was ten-fifteen. How long did these church services last anyway?

Still bored, still antsy, I decided to check my cell phone for messages. I'd turned off the ringer the minute I left Palm Springs. But I'd kept the phone charged up. I didn't want to talk to anyone, but I did want to know who was calling.

It's funny because for the first three days G.G. didn't call. Not once. That was because he was in New York, tweaking the details of his upcoming solo tour and CD release, and he had his manager and his handler and his producer there to keep him motivated and on schedule.

Once he got back to Palm Springs, though, and couldn't make his own coffee or find his shoes or remember which bank his money was in, then he'd started calling. I'd left him a short note, so he knew my absence was deliberate. But he must not have believed that I actually could dump *him*, the great Guitar God. He called me nine times the first day of his return, ten the next; eight and then four, and so on.

Up to now I hadn't listened to the messages, only counted the number of missed calls. As of yesterday I guess he'd figured out I wasn't returning his calls. That's when his manager, Coco, had started calling. Coco as in Cocaine Convert.

I stared at my phone now. A total of thirty-seven missed calls in the last five days. You'd think he missed me or something.

I cupped both my hands over my stomach. "Please don't have the addictive gene," I whispered to my baby. Then I started listening to the messages.

It didn't take long for G.G. to go from cajoling to pleading to frustrated to majorly pissed off. How could I do this to him right when he was about to launch the most important tour of his life? How could I abandon him this way after all he'd done for me? How could I be so mean? So selfish? Such a bitch?

I listened to them all, except for the ones when he was too stoned to keep his words straight. Those just made me mad. And sad. How many people in my life had ruined themselves with alcohol, drugs and the risky behaviors they encouraged?

Never again, I told myself. If the guy had one drink, my alarm system would turn on. Two and I would go into red alert. Three and they were out of here. No drunks needed. As for drugs, forget it.

I'd outgrown that phase at twenty-five. Yet I'd stayed on the fringes of that lifestyle for another fifteen years.

Well, no more.

I moved on to Coco's calls. More cajoling.

"Look, Red, just come back and help him through the tour. That's all. I'll put you on salary. But don't tell him that. Call me, okay? There's money in it for you, babe. Good money."

Yeah, right. There wasn't enough money in the world to make me babysit G.G. through another tour.

His next message was more specific. "Look, Red. I've got a big deal going here, and you're blowin' it. People are interested in doing a reality show with G.G. Him on tour, the little lady backing him up. Think Ozzie and Sharon without the brats. Jessica and Nick without all the cutesy bullshit."

A reality show with G.G.? I snorted with laughter. Who would want to see that? The wreckage of a major talent. At best it would be a cautionary tale: do enough drugs and you, too, could lose your mind. And girls, hook up with a super macho, self-indulgent prick, and you, too, can someday turn forty with absolutely nothing to show for it.

Then again, how much money *was* he talking about?

"No." I shoved the phone in a drawer and slammed it shut. This baby's future was more important than any amount of money. If I couldn't hang on to my sanity in

G.G.'s world, I sure as hell wasn't going to subject this innocent, impressionable baby to it.

"Come on, Tripod. Last call," I said, heading back down the stairs. "You, too," I called to Angel as she stood up on the couch, watching me.

But I guess the little dog didn't trust me any more than she trusted Tripod. I'd just sat down on the back step, waiting for him to do his business, when Alice's big van drove up, followed by Carl's big Oldsmobile. Daniel was out of the van almost before it stopped.

"Hey," he grunted as he sped past me and into the kitchen. In thirty seconds flat he had a glass of milk, a jar of peanut butter, a box of crackers and was headed up the stairs.

Out in the yard I could make out Alice and Carl standing beside his car. She didn't want him to come in. I knew it instinctively. Was it because of me and the undisguised animosity he and I aimed at each other? Or would she be fending him off even if I weren't here?

Who knew?

Who cared? I reminded myself. Certainly not me. Still, I couldn't help wondering how he'd got even this far with her. Then Tripod came around the side of the house and added another layer of threat to Alice's attempts to send Carl home, and the man finally caved.

He glared at me as he drove off. "Love you, too," I murmured, giving him a finger wave. "God bless."

"Have a nice evening?" I asked Alice when she reached the porch.

"Yes." She stared warily at me. "And you?"

"It was very productive. What I decided was that until the legalities of this whole mess are ironed out, you can keep living downstairs. I'll take the upstairs. But don't worry," I added before she could object. "Daniel can keep his room. In return I'll take full access to the kitchen. And yes, I'll buy my own groceries."

I waited for her reaction as we stood there in the silvery darkness. Would it be tears like she'd turned on for Carl? Or anger like most people caught in a lie resorted to?

Or would she admit her guilt like a good, God-fearing Christian should? *Yes, I sold your property. Yes, I owe you big-time. Yes, what's left of the farm is rightfully yours.*

Instead she opted to bargain. "Listen, Zoe. I know you're angry."

I crossed my arms. "Damned straight."

"But there's got to be a way for us to resolve this matter without having to sell the house."

"Of course there is. Just go to the bank, Alice. Get a loan and I'll sell the place to you."

She let out a ragged sigh and rubbed her arms. "Can't you understand? I don't earn anything working at the church. And Lester's Social Security isn't enough for me to qualify for a loan."

"Then get a different job. A real forty-hour-a-week job, like the rest of the world has to do," I added, losing patience with her.

She stiffened. "I happen to believe that raising children is the most important job a woman can do."

So do I! I wanted to shout. *That's why I need my inheri-*

tance, so I can afford to be at home and raise my child. But Alice didn't need to know my business.

"Nice try, Alice, but it won't work. First of all, Daniel is nearly grown. He doesn't need you hovering over him anymore. Second, part of raising a child is providing for him. Lots of mothers have to work, you know. And they manage just fine."

That's when she finally resorted to tears. "Isn't it enough that he's lost his father? Now you want to yank his home out from under him, too?"

"You can *buy* the place," I repeated in what I hoped was a maddeningly patient tone. "Get a paying job, buy the house and he won't have to move."

"You make it sound so simple, but it'll take years to save for a down payment."

"Then borrow it from Carl."

When she didn't respond to that, my sensors went up. "What's the matter? Carl won't pony up? I thought you two were getting married."

"I never said that."

"Well, Daniel sure seems to think so. Did you know—" I broke off. I wasn't going to break the kid's confidence just to make a point.

"Did I know what?" she asked, her voice sharp now. She might be easy to push around on other matters, but when it came to Daniel she developed a backbone. And fangs.

"Did you know that…" Tripod chose that moment to lumber up the steps "…that Tripod's not interested in eating your little morsel of a dog anymore?"

She looked down at Tripod, who was grinning and wagging his tail like a little boy who'd been having so much fun but was tired and hungry now and ready for bed.

"How did he lose his leg?"

"An ex-boyfriend hit him with his car. I took him to the vet but his leg was too bad to save. I kept the dog but got rid of the guy. Of course that was a couple of boyfriends ago," I added just to annoy her.

It worked if her thinning lips and flaring nostrils were any indication. "You're as bad as Mother," she muttered.

A big red flag slapped in a bull's face couldn't have roused a temper greater than mine. I sprang to my feet, shaking with fury. "Our mother was an emotional cripple who didn't know how to take care of herself or her children. She never held a job, never did anything but live in this place and use it to attract people to her. Who does that sound more like, you or me?"

Her face went pale, but I didn't quit. "Mom needed other people around her all the time, picking up the slack, petting her, telling her what a great person she was when the truth was, she was totally helpless. Who does that sound more like, you or me? *I'm* not the one who sold land that wasn't mine, Alice. You're such a wimp, I bet you didn't even get the full market price."

When she again started to cry, I rolled my eyes. "I knew it! So why'd you do it, Alice? Why'd you sell that land, probably for a song, to your church? So everyone would think you were such a great person? Such a great Christian? So good. So generous. How is that so different from what Mom did?"

"At least I never did drugs or…or slept with men I didn't even know!"

"No. You just prayed a lot and convinced yourself that your piety made everything else okay. Well, it didn't. And just for the record," I said as I opened the door to let Tripod inside, "I never did drugs or slept with men I didn't know, either."

I don't know why I told her that. I didn't need to justify myself to her. Let her think I was a drug-using slut like our mother. So what? I had quit caring about her opinion when she wouldn't leave this hellhole with me twenty-three years ago. So why had I defended myself to her?

I charged upstairs, slammed into my room, then just stood there, confused, pissed as hell, and…and sad. What a crappy childhood we'd had. Were we ever going to get over it?

You'd think after that confrontation, that I wouldn't have been able to sleep. And at first I couldn't. But then I went into my new study, pulled out the three books I'd bought on child rearing, and curled up on the daybed in my new sitting room. Tripod settled at my feet, and I put on a CD of Strauss waltzes. Waltzes are one of my secret vices. Romance novels, too.

Anyway, in the small pool of golden light cast by the bedside lamp, I started to read about the first three months of a baby's life, how babies are adventurers in a whole new world and how everything a mother does has an impact on her infant's perception of that world. Security, stability, comfort, stimulation. Those were the things I had to supply for my baby, every minute of every day. That's why I wanted my inheritance, so I wouldn't have to work outside the home, at least until my baby started kindergarten. So I could give her the best start a child could get.

Despite my blowup with Alice, I knew she'd tried to do that for Daniel. But it was my turn now. My baby's turn.

As I closed my eyes and rested the book on my chest, I imagined my baby, sweet and beautiful and smiling up at me with the most innocent, trusting look in the world. I wasn't going to fail her—or him. Jessie Anne Vidrine," I murmured as I sunk into slumber. "Or Jesse Andrew Vidrine. I'm your mom, baby heart. I'll always be your mom."

CHAPTER 6

Alice was gone by the time I came downstairs the next morning. The truth is, I stayed upstairs until I heard her leave. I didn't want to see her, accuse her or argue with her. I'd slept hard and heavy and awakened groggy, and the last thing I wanted was to start up with her all over again.

Tripod was anxious to get out. Call of nature. In his beeline to the front door, he didn't even pause to harass Angel, who lay in a patch of sunshine on the living room floor. I went into the kitchen, made a fresh pot of coffee, then went out onto the porch. Daniel was gone; it was just me, the dogs and my ghosts.

Maybe that's why I decided to call Coco. So I wouldn't have to deal with the nasty specter of my childhood that poisoned this house. I considered the fact that it was only seven o'clock in California but decided it was too bad for him.

"What?" he answered on the third ring.

"Hey, Coco. It's Red." To him I was Red. But to the rest of the world I was back to being Zoe.

"Red? What the hell?"

"Oh, dear, did I wake you up?"

"Shit, no. I haven't been to bed yet. Where are you? What the crap is going on anyway? G.G. is—"

"Look," I broke in before he could get up a head of steam. "Here's the deal. I've left G.G. for good this time, and I won't be back. I won't be going on tour with him. I won't be babysitting him from town to town. And I won't be on his stupid reality TV show."

"Now wait a minute, Red."

"No. You wait a minute. I'm done, Coco. I'm done."

"Well, that's just plain stupid. One season on that show could make you a very rich girl."

I closed my eyes against the temptation. "*If* it gets picked up, and *if* it's a hit."

"What 'if'? It's a shoo-in."

"You know what? I don't care if it is. I'm sure he can find some other bimbo to take care of him."

"But... But he loves you, Red. G.G. really loves you," Coco swore in this smooth, convincing voice. It was his best asset as G.G.'s manager. If he would lay off the booze and drugs, he could be a great manager. The sky could be the limit. But he was just one more sad example of talent and drive sabotaged by that scene.

"G.G. has never loved anyone," I retorted. "Except maybe that electric-blue six-string that he swears brings him good luck. He may need me for all sorts of reasons. But he damned sure doesn't love me."

"Is that what this is about? Because he doesn't say he loves you often enough? I thought you were a realist, Red. That you'd been around long enough to know how it works."

It's funny because, until I got pregnant, I *had* known how it works. I didn't love G.G. any more than he loved me. He'd been fun, and life with him had been exciting—except for when it was awful. But I'd managed for almost three years like that, being Guitar God Givens's main squeeze and feeling like the good outweighed the bad.

Then, all in one day I got tired of that life. And even though I didn't believe in love between men and women—I really think it's all a crock made up by Hallmark and the diamond industry—I had begun to believe in motherly love. Because God knows I already loved this baby growing inside me.

It scared me how much I loved this baby.

"You know what, Coco? I'm done with this conversation. Tell G.G. thanks for the three years. It was fun, but I'm moving on. And so should he."

"But Red—wait. That TV deal is almost wrapped up—"

"Bye-bye." I ended the call. And that fast I was done with him, with Coco and G.G. and the whole aging-rockers-who-don't-want-to-grow-up scene.

I tossed my phone on the bed, then took a long, steamy shower. Afterward, with my hair still wet and not a lick of makeup on, I hiked over to Harriet's house. I guess she was almost as lonesome as me because Tripod and I spent the whole day there. She was transplanting tomato, pepper, cucumber and squash seedlings from flats into the garden, and since it was hard for her to kneel down I volunteered to do it. She sat on a red-and-white metal lawn chair in the shade of a young pecan tree, while I dug and planted and generally ruined my already haphazard manicure.

It was the first day I didn't dwell on leaving G.G. or confronting Alice, my twin nightmares. I'd taken those two giant steps and was still standing. Now I was in wait mode. So I sat in the April sunshine, not worrying about getting sunburned and freckled, just savoring this very weird sense of freedom.

When I laughed to myself, Harriet looked up from her knitting. "That's good, you laughing. What are you thinking about?"

I chuckled again and lifted my face to the sun. "I was thinking about how free I feel, how unworried and content. Crazy, huh?" I opened my eyes. "Considering that I'm pregnant, unemployed and homeless, I shouldn't be feeling this good."

"That's one way of looking at it. Or you could say that you're pregnant and you've come back home. Maybe that's a truer picture."

I shook my head in fond exasperation. "Whatever. That place will never feel like home to me. But I guess it is better than sleeping in rest stops." I yawned. "Man, I slept like a log last night, yet I'm already sleepy."

"Take a nap, then. Lots of pregnant women do."

So I did. I stretched out on a glider on her front porch, and before I realized it the afternoon was gone and Harriet was inside watching *Jeopardy*. I could hear the distinctive theme song, and it only increased my sense of well-being.

This was the kind of house a child should grow up in, I

thought as I blinked back the cobwebs in my head. It was far from fancy—nothing like G.G.'s place in Palm Springs. But it was comfortable and warm. And safe. I put one foot on the porch floor and started the glider moving. I could smell the sweet, citrusy fragrance of roses vining up the corner of the porch, and another nutty, baked aroma from inside. Biscuits? Cookies?

I sat up, hungry as a bear. More pregnancy symptoms.

"Well, hello," Harriet said when I went inside. She was sitting with her feet up. "I have fresh bread in the kitchen. And butter from a farm up the road."

"I've died and gone to heaven!" Bustling around in her kitchen felt so good. A domestic goddess I am not. But even I can manage bread and butter and two big glasses of milk.

We were watching the local news with Angela Hill on CBS when I blurted, "Joe Reeves asked me out."

She looked at me over the top rim of her glasses. "Joe from the newspaper? How did you meet him?"

"I was going to the library. What do you know about him?"

"Not a lot, but what I know I like. He's lived here on the north shore for a few years with his son."

"What happened to his wife?"

"She's an actress, up in New York, I think. Just as he was getting sick of the whole celebrity scene—you know, he was a reporter in New Orleans—well, her career was taking off. She moved to New York. He moved here."

"They're divorced?"

"They are. And she's involved with some director. Or maybe he's a playwright. Anyway, I read about it in *People* magazine."

I groaned. "Not you, too."

She laughed. "It's entertaining. Besides, I always wanted to dance on Broadway."

"I think your USO audiences were a lot more deserving. So, has Joe been linked to any women around here?"

"So you're interested." She grinned at me.

"Not really. I just want to know if he's a regular jerk or a major jerk."

She chuckled and shook her head. "Such a cynic. But let me think. I did hear about him dating Marjorie Hammond. She teaches music at Covington High. But that was some time ago. I don't get out like I used to, so I miss out on a lot of local gossip. But I know I haven't heard anything bad about him."

I slathered butter on another slice of bread. "Damn this is good. I don't know why I agreed to go out with him. It's not really a date, though. We're going to the Strawberry Festival, and his son will be with us."

"I'm pretty sure he thinks it's a date, Zoe. The question is, do you?"

"No. Maybe. I don't know." I blew out a breath. "The thing is, I don't want him to figure out my connection to G.G. and that whole scene. I mean, you know how reporters are. Anything to sell more copies of their papers."

"So why did you agree to the date?"

I chewed my bread a long time, but eventually I had to

swallow it. "Because he's good-looking, I guess, and I need to feel attractive. Otherwise I start feeling useless, an unnecessary waste of space."

That brought her feet to the floor. "You are not a waste of space. But you know, one day you *are* going to be fat and old."

I snorted. "I'm going to be fat in another month or two. And right after that I'm turning forty. Official middle age."

Harriet shook her head. "You need to realize that there's a lot more to you than your long legs, red hair and green eyes."

"Don't forget the boobs." I stuck out my chest. "Men love the boobs."

She frowned at me. "Can't you be serious for one minute?"

I blinked at her stern tone.

"Look, Zoe. You are so much more than just how you look. Do you think that baby is going to care how pretty you are or aren't? Of course not. How you care for her, love her and hold her—that's what will prove your worth to your child. Let me ask you this," she said when I didn't respond. "Was your mother pretty?"

I stiffened. My mother had been beautiful. Ethereal. The quintessential hippie girl, a fey sprite with her long blond hair, clear blue eyes and pert, unfettered-by-a-bra breasts.

I shot Harriet an aggrieved look. "That was a low blow. But you're right. She was beautiful. She was also the world's worst mother." I took a suddenly shaky breath. "What if I'm just like her?"

"Oh, honey, you're not. Of course you're not. The fact

that you're worried about being like her only proves to me that you won't be."

I held on to that thought as I walked down her long driveway, then across the road and down the path that cut through the woods. Tonight I would read further in that baby book. By the time Jessie/Jesse arrived I would be on top of things, the best mom I could be.

It had been a good day, a normal day. The first in a very long time, and I decided not to spoil it by arguing with Alice tonight. Instead I'd talk to Daniel about that article, or take a drive down to the lakefront. Something peaceful.

Unfortunately Carl's maroon Oldsmobile sat in front of the house like a warning sign: Danger; Keep Out.

Of course, I walked straight in. "Hey, Alice. Hi, Carl," I said. They sat at the dining room table with papers spread everywhere.

"Hello." At least Alice pretended to be civil. Carl just flatout glared at me, then grabbed a piece of paper and shook it at me. "Alice got this letter from your sleazy lawyer."

"Good," I said, almost chortling at how much he despised me.

"How you can do this to your own sister is beyond me!"

"I'm just claiming what is mine, Carl. Which isn't your business, anyway." With that I sauntered up the stairs. But later as I sat in the bathtub I realized I had made a tactical error. Instead of aggravating Carl for the pure fun of it, I ought to be encouraging him to marry Alice and buy this house with her. That would get me my money a hell of a lot faster than going through the courts to establish my claim and *then* putting the house up for sale.

Only later as I was settling in with my book did I realize that I hadn't heard a peep out of Daniel. When he didn't answer my knock I peeked inside. Empty.

Downstairs I found Alice alone in the dining room. "Carl left?" I asked.

"Yes."

"Where's Daniel?"

"A friend's house."

Not Josh's, I was willing to bet. I glanced at her papers. "So. Are you and Carl figuring out a way to buy the house from me?"

Only then did she look up at me. "The whole world doesn't revolve around you, Zoe. I do have other things going on in my life."

Ooh. The kitten was spitting and hissing. "Something more important than your home and Daniel's? More important than being charged with fraud?"

"How can you do this to me?" she shouted. "Why do you hate me so much?"

I planted my fists on my hips. "I don't hate you. I basically don't give a damn about you one way or the other. All I want is what's mine. But while we're on the subject of hate, what am I supposed to think about someone who tells everyone that I'm dead? Maybe that *she* hates *me?*"

"I don't hate you. You're twisting everything around to justify what you're doing."

"Really? Well, tell me, how do you justify what you did

to me? How do you justify selling property that wasn't yours to sell?"

"I didn't know where you were!"

I just stared at her. "You could have found me. You saw me in that video—it wouldn't have taken more than a few phone calls. And even if you couldn't find me, you could have sold the land for its fair market value, then put my half aside in a bank account."

She shoved away from the table and stood. "The last two times I called you, you said you didn't want anything to do with this place. First, you wouldn't come home when Mom was dying—"

"You never said she was dying. You said she was sick. And you never said it was AIDS!"

"—then you wouldn't come here for her funeral."

I crossed my arms, trying to squash any guilt I felt over that. "This is all a smokescreen, Alice, and you know it. You loved Mom—I didn't. That doesn't change the situation. You *gave* that land away to your church when it wasn't yours to give."

She looked away and I was smart enough, for once, to just let my words hang there over her, smothering her with guilt.

"It was for a good cause," she finally said in a more subdued tone.

"You mean your church? The problem is, that's *your* good cause, Alice. Not mine."

"I know," she admitted, to my great surprise. She looked up at me with this earnest expression on her face. "The thing is, Zoe, it really is a good cause. We do so much good work in the community. Tutoring. Play groups. Pastoral counseling. All kinds of community outreach like—"

"Alcoholics Anonymous? Al-Anon? That sort of thing?" I threw in. But I already knew what her answer would be.

"Well, not those. But we have grief counseling."

"Domestic abuse or suicide hotlines?"

"No," she answered more slowly.

"You see, that's my point. My money should be spent on *my* charities, not yours."

"But we do a lot of good, Zoe. We're a small church but we do what we can. If you would just come over there with me you'd see. We have this—"

"Okay."

That stopped her with her mouth open. "What?"

"Okay. I'll go over there with you. Maybe tomorrow."

"You'll go to church with me? But…we don't have any services tomorrow."

"That's okay." I was being devious, but what the hell. It wasn't the church service I was interested in or their play-acting at counseling services. They weren't involved in substance abuse counseling or suicide or domestic abuse, which said to me they didn't really want to get their hands dirty. No druggies or drunks or beat-up women for them. Uh-uh. But I just kept my mouth shut. Let Alice think I was interested in her church and its "outreach" programs. All I wanted was to see the place and calculate its worth. Because if Alice couldn't pay me, maybe they could.

"So," I went on, wanting to change the subject. "What are you working on here, church business?"

I could tell she didn't really want to say. But using my most sincere smile, I sat down across from her and waited. Pushover that she was, she quickly caved in.

"I've been working on a book."

"A book? You mean like a novel or something?"

"No." She hesitated. "It's sort of a guidebook. For women who are married to ministers."

Didn't that just figure? "Is there much demand for a book like that?" *Can you make enough money on it to buy this place from me?*

"I hope so."

I scanned the table with its separate piles of paper-clipped papers. "Is it all written?"

"Mostly," she said, beginning to warm up to my interest. "I started it before Lester got sick. Then after he passed on, I just lost interest. But Daniel's been encouraging me."

"And Carl? What does he think?"

When she stiffened, I had my answer. He wasn't encouraging. What a surprise. But I waited to hear her version of it.

"Carl thinks it's a good idea," she said. "But, well, he has a lot of suggestions that I hadn't thought about."

Yeah, I bet. "What's the title?"

"I was calling it *The Minister's Left Hand*. You know, God is at his right hand and his wife—his helpmate—is at his left."

"I like it." I had to admit it was a good title.

"But Carl thinks it's better to be straightforward. *The Minister's Wife: How to Support Your Husband's Ministry.*

"Boring," I said, stretching out the word. "Yours is much better."

"You think so?"

It was pitiful how easily Alice could be manipulated. Not that I was manipulating her about the book title. I meant that. But it was obvious she yearned for approval, if not Carl's, then she'd take mine. That was our mother's doing, of course. She'd trained us both to yearn fruitlessly for love and approval from others.

But though I'd got over it, Alice obviously hadn't. It made me sad for her. She was the kind of person who took care of everyone: sick mother; sick husband. And now she was taking on another old man whom she'd eventually have to nurse.

Still, what could I do to change that? Nothing.

Feeling awkward now, I wrapped my arms around me and gave her a halfhearted smile. "Well, I guess I'll turn in."

Later I sat up in bed reading, listening for the faint sounds of Alice moving around the house. She went outside on the front porch for a while. Then she came in, and soon the hall light winked out.

It was weird. This was my third night here, but there was something about being here alone with Alice that brought back a new flood of memories. And for once they weren't all bad.

I remembered when I was nine and she was twelve, and we finally claimed one of the upstairs bedrooms as ours. Up till then we'd slept wherever we could find a bed. On a couch or in a sleeping bag on the porch. An old mattress on the floor in any one of the bedrooms. I hadn't cared back then. I mean, I didn't like it, especially when there were all kinds of people sleeping here and there. But back then I didn't understand any other way of living.

But Alice did. She'd been to the homes of a couple of girls from town, and she'd seen their canopy beds and eyelet curtains and Barbie doll collections. It was her idea to take one of the upstairs rooms just for us. Only she didn't know how.

That's where I came in.

First I stole a padlock from the hardware store in Oracle. The next week I stole two pairs of hasps. It took us all day to install the hasps—one set on the inside, one on the outside—but we did it. Since Mom hardly ever came upstairs, we took two mattresses from the High Way Room, a set of venetian blinds from another room and an old dresser from the hall.

From then on we scrounged everything we could: a torn rug from someone's trash pile, a broken lamp that Harriet helped us rewire. We could be really cute and appealing when we wanted to be, and we learned that in the world outside our farm, cuteness counted for a lot. Nobody likes a scruffy, dirty ragamuffin. But when we were clean and combed, and yes-ma'amed and no-sirred people to death, they would go out of their way to help us. Especially old people.

I stared out the open window and stroked Tripod, who'd snuck up onto the bed—as if I wouldn't notice. Alice had been a plump, golden-haired angel of a child, small for her age, and once I'd turned ten, shorter than me. I'd been skinny and freckled with clouds of red, wavy hair. Put us in gingham dresses with ribbons in our hair, and we looked like we'd stepped out of a 1950s photograph.

Those dresses were the only good thing our mother did for us. Every now and then she liked to dress us up and show off how pretty we were, like that was some great reflection on her. Whenever she had a few bucks she would order clothes for us from catalogs.

Yeah, the dresses came from Mom, but the ingenuity was all ours.

I wondered if Alice remembered those days. On impulse I sat up and swung my legs around to get up. Then I stopped. I wasn't going downstairs to talk to Alice. No way. All that would accomplish was to show her my weak side. And I couldn't do that.

Maybe one day when I was settled in my new life with my new baby, and things were calmer, she and I could talk about those days. I'd watched *Oprah* and *Dr. Phil* enough to know that she and I both had unresolved issues from our childhood.

Unresolved issues. Now there was an understatement.

But now was not the time to resolve them.

So I swung my legs back into the bed and pulled the covers up to my chin. And when I still couldn't sleep, I got up, found my CD player and put one of Daniel's CDs on. The most lyrical one.

The message was too hokey for me. Prayers didn't do any good except for building up false hope. And looking up to the heavens too long would only get bird crap in your eyes.

But the melodies were soothing, and the harmonies were good. I'd give the band that much.

I yawned and turned my back to the window. I needed to work on that article. Maybe tomorrow…

CHAPTER 7

I woke up nauseous. It didn't happen every morning, but it was happening today, worse than any other time so far.

Sitting up made it worse, so I lay back down, breathing through my nose, praying it would ease enough for me to at least make it to the bathroom.

Of course, that's when Tripod chose to start up. He stood at the door whining. I understood that he needed to get outside to take care of business, but for the moment he had to wait. Then he started to bark.

"Please, Tripod," I pleaded, until a fresh wave of nausea hit me. But he had his own miseries. If I didn't let him out soon...

"Zoe?"

Alice. Thank God.

At the sound of her voice, Tripod's barking became more desperate. I closed my eyes and waited. Sure enough, her knock sounded on the door. "Zoe? Are you there?"

"Yes," I croaked out.

"Are you all right?"

"No."

She opened the door. Tripod bolted out. "Could you let him outside?" I asked.

"What's wrong?"

"I don't feel well. Just…let him out. Please?"

From downstairs Tripod was raising a racket, with Angel joining in. That sent Alice down after him. But she was back in less than a minute. "What's wrong? You look terrible."

"Thanks." I kept my eyes closed. "I think maybe I caught a bug or something."

"Do you have a fever?"

"No. I mean, I don't think so."

"Let me see."

I opened my eyes just in time to see her coming toward me with her hand extended to feel my forehead. Full mothering mode. Only I didn't need mothering.

"Get away," I muttered, turning my head aside. Just that little movement and my stomach lurched.

Her eyes narrowed. "Are you hungover? Have you brought alcohol or…or *drugs* into my home?" Her voice got high and screechy.

"No!" I jerked upright. "I told you, I *don't* do drugs, and I *don't* get drunk!"

But I *was* going to throw up. I tossed the covers aside. "And this is *my* house now, not yours," I swore as I bolted for the bathroom.

I managed to reach the toilet before I lost it. But as my stomach clenched and revolted and tried to spew out every meal I'd eaten for the last three months, I wasn't so sure I was going to survive the next ten minutes. I retched and choked and retched some more until my body was a limp rag and my face was wet with tears and snot and disgusting drool.

After the worst was over, Alice handed me a damp facecloth and then a glass of water to rinse out my mouth. I didn't want her help. Anyone's but hers. But I was grateful all the same. I hate throwing up worse than anything. And pregnancy throw-up is worse than regular throwing up. At least with normal vomiting you feel better afterward. But not when you're pregnant. Nothing helps. Nothing except time.

Alice left as I cleaned up. She came back with crackers. "You're pregnant, aren't you?"

Shit, shit, shit! "Me, pregnant? Yeah, right," I scoffed, stalling for time. "It's probably food poisoning."

"Yeah, right," she echoed. "Here." She thrust the crackers at me.

"Ugh," I mumbled, turning away from the sight of food.

"Keep them by the bed, then," she said. "Nibble on one or two of them before you get up in the morning. It worked for me."

"I'm *not* pregnant," I repeated. But even I knew it was a useless lie. She followed me across the hall, then stood in the doorway as I stared at the bed. I wanted to crawl back in, pull the covers up and go back to sleep. But I suspected I wouldn't be able to.

"How far along are you?"

I ignored her and turned to the dresser, looking for my hairbrush.

She cleared her throat. "You're not going to, you know, get rid of it, are you? Because I can—"

"No!" I whirled around, then grabbed the dresser

when my head spun and my stomach turned over. "Hell's bells, Alice! Do you think you're the only person in the world with any sense of morality? Do you think you're the only person who knows right from wrong? But of course you think that," I went on. "Anyone who doesn't look and talk and think like you is in league with the devil, right?" I was fading fast. "Just…just get the hell out of my bedroom."

When she hesitated, my voice turned vicious. "Get out of here, Alice, before I have you evicted from my house. Now!"

She went, and for about two seconds I basked in satisfaction. I'd sure shown her. Then depression set in bigtime.

I was sick; I was pregnant; I was alone.

I sat on the side of the bed, wanting to call someone, but who? My friends from my old life were not real, to-the-bone friends. And most of them were friends of G.G.'s.

As for my new life, it hadn't really started yet. It couldn't until I had my money and split this town.

There was no one for me to call, except maybe Harriet. Cheered by the thought of her serene spirit and welcoming kitchen, I sat down on the bed and began to nibble on a cracker. Maybe I'd go to the library for a while, then drop by my lawyer's office. After that I'd go see Harriet.

But an hour later when I had showered and dressed and come downstairs, Alice was waiting for me. "Feeling better?"

I hated that she was being so nice to me. "I feel like crap," I said. "But I'll live."

She pursed her lips, and for a moment I was reminded of the Church Lady on *Saturday Night Live*. Sensible outfit with a mid-calf shirt and a nondescript blouse. Ugly shoes and her hair in a ponytail low on her neck. Her only jewelry was her wedding band.

"You're not working at the church today?" I said as I headed for the kitchen and more crackers.

"I was waiting for you." At my confused look she added, "Yesterday you said you wanted to go visit the church."

Oh, hell. "Did I say this morning?"

"Well, no. But I thought…"

"Fine. We'll go," I snapped. I already felt like crap; why not get the torture over with? Plus, when I saw my attorney, I might be able to sic him on the church as well as Alice.

I made myself two slices of toast. No butter. She wisely kept her mouth shut about my pregnancy. But when we left the house and started toward the garage, I balked. "Let's walk."

"Walk? You mean through the woods? But I have on my good shoes."

Those were her good shoes? "The path isn't muddy. I walked it the other day. Besides, I want to see exactly where the dividing line is between the church property and mine."

She didn't like that. But again she kept her mouth shut and followed me.

It was a pretty day, warm with a vivid blue sky and no hint of the humidity the coastal south was famous for. Wild azaleas were blooming gold and orange, so unlike their hot-pink cultivated cousins. "I bet Harriet would like one of those in her garden."

"Harriet?" Alice said. "You've been to see Harriet? You know, she goes to our church, too."

Harriet went to Alice's church? I tried to hide my disappointment, but it was hard. Why would free-spirited Harriet join any church, especially a homeschooling, hide-our-kids-from-the-world kind of place like that? And why hadn't she told me that before?

Needless to say, I was in a pissy mood by the time we reached the church. "So you sold everything past the creek," I stated. "How many acres was that?"

"Twenty-three or so," she said in this low, guilty voice.

"Leaving fifteen with the house."

"Yes."

"I need a copy of the act of sale with any surveys, appraisals. Stuff like that."

"Please, Zoe. Can't we figure this out ourselves without any lawyers getting involved?"

"So I can get screwed? I don't think so. I want to know what that land was worth when you sold it and what it's worth now." I opened the church's front door. "This place is bigger than it looks."

Alice showed me everything. She didn't have much choice. But while she introduced me to the church secretary, expounding on the Sunday school classes, the homeschooling center and study rooms and the pastoral counseling center, I was doing mental calculations. They'd sunk a lot of money into this place. While I didn't want the land back from them, I sure wasn't about to let them get away with robbery either.

"I've saved my favorite spot for last," Alice said. Good thing, because I was beginning to poop out. Between getting sick and not eating a decent breakfast, I was seriously lagging. And we still had to get back home.

I meant get back to the *house*.

But I wasn't letting Alice see my fatigue, especially since I'd been the one to insist on our walking.

"The grief group built it," she said. "They were planning it even before Lester got sick. After he died, more people joined in." She led me behind the church annex with its offices and kitchen and meeting rooms, past a small fenced playground and into a shaded area where the trees hadn't been all sliced down. I remembered this area, a low spot with the only stand of cypress trees on the farm.

"I call it Cypress Cathedral," she said in a hushed voice.

I could see why. The same group of towering cypress trees plus a group of younger ones made a compact semicircle that had been cleared of all the underbrush. It was a small space but very tall, like an old Catholic church, only floored with red cypress needles and scented with wildflowers, bog and the faint biting scent of cypress. Two benches had been fitted beneath low-hanging branches, each one angled to look over the undisturbed woodlands.

It was…strange. The church buildings had been steel and glass and concrete block. Nothing appealing or affecting about them. But this simple place felt almost holy.

I shook my head against the feeling. I was tired; I was

hungry; I was light-headed. Yeah, the place was pretty, but most woods were. It wasn't any more holy than any other place on the planet.

"I'm heading back," I said. "I have things to do. Places to go. People to meet."

"Wait, Zoe." Alice caught my arm. "Can't we…can't we find a way to get along?"

"Sure we can. You can announce to the world that you lied about me being dead. Then you can give me my share of our inheritance. It's easy, Alice. And it's fair. If the tables were turned, you'd want the same thing from me."

Her hand fell away from my arm. "Yes, you're right. I would."

Well, well, well. We were making progress.

I left it at that. As a child I'd fought and argued and butted my head against the brick wall of my mother's self-involvement, all to no avail. I'd learned the hard way to bide my time, to make my plans and keep my own counsel until I was ready to act. It was a talent that had served me well in L.A., too, dealing with illogical musicians and temperamental boyfriends. Alice was just more of the same: impulsive and unwilling to take responsibility for her poor decisions and bad behavior.

But she wasn't getting out of this. Besides, now that she'd figured out I was pregnant, I didn't have to be in such a hurry. I mean, I still needed my money, and I wanted to be settled somewhere else before Jesse/Jessie was born. But I could afford to wait her out, to force her hand.

We walked back to the house in silence but not an ugly

silence. A spring breeze had the branches swaying and the leaves dancing. A pair of squirrels raced around the thick trunk of a water oak, and a cardinal flitted through the low hanging branches of a sweet gum tree.

Eden. That's the word that came to mind. Eden couldn't have been prettier than springtime in south Louisiana. Amazing how fast people could mess up such an idyllic place. My mother had pretended our farm was a modern-day Eden. People free to behave as they wanted. Unfettered by rules. Free from conventional mores.

She'd used those two words a lot, free and unfettered. But I'd never felt free or unfettered in this place. More like trapped. Kids were always trapped by their parents' bad decisions. My father hadn't known or cared about my existence. For my mother I'd been like a toy, entertainment to be shared with her friends. So had Alice. Then as we grew, we'd been alternately her servants or her scapegoats.

Eden? As we emerged from the woods and spied the back of the house, I snorted. More like the bowels of hell.

I stayed only long enough to grab my keys and go. On the way to town I passed Sara Mae's. I flipped it off as I sped by. No way was I ever setting foot in there again.

Once at the library, I buried myself in the microfilm. My mother had died at home with only Alice to nurse her. There hadn't been hospices for AIDS patients back in 1986. They were the unclean, the untouchables of their day.

I stared at the article that announced her death, at the photo some unscrupulous creep had taken of her close to the end. My beautiful mother, so skinny her head looked like a skull, with bruised-looking eyes and thin, patchy hair. Without the caption, I would never have known it was her.

Again the letters to the editor had been vile. The wages of sin. Cavorting with the devil. God's retribution.

I closed my eyes, trying to remember her in better days. What I saw, though, was Alice's face superimposed over hers. Blonde hair, blue eyes, pretty smile.

How much of the anger I threw at Alice was really left-over anger at my mother?

That sobered me up. I needed to keep things straight. Alice's only real sin was to sell my land—and to tell people that I was dead.

And not to leave with me when I'd begged her to.

But no. I couldn't hold that against her. She'd wanted to stay and that was her decision to make.

Damn, but I hated to be fair about things when all I really wanted to do was strike fast and hard and then leave. I turned off the microfilm machine, removed the film and put it away. My life history as reported by the *Northshore News*—and occasionally by the *Times-Picayune*.

That made me think of Joe and our date for tomorrow. I shouldn't have accepted, but now that I had I meant to have a good time. I walked down the stairs, waving to Kenyatta, who was checking out books for a lady and her two toddlers.

I stared at the little boy and girl. Were they twins? Their mom looked up at me and smiled. I smiled back and felt better as I left the library. Soon I would be just like her, taking Jesse/Jessie to the library, listening to story hour, checking out books. I could hardly wait.

My good mood lingered even when my lawyer's secretary informed me that he was out. But she did have an envelope for me since I'd told him not to mail anything to the farm. I sat in Jenny Jeep and scanned the documents. He'd found the act of sale recorded at city hall. Twenty-three thousand dollars! Only a thousand dollars an acre? He also showed an act of sale for a property not far from there that had sold for eighty-five hundred an acre.

I did a quick, mental calculation. That would make our twenty-three acres worth nearly two hundred thousand dollars! Damn! That would get me started off in a new life pretty well.

He'd also included a note saying that an appraisal of the remaining house and property would cost three hundred and twenty-five dollars. I went back into his office and wrote the check right then and there.

Afterward I cruised down Main Street until I found a little lunch spot. But instead of eating there, I ordered two lunches to go. Then I headed for Harriet's.

It's funny how just one person's smile of greeting, so utterly sincere, can make everything that's wrong in the world seem right. "You brought me lunch? Why, thank you, my dear. How sweet of you," she exclaimed.

"It's my bribe, a way to make it okay for me to hang out here."

"Now, Zoe, you know you don't have to bribe me. I'm

pleased as punch to have company." She folded her newspaper and put the crossword puzzle aside, making room at her kitchen table. "Napkins are in that drawer. Forks are by the sink."

Such a simple thing, sharing a meal at a kitchen table. The only time G.G. and I ever ate a meal together was either at a restaurant, mainly when we were on the road, or else side by side in bed with the TV on. And even that was rare. Mostly we each grabbed a meal or a snack on the run alone.

An article I'd read in *Parents* magazine while waiting to see my ob-gyn in L.A. had stressed the importance of families eating meals together every day. I planned to do that with Jesse/Jessie. Every single day. All three meals.

Feeling amazingly contented, I put a hand on my stomach and smiled at Harriet.

"You're in a good mood," she said. "Ooh, gumbo and garlic bread."

"Alice figured out that I'm pregnant. I was sick as a dog this morning, and she saw me, so…" I shrugged.

"How do you feel about that?"

"Spoken like a psychotherapist," I retorted. "But actually… I don't know. I guess its okay. It doesn't change anything, though. She's trying to be real nice to me, but today I found out that she sold the back acreage for a fraction of its true worth."

"To the Victory Church," Harriet said.

"Yeah." I paused and stared at her. "Your church."

"That's right."

"You were a member when Alice's husband was the pastor?"

"Oh, yes. He was an excellent speaker. Even when I didn't agree with him, I always enjoyed listening to him."

Suddenly my gumbo lost its appeal. "You don't think he was too old for Alice? Too, I don't know. Old-fashioned? Uptight?"

She laughed. "Lester Collins was too old for *me*, and I was nearly twenty years older than him. But he and Alice seemed well matched. She wasn't unhappy, Zoe. And when he died, she was devastated."

I shook my head. "I don't get it. And now she's got this guy Carl sniffing around after her. Daniel doesn't want them to get married, you know."

She wrinkled her nose at me, then swallowed a spoonful of gumbo. "That doesn't surprise me. Carl's not a bad man. But he's awfully rigid."

"You don't say."

"But Joe isn't. Or so I hear," she added with a teasing smile.

I started in on my gumbo in earnest. "I guess he *isn't* rigid. He's a reporter, isn't he? And they're known for contorting themselves every which way to get a story."

"So why go out with him?"

I considered a long moment. "I guess I just like living dangerously."

She gave me a knowing look. "Plus he's a very good-looking man."

"Gee, I hadn't noticed."

She laughed and we ate in silence for a while. Then out of the blue she said, "You could stay here, you know. Have your baby and live here with me."

I stared at her with my mouth opened. "I couldn't do that."

"Of course you could."

I wanted to. Every single cell in my body reacted with a resounding *Yes!* I would absolutely love to have Harriet with me when I had my baby and afterward at home to help me figure out how to be a good mother. But that would mean staying in Oracle.

"Or you could come with me," I ventured. Even as I said the words I knew it was a stupid suggestion.

"Go with you where?" she asked.

Was she actually considering it? I leaned forward. "Anywhere you want. Florida. The Carolina coast. I don't care where."

"If you don't care, then why not here?"

I tilted my head to the side. "C'mon, Harriet. You know why."

"Does my house hold bad memories for you?"

"Of course not. I loved this place when I was a kid. I still do. But…it's too close."

"Yes, I understand why you feel that way. But in time you might not feel so strongly about your old home. You've been gone twenty-three years, remembering it like it was and hating it. Right?"

I nodded.

"You haven't even been back a week," she went on. "Maybe you should just relax a little. See what happens."

When I didn't respond she said, "The offer still stands, Zoe. You're welcome to move in here if you ever want to. Okay?"

I shrugged. "Okay." But as generous as her offer was, I'd lost the optimism I'd arrived with. Only as I drove back to the farm a couple of hours later did it occur to me how important a part Harriet had already assumed in my life. I'd loved her as a kid, then abandoned her when I'd abandoned everyone else in Oracle, Louisiana. As eager as I was to ditch this place once more, the fact was, I didn't want to lose her again.

I pulled up in front of the house and spied Daniel, Tripod and Angel on the porch. It's funny. After vowing to Harriet that I hated the place, for that brief moment I saw it in a different light. A venerable old house. A kid and his dogs. How normal. How wonderfully ordinary.

The kid had already started to get to me. Now Harriet was, too.

I closed my eyes against the pretty scene. I had to remind myself that the only thing that mattered to me was how much the house was worth. Nothing else.

I opened my eyes, and this time I studied the house with a cold, calculating stare. At least two thousand square feet, with fifteen acres, backed up by a stream. In a booming parish like St. Tammany, it had to be worth at least a quarter of a million.

Hell, at that price, even after I sold it, Alice would be entitled to a small portion. Enough for her to put a down payment on a little subdivision house for her and Daniel

She might not like that scenario, but she ought to be grateful. It was a better deal than she'd given me. And she'd have to admit that I wasn't trying to cheat her. She'd tried to screw me over—in the name of God and church and religion. But I wasn't doing anything but getting what was legally mine. Then I'd be gone, out of her hair forever this time.

Somehow, though, the prospect wasn't nearly as appealing as it had been before.

CHAPTER 8

I decided to meet Joe at the Strawberry Festival outside of Hammond instead of at the house. I already regretted agreeing to this "date." What had I been thinking? I should have stayed at the farm and worked on the article I'd begun last night about Daniel and his friends and their musical tastes.

But, instead, here I was, wearing an apple-green halter-top and a green-and-white-print flared skirt with white plastic platform flip-flops. My hair was up in a loose French twist. I had on dangly peridot and coral earrings, a gold ankle bracelet and Coral Seduction polish on all twenty of my nails.

Add to that my retro Chanel sunglasses, and it wasn't a particularly subtle look. But the fact is, I don't know how to do subtle. When your hair is red and you're five foot nine, it's hard to blend in with the crowd.

I sat in Jenny Jeep at the edge of the parking lot, watching for Joe. He hadn't been too thrilled about me driving here myself. But no way was I making myself dependent on a man for anything. Even just a twenty-mile ride home.

He saw me first. I guess my red Jeep with her giant eyelashes painted above her headlights was easy to spot. As he parked and got out with a slender kid of the same dark hair and coloring, I blew out a nervous breath. I'd only had a little nausea this morning. That was a good sign.

I climbed down from Jenny, slung my little Monica Lewinsky bag over my shoulder, and lifted my chin. This wasn't really a date so I didn't need to feel nervous about anything. I was just whiling away the days, passing time until this whole inheritance thing could be settled.

"Glad you made it," Joe said, giving me a quick once-over. Not leering, just…thorough. I ignored the stupid little thrill that shot through me. Old habits die hard, but they *do* eventually die. Certainly my need for male appreciation was dying. If it didn't die on its own, I planned to kill it myself.

"Yes," I said. "Your directions were great." I smiled at the boy slouching beside his dad's Ford Explorer. "Hi. I'm Zoe."

He shook my hand, grinned, showing a mouthful of braces, and turned a faint pink. "Hi. I'm Pete," he said in this voice that cracked on the third word. He blushed harder, but I just smiled. He was skinny and gawky with a mouth full of metal. But give him two or three years and he would be a heartbreaker.

Just like his father.

Pete was saved from further embarrassment when a kid across the parking lot hailed him. "Okay," Joe said. "Keep your phone on and plan on meeting up with me in about an hour and a half. Okay?"

"Sure," Pete said. Then he was off, joining up with three other boys. So much for him chaperoning me and his dad.

Joe waved at the other boys, then turned to me and grinned. "Ready for a real small-town experience?"

We fell into step together. "I don't remember this festival from when I was a kid."

"It's grown a lot in the last fifteen years or so. Do you want to start with food, music or the craft booths? Or are you into carnival rides?"

"No rides," I said. "But yes to all the rest."

So we bought strawberry shortcakes and, while we ate, strolled through the crafts booth. If you like strawberries, this was definitely the place to be. Strawberry pottery, place mats, aprons, art, clocks, linens, clothing, sandals, watches, barrettes and on and on and on.

"You have to let me buy you something," Joe insisted as we laughed over a pair of sunglasses shaped like strawberries, with red frames and rose-colored lenses.

"No, I don't. I'm not really the cutesy type."

He raised his eyebrows. "You have eyelashes painted above your car headlights."

I laughed, too. "You've got me there."

"So a strawberry ring is not completely out of the question," he said, stopping at a jewelry booth. The proprietor, a pretty, dreadlocked woman with beads sewn into her hair, had a wide assortment of silver jewelry, some of it really striking. But she also had a tray of children's jewelry, bright fun stuff, plastic one-size-fits-all kind of stuff.

We settled on a pinkie ring for me. "What about you?" I asked. "I think you need a little strawberry stud earring. Just one, of course."

"But my ear isn't pierced," Joe said. "It was once, but I let it close up."

"When you became a father?"

He shrugged and gave me a one-sided grin. "I was moving into a different stage of my life."

I guess I understood about that.

From somewhere the amplified whine of a guitar rose up, and I heard a roar of approval.

"Looks like the country music is giving way to rock and roll," he commented.

"Which do you prefer?"

"Me? I'm a Tom Petty, Lynyrd Skynyrd, Bruce Springsteen kind of guy. How about you?"

"Oh, I like everything. Except for modern jazz. They try to play the music too—"

"—darned fast," we finished the old lyrics in unison, then laughed.

"I'm sure Pete and his friends are over at the stage," he said.

"Who's playing?" I asked. You can take the girl out of the music industry, but you can't take the music out of the girl.

"Nobody you've ever heard of. Mostly local cover bands. Rock, country, Cajun and blues. Let's check it out."

Whoever they were, they were pretty good for a cover band, playing Rod Stewart's "Maggie May," an old favorite of mine. It was a raised stage, shaded by a giant awning. A crowd of teenagers pressed up against the stage. I couldn't pick out Pete, but Joe pointed him out.

"Does he play?" I asked as the band finished the song with a flourish.

"Who, Pete? Oh, yeah. His mother started him on the piano when he was only seven. Then a couple of years ago he jumped to the guitar."

"Ah, yes. Boys and their guitars."

As if on cue, the lead guitarist let out another soaring note, a searing, quivering whine that morphed into a riff that was a rock classic. The crowd erupted with approval.

I stiffened in recognition. "Harley Nights." One of G.G.'s best-known songs. A guitar player's nightmare that only the best players could do justice to. And this guy was doing it up right.

But that didn't change my reaction. G.G. loved that song. It had made him sinfully rich. But he hated it, too, especially when it continued to get more airplay than his later releases.

I'd met G.G. when "Harley Nights" had first hit the charts and put him on the map. But we hadn't got together then. I'd been with Dirk, and G.G. was too busy plowing his way through the fields of nubile young groupies sprouting in his path. One thing I'd never gone along with was infidelity, sharing my man with anyone else. No way was I following in my mother's insane, self-indulgent, self-destructive path. By my reckoning, she'd never been happy more than a day or two at a time. So why would I follow her example?

One woman, one man. That was my way. Not for life, of course. Monogamy sounded good in theory, but how many people were faithful for their whole lives? But serial monogamy worked for me.

It had taken almost five years until G.G. and I hooked up, and we were together for almost four years after that. So far as I knew, he'd been faithful to me. But I'd connected with him during his decline, both professionally and personally. As his drug problems had increased, his creativity and productivity had plummeted, which in turn had pushed him even deeper into drugs. He'd needed me on so many levels, and I'd jumped right in. But I could see now that trying to rescue him hadn't worked for me, or for him. It had taken my pregnancy to wake me up to how bad things really were.

I listened to the band now, doing a credible version of G.G.'s classic. He would love it, hearing them do justice to his rock-and-roll anthem. If he were here, someone would surely recognize him and the crowd would start chanting his name, forcing him, despite his token reluctance, onto the stage. He would take a guitar and wow the fans and the band with his guitar virtuosity.

Yeah, on stage he was the consummate showman. But afterward in the car going home, in the hotel room, in private where no one but me or Coco or one of the others whose paychecks depended on him could see, he would rage, cursing the idiots who stayed stuck in the past, who couldn't move on or recognize the next big thing. Recognize true musical genius like his. Then he'd get drunk or stoned, find his favorite guitar and try to write something new.

Over and over he had gone through this pattern, and

the new songs had only got worse and worse. He'd blamed his band of course and struck out on his own. I didn't hold out much hope for the new CD's success. But at least now he would be able to console himself that it was *my* fault, not his. I'd left him and he'd fallen apart. That's why his new songs would be a spectacular flop. Then he'd get loaded, write more bad songs, until one day he'd either get sick of the pattern and stop, or else take an overdose and die.

Either way, I wasn't exposing my baby to it.

I stood there, staring at the stage, swaying to the music. "Harley Nights" was, after all, a truly great song. My hand stole down to my stomach. *I hope you have his creative genes. But please, please, don't turn into an insane addict.*

When the final note ended with an explosion of sound, the crowd exploded, too. It was always like this at the end of "Harley Nights," and I wasn't immune to the excitement. But this time it also left me sad. For a while I'd hoped G.G. would be the one. Stupid, I know. If anyone should understand how transient rock star romances were, it was me. But still, I'd hoped.

I didn't hope for such things anymore.

"That was great!" Joe exclaimed, jolting me back to the present. "You know, I saw G. G. Givens play once. It was Houston, about ten years ago. He was really something. He's Pete's guitar idol, you know."

"And every other teenage boy's," I said, pasting a determined smile on my face. "They don't call him Guitar God Givens for nothing."

Next to us a beefy guy guffawed. "Guitar God, maybe," he said to us. "But his girlfriend's apparently not too crazy about him."

His girlfriend? That was me. I froze. On stage the band was firing up on Duran Duran's "The Reflex." But I couldn't move. What did this guy know about G.G. and me?

"What do you mean?" Joe asked him.

The guy guzzled the last of his beer, then wiped his mouth with one wrist. "She dumped him. It's in the *National Star*. She ran out on him. And the hilarious thing is the stupid jerk took out an ad in *People* magazine trying to get her back!" He cracked up over that. "Can you imagine? Paying big bucks for an ad to find the stupid broad who dumped you? I think he must've fried his brains. Or else the broad is the best lay around. Sorry," he added when he saw me staring at him with my mouth sagging open.

But I didn't care about his sexist remark. The music cascaded in waves over us. The guy turned back to the stage, and so did Joe. But I just stood there trying to process what he'd said. G.G. had talked to the gossip rags about me? And he'd taken out an *ad*?

No way.

"Excuse me," I muttered to Joe, then turned to leave.

He caught up with me near the food tents. "Zoe, wait. Are you okay?"

"I…I have to go."

"What's wrong?" He caught my elbow in his hand, but I wrenched it free.

"I have to go." I needed a newsstand and fast.

Joe followed me back to my car, but when I tried to open the door he planted one hand firmly on it. "What's going on, Zoe? One minute we're having a nice time. The next minute you're running away like I did something terrible."

"It's not you," I managed to say. *Now get out of my way!* I wanted to scream.

But he was right. I was acting crazy, when he'd been nothing but nice to me. He deserved some sort of explanation, even a totally made-up one. "I haven't been feeling that well."

He stared at me like he was trying to figure out whether I was lying or not. "I noticed you rubbing your stomach earlier."

He'd seen that?

"Was it the strawberry shortcake?"

"No. Maybe." I pressed my lips together. "It started this morning. Actually last night," I amended. No need for him to suspect morning sickness. "I thought it was over with but maybe the strawberries got to me. Or more likely the whipped cream."

"And at Sara Mae's it was too much mayonnaise. Seems like you have a mighty delicate stomach."

He had me there, but I squelched any further tendency to justify myself. So what if I was making a fool of myself? Joe Reeves was only a momentary distraction, someone I would forget as soon as I left Louisiana.

And if G.G. really was making a big thing about my disappearance, then I had just become news to Mr. Joe Newspaper. And the worst kind of news from his perspective: stupid celebrity news.

"Look, Joe. I'm sorry. You're a really nice guy and…and your son is so cute. Only…I guess it's too soon for me to be dating again."

How lame was that? But it had the desired effect.

"Fine." He backed away from the car. From me. "I guess I should have figured out your game when you insisted on taking your own car."

"You think I planned this?"

"Then explain what's going on."

I shook my head. "It doesn't matter."

He didn't stare after me as I drove away. It would have been easier to blow him off if he'd been some sappy, clingy guy, mooning over a woman he'd only met three times. Instead he'd opened my car door, then once I was seated closed it—only a *little* too hard. Then he turned away and strode back to the Strawberry Festival.

Not until I pulled onto I-12 heading back to Oracle did I realize I was obsessing more over what Joe Reeves thought of me than what G. G. Givens was up to.

"I hate all men," I muttered. Then I screamed out at the universe. "I hate all men! They're a pimple on the ass of women everywhere! The Black Plague. The Asian flu! SARS! AIDS!"

AIDS, which my mother had died of. Probably contracted from some man. Through sex or shared needles, it didn't much matter. Men made women's lives hard. Even men like Joe Reeves who weren't trying to make life hard for us but did so anyway.

If only I'd been born a lesbian.

Except then you wouldn't be pregnant.

Okay. Men did have one use.

I exited the interstate and pulled into the first drugstore parking lot I saw. They had both publications, a fat handful of each, in fact. With my sunglasses firmly in place, I paid for them and ran for the car. Then I sat there frantically turning pages until I found the article and the ad.

Thank God one of Hollywood's newest starlets had been arrested for driving drunk. Otherwise G.G. and I might have been on the *National Star*'s front page. As it was, we weren't that far behind.

But we wouldn't even have been there except for the ad in *People*. The fact is, I'm a nobody and G.G. is pretty much a has-been, despite all his efforts to revive his career. But advertising to find your lost girlfriend? How pathetic was that?

Didn't G.G. realize what a laughingstock he was making of himself? Everyone would be making jokes. And once Letterman and Leno and Conan got a hold of it—

Holy hell! I straightened up as it hit me. I stared at the ad in *People*, at the picture G.G. had put in it of him and me getting out of a limo.

That was the whole point: to get everyone talking about us—about *him*. Let David Letterman and Jay Leno make their barbed remarks. That would only expose G.G. to a wider audience—at no cost to himself. He'd tried to get on Letterman's show last year, to no avail. I remembered how furious he'd been.

I bet he could get on now.

"You slimy bastard," I swore.

The woman getting of the car next to me shot me an outraged look.

"Sorry," I mumbled, rolling up my window as she herded her three kids away from me. "Sorry."

But he *was* a slimy bastard. And so was Coco. He was the one who'd probably come up with this horrible but brilliant idea. G.G. wasn't savvy enough to. Free PR. That was the name of the game. And if beer-guzzling festival-goers in small Southern towns were any gauge, they'd hit the bigtime. Free PR out the wazoo.

Trying to calm myself, I studied the ad. "Have you seen this woman?" the headline said in bold letters across the top. I wasn't familiar with the photo beneath it, but I was pretty sure it had been taken last year at some music industry function in San Francisco. I'd bought that dress at the last minute, and G.G. had loved it. With a neckline cut almost to my navel, it had boasted the most incredible hidden substructure, holding my breasts up like they were a seventeen-year-old's.

G.G. was grinning at me with heavy-lidded eyes. He'd been stoned, of course. Happily stoned. But that's not how it looked here. In the photo he looked heavily smitten. Giddy in love.

Yeah, right.

Then I read the handwritten letter beneath the photo, and even I had to wonder if maybe he *did* love me.

I've lost her, it began. I've lost the most beautiful, wonderful woman in the world. I'm a fool. I took her for granted when I should have cher-

ished every moment with her. And now she's gone and I can't find her. If you see this, Red, then call me. Please. I love you. And if anyone else has seen her, please, please call 1-555-Find Red.

It was powerful stuff, and some stupid part of me wanted to believe G.G. After all, I was pretty sure he'd been faithful to me. He deserved some credit for that. And he probably *did* miss me, considering that I took care of every aspect of his life that his manager didn't.

But the whole thing still stunk of cheesy PR. It stunk of Coco.

On the other hand, just because Coco seized an opportunity didn't mean G.G. wasn't sincere.

I frowned at the handwritten message. It was G.G.'s handwriting all right. And G.G.'s signature. But the crummy idea was all Coco.

The question now was, what was I going to do about it?

CHAPTER 9

As I drove back to the farm, I passed an old school bus
with the name Simmons Creek Victory Church printed on
the side. It was full of kids and heading in the opposite direction, probably to the Strawberry Festival. Clean, whole-
some, family fun.

Except that those innocent ears would be exposed to
music created by drug users, wouldn't they? I rolled my eyes.
Dear, dear me. The poor children were certain to turn out
depraved if they listened to that filth. Never mind that
"Harley Nights" was a love song. The fact remained that
G. G. Givens was an alcoholic drug-user. Therefore any
message he had to give must be tainted. I hoped the chap-
erones of that church group had brought enough earplugs.

You might say that I was in a very bad mood by the time
I got home, so it was unfortunate that there were several
cars parked in front of the house. If I hadn't been feeling
so pissy, I might have made a big U-turn in the driveway
and driven over to Harriet's house. But I was spoiling for a
fight, and Alice and her church friends who'd obviously
come over here the minute I left were as good a target as I
could hope for. No doubt she was rallying her troops to

defeat me. Never mind that *she* was the one who'd betrayed me.

I jerked to a halt, scattering gravel, then jumped down before the car had even stopped rocking. With a shrill whistle I summoned Tripod, who came lumbering from around the back of the house. "Let's go, baby. Let's go stir some sh—Crap," I amended, lightly touching my stomach.

The women sat in the living room, Alice and four of her friends holding delicate coffee cups and saucers, with embroidered cloth napkins draped over their laps. Very la-di-dah.

It drew out the very worst in me.

"Oh, my." I halted in the doorway. "Am I interrupting some sort of prayer group?"

Alice's eyes got big and she glanced nervously at her friends. "No."

One of the women, a brittle-looking beanpole with ugly brown hair, scowled at me. "I thought she wasn't going to be here."

I swear the hackles on my neck rose up. If I could have, I would have snarled at the bitch. "I'm afraid *she* comes and goes whenever *she* wants to," I retorted. "After all, it is *her* house."

Alice stood up abruptly. "Please, Zoe."

But I was in no mood to be placated. I was mad at the world, and I wanted somebody's blood. Ugly hair would do just fine. I stared at her. "What's your name?"

A frightened silence fell over the mealymouthed crowd. "Well?" I persisted. "Cat got your tongue? Or are you early-onset Alzheimer's?"

Her nostrils flared. "I'm Beth Ann Theriot, if you must know."

"And you?" I glared at the round-faced brunette beside her.

"Toni Short."

"Amber Higgs," the next one said before I even asked.

"And you?" I demanded of the last woman.

She was the only one who didn't look like she hated me. She did look kind of alarmed but not really mean. "I'm Vivian Nunez."

"Well, Beth Ann, Toni, Amber and Vivian. I'm Zoe Vidrine, as I'm sure you already know. I'm half owner of Vidrine Farm, a good portion of which was fraudulently sold to your church. You all *do* go to Alice's church, don't you?"

Three of them nodded, but Beth Ann refused to respond. She just folded her arms and scowled.

Aha. Ugly hair was a worthy opponent. So I smiled at her. "Not only was it sold fraudulently—a felony, I might point out—but it was also sold for a fraction of its actual worth. Do you see where I'm going with this? Since I don't really want to stick it to your church, I have no choice but to stick it to my sister. What I'm trying to say is, she sold her half of our inheritance to *you*. My half is what's left—this house. So you see, Beth Ann, y'all are sitting in *my* house, enjoying *my* hospitality. The least you could do is be civil to me."

Her eyes burned black with fury. "I do *not* have to be civil to a lying witch with a capital B, one who's torturing my dear friend Alice. Especially when that witch is known to be a loose-moralled, drug-using slut!"

"Beth Ann!" Vivian exclaimed.

"A witch with a capital *B?*" I pressed one hand to my chest as if taken aback. "You mean a…a Bitch?"

Then I strode into the room and stopped just in front of her. "How astute of you, Beth Ann. I *am* a bitch when I need to be. But I'm not a drug user. Nor am I loose-moralled, as you put it. But even if I were, as I recall, Jesus was a hell of a lot nicer to Mary Magdalene than you and my sister have been to me. Of course, what do I know about Bible stories? For all I know *The DaVinci Code* had it right, and Jesus married her, loose morals and all."

There were a couple of gasps, but I didn't wait for them to recover. "Enjoy your visit to my home, ladies." I gave my sister a thin smile. "See you later, Alice."

It was a great finish, and I was proud of myself. But by the time I reached the kitchen my knees had turned to Jell-O. I have a smart mouth and I can square off with the toughest customer. Afterward, though, I always dissolve. I hate having to be belligerent, but sometimes there's no other way.

I grabbed a glass and filled it with water, but my hand shook almost too much to drink it. Alice was lucky I didn't evict her from this place. If it wasn't for Daniel, maybe I would.

But I *could* go ahead and list the house for sale.

I set the glass on the counter. That would really rattle Alice's cage. It would show her I was serious, and by the time a sale could be finalized, my lawyer should have the inheritance issues resolved. With the baby coming and now with G.G.'s insane campaign to find me, I didn't have time to waste.

I searched the kitchen for a phone book. Instead I found an issue of the *Northshore News*.

For a moment I paused. I'd really ruined things with Joe. If I'd just stuck with my instincts and turned him down in the first place, none of this would have happened. Not that what he thought really mattered to me. Besides, with this G.G. business and the ad in *People*, Mr. Ex-Celebrity Newshound would eventually find out about me anyway. Whether we'd dated successfully or never previously met, the results would have ended up the same.

First things first, I told myself, before I could get all depressed about Joe. First list the house; then light a fire under my lawyer. After that just lay low and wait for G.G.'s little PR campaign to fade away.

But anger seethed just beneath the surface of my enforced calm. And I knew it would take only one wrong word from Alice and her gang of hard-hearted church ladies to set me off again.

Fortunately, they avoided me, moving their evil plotting to someone else's house. It was the first time since I'd returned to Oracle that I was actually glad to be alone in the house. Even Angel was gone. God forbid she be corrupted by the three-legged mutt I'd inflicted on their household.

I called a real estate agent to discuss listing the house.

The man told me I needed to find a survey and any perti-
nent title information. So I called my attorney's office and
left a message about that.

After that Tripod and I walked to Harriet's, but she
wasn't there. Feeling bereft, I sat on her garden bench, just
admiring her garden with its day lilies and gardenias, zinnias, daisies, bachelor's buttons and lantana. It was a rau-
cous riot, cheerful and exuberant. Like Harriet.

Compared to Alice's clean, green-and-white foundation plantings, it was practically a kaleidoscope.

That's when I got the idea. I was stuck here for a while.
Why not entertain myself by learning from Harriet how to
make a warm, loving home, one perfect for a child to grow
up in? And what better place to practice on than Alice's
too-sedate garden?

You'd be amazed how many plants you can buy for
$129.72. Flats of orange petunias, coral impatiens and
rusty-leaved begonias. Six-packs of lime-green-and-purple-
leaved coleus and brilliant zinnias and an old-fashioned
ham-and-eggs plant.

For good measure I splurged on two vivid yellow man-
devilla vines, which the sales clerk assured me would twist
and climb up the porch columns and put on an amazing
floral display.

I looked at Tripod as we headed home. "Yes," I said. "I
know I'm insane." But I was used to being busy. If I had to
hide out at the house until this mess with G.G. and *People*
blew over, at least I'd have something to do.

When I got home Daniel was there, but Alice's car was

still gone. "What are you doing?" he asked as he helped me unload Jenny.

"Isn't it obvious?"

"Well, yeah. But, I mean, does Mom know?"

The bigger question was, did he know my reason for coming back here? I decided it was time to let him know. I set the lantana beside the steps. "Your mother and I inherited equal shares in the farm, Daniel. You understand that, don't you?"

"Oh. Yeah. That makes sense. So this house is, like, half yours?"

"The whole farm was half mine, but since Alice sold a big chunk of it—more than half the acreage—without my consent, it's a pretty safe bet that I'll become owner of what's left."

Beneath his shaggy hair his brow creased. "You mean, like, this house is yours?"

I pressed my lips together and nodded.

He set down the tray of petunias. "So, you're gonna own our house?"

"It was half mine to begin with. You told me you were good at math, so I know you can figure this out."

His young face pulled down in a frown. "Does that mean—" He broke off but I knew what he was asking.

"Does that mean that you have to move?" I shrugged. "I'm hoping your Mom can buy the house from me. In the meanwhile, don't worry. You don't have to move out. Nothing's changing."

I could see the relief in his eyes, and it really got to

me. Damn Alice for being so helpless and unable to provide for her child.

Daniel gestured to the plants. "Nothing's changing except that you're planting whatever you like."

I smiled at him. "Yeah. I'm settling in here for a while and, no offense, but I like things a little livelier than your mom does."

Apparently appeased, he went back to the Jeep for a flat of zinnias and brought them to the front steps. "Is it some kind of girl thing, all these flowers? Mom says Grandma liked to grow stuff, too."

I stifled a snort. Yeah, stuff like weed and poppies and angel's trumpet. "Maybe so. I was influenced more by Harriet, though. She's got a spectacular garden."

"Oh, yeah. I shoveled, like, a ton of manure into her garden last year."

"That was nice of you. I guess you know her from church."

"Yeah. She and my dad used to have these debates." His face clouded again. "About God and theology. Stuff like that."

"Debates? Did she disagree with him?"

"I guess. I mean, not about big stuff like God and heaven and hell and the Ten Commandments. But things like the Bible and how to interpret it."

I could just picture it, and I suppressed a grin. "You mean things like a woman's place in the patriarchal society of most churches?"

He shrugged. "I guess. She believes in evolution, not creationism."

"You know about evolution?"

"Yeah. We learn all the theories."

"So, did either Harriet or your dad convince the other to change his mind on that one?"

He chuckled. "I don't think so."

"I don't get it. Why does Harriet continue to go to a church that she disagrees with?"

"I don't know."

I shook my head. "I'm surprised your father didn't excommunicate her."

He grinned. "That's a Catholic thing. Actually, I think Dad liked their debates. She was, like, the only person in the whole church who challenged him. Everybody else took everything he said as gospel."

"Including you?"

His face clouded over, and though he didn't answer I knew what he was thinking. "Listen, Daniel. No kid who ever lived agreed with everything his parents told him. It's the nature of the beast. Teenagers are supposed to challenge their parents. It's how they figure out who they are."

He grunted—such a guy sound. "Maybe."

We finished unloading the Jeep. Then he moved a chair from the porch out to the front yard so I could just sit there, look at the house, and figure out where I wanted everything put.

But instead of thinking about zinnias and begonias, I found myself thinking about Daniel's father. He'd enjoyed Harriet's company, and she must have enjoyed his, otherwise she wouldn't have continued at his church. To hear

Daniel's version, it sounded like he was this smart minister surrounded by a bunch of yes men, including his wife.

I wondered what he would have thought of me.

Not that it mattered, of course. I didn't care what anyone thought of me. *Except for you*, I sent the mental message to my Jessie/Jesse.

And Joe Reeves.

"Get over it," I muttered out loud.

Tripod lifted his head and thumped his whipcord tail.

"Okay," I told my loyal mutt. "Let's get to work on this garden." But first I needed something to eat. I was ravenous these days. The second trimester was well underway. I hoped that meant the end of the nausea.

I stood up and unhooked the waistband of my capris. I needed to buy some new clothes, and soon. But I probably shouldn't go into town—or anywhere for that matter—until the current issues of *People* and the *National Star* were off the stands and some new scandal had become front page news.

CHAPTER 10

I didn't see Alice the rest of the day, nor most of Sunday. While I worked like a crazy woman in the front garden, she came and went via the back door. By the time they came back from church it was late afternoon. Even then it was only Carl dropping off Daniel.

Daniel raced by me onto the porch. "Hey," he said, then disappeared inside. That left Carl sitting in his maroon Olds, waiting for Daniel to return, I guess.

I decided it was time to make nice with Carl and maybe encourage him to help Alice buy the house from me.

Believe it or not, as I sauntered up to his car, he rolled the window three-quarters of the way up. What a wuss! But I kept a pleasant smile on my face and forced an apologetic tone into my voice. "Look, Carl. I know we got off on the wrong foot, and I'm sorry for that."

His bushy eyebrows shot up in surprise, but he didn't roll the window down.

"The thing is…" I continued "…you and I really want the same thing—for Alice and Daniel—and eventually you—to live happily ever after in this house."

I waited and, sure enough, the window began to lower.

He was a creepy old guy, and I couldn't understand Alice's interest in him. Then again, he'd probably been a creepy young guy once. It wasn't his age that most bothered me; it was his creepiness.

"Does this mean you're getting out of her house?" he barked out.

"Tell me this, Carl. If you were me and Alice was your estranged brother, would you just hand over that house to him if legally it were yours? Pick up that Bible," I said, pointing to the well-worn volume lying on the bench seat beside him. "Swear to me and God that you'd give up a two-hundred-thousand dollar property out of the goodness of your heart if that's all that stood between you and living on the street."

He wanted to say yes. I know he did. But that Bible wouldn't let him.

I placed one hand on the car and leaned my head down to face him. "Here's the deal, Carl. If you're serious about Alice, great. I don't want to live in this house. But I can't afford to give it away. Surely you and Alice can figure out a way to buy this place from me. I'll even give you a good deal. Not as good a deal as Alice and her late husband gave the church. But I'm not going to gouge you either."

I had his attention now.

Actually, I had more of his attention than I wanted. His squinty eyes kept dropping down to my chest. Up to my face; down to my chest; past me to stare at the house. Then the whole circuit started over again.

"That's a lot of money," he finally said. "And you're assuming it's all yours."

"Consult a lawyer, Carl. You'll get the same answer I did. That land wasn't Alice's to sell, but I'm not trying to punish her over it. I just want what's mine, and then I'm gone. She can get a paying job instead of volunteering all the time at the church. And you already have a job, don't you?" *Didn't he? I sure hoped he did.* "Between the two of you surely you can pay a mortgage, just like the rest of your church members do."

Except that he didn't want to pay a mortgage. I could see it when his expression turned sour. "Or maybe…" I went on "…the church could buy the house for the minister's residence and you could live there for free."

His eyes darted back to me. "They haven't selected a permanent minister yet."

"Then how about I won't sell to the church unless I know you get the job?"

I guess he liked that, because he blinked several times before peeking at my chest again.

"How soon until the church decides?" I asked.

"Soon," was all he said.

I heard the front door slam. Daniel was coming out. When he paused on the front steps to pet Tripod, I leaned nearer the car window. "There's one more thing, Carl. If you plan to marry Alice, you need to try harder with Daniel. He's a good kid. But right now you're a long way from measuring up to his father. Try harder to be nice," I finished. "Okay?"

As Daniel ran up, Carl glanced over at the kid, then nodded.

I tapped the roof of his car. "We'll talk later."

"Right," he muttered. "We'll talk."

I watched them drive away. "Well, it's just you and me," I said to Tripod. "Just like always. And you," I added to Jesse/Jessie.

That held true for about twenty-five minutes. Long enough for me to take a shower, wash my hair and put on a pair of cutoffs and a comfy old T-shirt without a bra. I was in the kitchen rustling around for the ingredients to soothe my sudden craving for a grilled cheese sandwich or two—or three—when I heard a car door slam. They were back already?

But it was only one car door. And only one silhouette on the front porch knocking on the door. Carl?

No. It was Joe Reeves. I'd recognize those shoulders anywhere.

Shit, shit, shit!

Shoot, shoot, shoot.

I stood in the hall, frozen with indecision. For whatever reason he'd come, it couldn't be good.

"I know you're there, Zoe. I can see you in the hall. So come answer the door."

"Alice isn't here," I called out to him, not budging an inch.

"I'm here to see you."

"Why?"

"Open the door and I'll tell you."

I drew myself up. "Okay," I muttered to myself, "You can do this." Whether he'd come because of the ads or my peculiar behavior at the Strawberry Festival, either way I could brazen my way through it.

I opened the door. Not enough to let him in. Of course that idiot Tripod slipped out and immediately began to wriggle for joy, as if he'd known Joe Reeves all his life. The fact that Joe went down on one knee and fondled my traitorous mutt, establishing himself as Tripod's newest lifelong friend, didn't improve my mood. Beloved by children *and* dogs. Why did Joe have to be such an all-around good guy?

When he finally stood up and faced me, though, Joe's good-guy image was tarnished by his eagle-sharp gaze. A newsman's penetrating stare. "Can we talk?"

I held on to the doorframe. "Can we talk? You sound like Joan Rivers."

He just waited.

I broke first. "It depends what you want to talk about."

"I know now why you ditched me at the Strawberry Festival," he said. "I saw *People*, and the *National Star*."

My jaw tightened. "I don't do interviews." I tried to close the door, but he blocked it with his foot. Such a cartoon move.

"I found a lot of interesting information about you. Though I doubt most people outside of Oracle will associate Red Vidrine with Zoe Vidrine."

"And you can't wait to expose that fact to the world," I snarled. "Once a paparazzi, always a paparazzi. Now get your foot out of my damned doorway before I break it!"

"This is your chance to tell your side of the story."

"There *is* no story. G.G.'s an idiot and I left him. That's it."

"But you came back here, to Vidrine Farm where you

grew up. I researched it, Zoe. It's all online, in the archives of my newspaper. Even the *Times-Picayune* has articles about your mother and what went on here."

"What's already out there is out there. That doesn't mean I have to bare *my* soul to the world." Suddenly I was exhausted, completely drained and on the verge of tears. "Leave me alone, Joe. Just…leave me alone."

I didn't think he would. His eyes were this dark, ice-blue color. Like flint. And his face was set in lines that revealed nothing of his thoughts or feelings. But just when I thought I might have a fight on my hands—one I probably wouldn't win—he pulled his foot free of the door.

But I didn't slam it closed.

"You can't hide out forever, Zoe. I figured out who you are—other people will, too."

I hated that he was right. Damn G.G. to hell and back!

"How did you figure it out?" I asked.

He shrugged. "I was pretty p.o.'d after you left me flat. So when I got home, I Googled you, and there you were. There were only a few listings for Zoe Vidrine, mainly from when you were a kid. After that, nothing. So I cruised a couple of other Vidrine listings. I found two veterinarians. A romance author. A car dealership. And then I found Red Vidrine. Magazine listings, videos, news clips. Lots of photos of tall, red-haired Red Vidrine, who just happened to look exactly like the Zoe Vidrine who'd just ditched me."

I swallowed hard. God, I hated the Internet. "There's no story here, Joe."

"Sorry to disagree. Your boyfriend made it a story when he took out an ad to find you in a national magazine."

"I thought you gave up so-called celebrity news. Isn't that why you moved here? And just for the record, he's not my boyfriend anymore."

Call me stupid, but despite Joe's self-serving purpose for being here, I wanted him to say something like, "I'm glad he's not your boyfriend anymore." Or, "His loss is my gain." Pure idiocy, I know. But then, I have a great record at being a pure idiot, especially when it comes to men.

What Joe said was, "He obviously thinks he's still your boyfriend."

"He also thinks he can climb back to the top of the charts while he's strung out on—" I broke off. This was a newshound I was talking to.

Sure enough, his gaze sharpened. "Did you leave him because of his drug use?"

I just shook my head in regret. "Goodbye."

"Drug use by rock stars isn't exactly breaking news, Zoe."

"Then why ask me about it?"

He pursed his lips, his gaze never wavering. "When a woman flees a man, there's usually some sort of abuse involved. Or else another man."

I snorted with laughter. "Tripod's my only other man."

"So I figured. That leaves us with abuse."

"Oh, no, you don't." I shook my head. "G.G. has never laid a hand on me in anger. He wouldn't dare. And as for verbal abuse, I guarantee I'm a lot better at it than he is."

"Which leads us back to the drug question."

"Which I'm not answering." I crossed my arms.

That's when he smiled, that same half smile he'd given me the first time I'd seen him. "But at least you're still talking to me."

I scowled. Anything to squash the answering smile that threatened on my lips. "Not for long."

"Maybe you should, though. I'm a hell of a lot more likely to get the story straight than any of the bozos who are already on your trail."

I wanted to believe him. But he was a man, and a newsman at that. "Nice try, but I think I'll just lie low. There is one fact you can spread about me, though."

"What's that?"

"That I have a shotgun, and I will use it on anyone who trespasses on my property."

Amusement glinted in his eyes. "Even me?"

I stiffened. *Even me*. Like we had some sort of relationship that exempted him. "Even you, Mr. Northshore News."

We stared at each other, one long moment that pulsed with all the possibilities between us. Possibilities that were now being dashed. His eyes flitted over me once. It was brief, just long enough to make me wish I had dressed nicer—and to remember that I didn't have on a bra.

Sexual attraction crackled in the air.

Then Tripod yelped, the connection was broken, and I finally closed the door.

I watched through the front windows as he drove away. How I wanted to trust him. But I didn't dare. I rubbed the little round tummy that protruded beneath my navel. It wasn't just about me anymore.

And anyway, I had bigger problems than Joe Reeves. If he could Google me, then so could every other newshound in America.

I decided to Google myself.

As I sat at Alice's computer, I wondered if she'd ever looked me up this way. After all, she'd known I wasn't dead.

What I found online relieved me just a little. Zoe Vidrine existed mainly as the daughter of Caroline Vidrine, and the listings all dated from the eighties. And there were no photos.

Red Vidrine was a whole 'nother thing.

I'd got the nickname, Red, from Woody Terrence, a small-time agent who'd booked me in commercials and bit parts in television pilots that never made it to the boob tube. I'd kept it as my professional name, and that's how everyone knew me.

So there was Red Vidrine, pages and listings and references, all of them from gossip rags and celebrity magazines. But none of them connected to Zoe Vidrine.

As I scanned down the sources and dates, a leaden weight settled in the vicinity of my chest. After almost forty years on this planet, was this all I had to show for it? A train wreck of a childhood followed by twenty-three years of spinning around in place. A lot of flailing around, but going nowhere.

"Until now," I whispered.

I turned the computer off without bothering to shut it down. I had to get out of here before G.G.'s bloodhounds found me out. But how?

I grabbed *People* and the *National Star*, and stuffed them into one of my suitcases. I always wore my hair long and loose. After all, it was my namesake. Easy enough to remedy that.

Without giving myself time to think, I found a pair of scissors in a kitchen drawer and cut off all my hair. First shoulder length. Then chin length. Then finally, about three inches long all around.

I looked like a badly shorn sheep, shaggy and spiky with sprigs of hair sticking out everywhere. I turned away from the mirror in horror. "I'm doing this for you," I murmured to Jesse/Jessie. "For you."

Then I jumped in the Jeep and tore out of the yard, looking for an open store. I had to drive all the way to U.S. 190 to find a twenty-four-hour Walgreens, where I bought hair dye. Blonde or brunette? I bought both. Tomorrow I needed to buy some baggy, nondescript clothes and sensible shoes. Something Alice would wear.

As I headed to the checkout counter, I grabbed a pair of generic reading glasses. All I needed to complete the look I had in mind was to knock out one of my front teeth. Then I saw the stack of *People* and the *National Star*, and I bought them all. The checkout clerk gave me a funny look but didn't say anything. I threw them in the back of the Jeep, then sighed. I could buy all the copies all around town, but that didn't mean I wouldn't be found out. Still, it was worth a try.

Alice and Daniel were home when I finally returned with my stash of trash reading. Daniel was in his room; I could hear his music. Alice was in the kitchen.

"Good grief!" she exclaimed when she saw me. "All your beautiful hair!"

"I'm tired of it," I muttered even as it occurred to me that her comment was the closest thing to a compliment I'd ever received from her. "It was too much trouble," I went on. Should I tell her the truth? "I'm going to color it, too."

She stared doubtfully at the mess I'd made of myself. "What color?"

Why that simple question got to me, I don't know. Maybe because it was such a normal sister-to-sister thing to discuss haircuts and hair color. Whatever the reason, I could feel myself starting to unravel. "You choose," I said, dumping the boxes of L'Oréal Preference on the table. Then in a mad outburst I told her everything: about G.G. and the ad, and my fear of a media feeding frenzy. Everything except about Joe's visit.

"I have to disguise myself," I finished up. "And unless you help me, or at least keep quiet about it, you're going to be deluged by the same bloodsuckers who'll be looking for me."

Her forehead creased as she considered her options. "Maybe this is a sign that you should leave here."

So much for us behaving like sisters. I glared at her. "Or maybe it's a sign that your fraudulent sale of my property needs to be made public information."

She sucked in a frightened breath. I went on. "Or maybe

it's not a sign at all, Alice. Maybe it's just one of those pre-dicaments of life that God throws in front of us. A test, as it were, to see how truly moral we are."

She swallowed hard. "You're hardly the one to be preaching to me, Zoe."

"At least I'm willing to admit my life hasn't been ideal. And I'm trying to change it. What are you doing? Trying to hang on to your mistakes and get out of any atonement?"

I guess maybe she heard that because instead of arguing any further, she reached for the two boxes of hair color, stood them side by side on the table and studied them. Finally she looked up at me. "I think…brunette."

My spine slowly began to unkink, and I sat down in my chair. "Why? I was leaning toward blond."

She shook her head. "Too flashy. You'll look different, but you'll still be noticeable."

"True." I stared at the woman on the brunette box. "I need to make myself invisible. Dowdy."

"Like me?" she asked.

Bingo. But I couldn't say that to her. "You're not a bru-nette."

"But I am dowdy in your eyes. Right?"

I studied her—her face, her hair, her only slightly plump figure. Yeah, she was dowdy, but she had lots of potential. "The thing is, you actually look a lot like Mom. And every-one agrees she was gorgeous."

She rolled her eyes as if that was too preposterous to believe. And yet it was true. She *did* look like Mom; she just didn't have that attitude that said, "I deserve everyone's attention, all the time.

"Yes, Mom was beautiful," Alice finally said. "Even up to the end when she was so thin and pale…"

I barely stifled a snort. "Beautiful on the outside, maybe. But face it, Alice, she was the most self-indulgent person that ever lived."

"Like you haven't been?"

I leaned forward and just stared at her. "You don't know a thing about me and how I've lived my life. I may not have much to show for my first forty years, other than a great wardrobe and half ownership in this farm. But you have even less."

"I have this—" She broke off.

"This house? I don't think so. You have a son—but I'll have a child soon, too. So you see? It comes down to the fact that my clothes are nicer than yours. That's why I win."

She shook her head, not appreciating my humor at all. "I have a community of friends, people who'll stick by me. Who do you have?"

"I have…myself. I'm not as helpless as you are. I can make a life for me and Jesse/Jessie just fine."

She made a face. "What kind of name is Jessie Jessie?"

"It's just Jesse or Jessie. Different spellings depending on whether it's a girl or a boy."

"Do you have a preference?" she asked.

I shook my head. "I want a healthy baby. And I want to be a good mother."

"That's why you left your boyfriend? This G.G. guy?"

"He's a cokehead. Not exactly promising daddy material."

"So, you're not going to tell him about the baby?"

I thought about it. "If he ever cleans up his act, sure. But until then, no. And in case you're considering contacting him as a way of getting rid of me, first consider the hell you'd be subjecting this innocent child to. Your spite would hurt this baby more than it would hurt me."

Her mouth gaped open in outrage. "I am not a spiteful person! Jesse/Jessie will be my niece or nephew. Daniel's only cousin. I'd never hurt your baby."

It's funny, but her words reminded me of what Harriet had said when I'd asked her to be my baby's grandmother. She'd told me that Jesse/Jessie already had a cousin and an aunt, and not to take them for granted.

"I know you're not spiteful," I conceded. "But it's hard to know who to trust these days." Then I leaned back in my chair. "Okay. Enough of this heart-to-heart stuff. Tell me, are you and Carl working on a plan to buy this place?"

She sighed. "Could we not talk about that right now?"

"Fine." I place my hands flat on the table and pushed to a stand. "But you can't avoid it forever."

I started to leave the room, then some imp made me stop in the doorway. I turned to face her. "Do you want to help me dye my hair?"

She looked as surprised by the question as I was. "Okay." She stood up, too. "What do I have to do?"

CHAPTER 11

Who was that woman in the mirror?

At least as a brunette the haircut didn't look quite so bad. With no makeup on, or jewelry, and only a pair of dark sunglasses, I didn't look remotely like myself.

"What do you think?" I asked Alice.

"Well…you don't look like you, and that's what you want, right?"

"What are you saying? That I look hideous?"

"No. Not at all. You couldn't look hideous if you tried."

"Why, Alice, I do declare." I pressed one hand dramatically to my heart. "That's the nicest thing you've ever said to me."

She wrinkled her nose. "You couldn't look hideous. But some of your outfits are tacky beyond belief."

It was such a smart-aleck quip, not what I expected from her, that I laughed before I could stop myself. "You ain't seen nothing yet, babe. I have this leopard-print and pink-lace outfit with a black leather bustier and matching stiletto ankle boots that makes men drop dead in their tracks and women snarl and grow claws."

She covered her eyes in mock terror. "Spare me. Please!"

I grinned at her and miracle of miracles, she grinned

back. "You know, I'm not quite as awful as everyone thinks," I told her. "And just maybe you're not quite as good. Don't frown," I added when her eyebrows drew together. "I'm kind of glad you have a secret, selfish side. All that saccharine goodness was wearing on my nerves."

She managed a sour smile. "Well, thanks. I guess."

An awkward silence fell between us. She shifted as if to leave, and I said, "How about we cut your hair, too?"

"Like yours?" she gasped.

"I *knew* you hated it!"

"No. I mean, it's just not me." She tucked a strand of hair that had come loose behind her ear.

"I didn't mean to cut it as drastically as I did mine. I just thought…I don't know. Something a little jazzier. Something that would play up your eyes. And highlights wouldn't hurt either. Professionally done, of course."

Her gaze cut to her reflection in the bathroom mirror, then met mine. "Maybe," she said.

"I bet Carl would like it."

"Maybe," she repeated. But there was more doubt on her face than before.

What was it with her and Carl? There was like this weird ambivalence between them. It seemed to me they needed either to piss or get off the pot. But I kept my thoughts to myself. And, anyway, who was I to advise anyone else on her love life? If I wasn't wasting my time with some rock-and-roll fool, I was dancing around some celebrity-chasing newshound.

But not anymore. From celebrities to celibacy. That was

my new mantra. As I went off to my lonely bedroom and Alice down to hers, I decided it was as good a plan as any.

I woke up with an entirely different agenda.

Actually, I woke up fine, except for the first shocking moment when I stumbled bleary-eyed into the bathroom and spied my new self. "What the hell?" I muttered, stumbling backward against the wall. Still, the hair was okay, a part of my plan. I showered and put on a pair of jeans and the loosest T-shirt I had—which wasn't all that loose due to the hormonal-related growth of my breasts. Oh, well.

No, the change in my agenda came a half hour later when I moseyed on down the stairs. The first face I saw was the skinny woman with ugly hair. Not that my own hair was looking so good. Still…

"Why, if it isn't Barbara Ann," I cooed.

She sent me a withering glare. "It's Beth Ann," she snapped. "Mrs. Theriot to you."

She and her little entourage sat in the parlor. Alice came though the dining room holding a silver tray with her coffee service on it. Very Old South. Very genteel.

Though I shouldn't have, after that teeny-weeny bonding between Alice and me last night, I felt terribly betrayed now. My first reaction, of course, was to strike back. I gave Alice an arch look. "Got the prayer circle going, I see."

"Someone's got to intercede for dear Alice," Beth Ann snapped before Alice could answer. "And God certainly seems like the right candidate, though I doubt you'd ever understand that."

"My, my. What big teeth you have, Grandma."

Alice sent me a pleading look. "Please, Zoe."

"She started it."

"No, you did. This is not a prayer circle," Alice said. "Not that a prayer circle would be a bad thing. We're working on my book. You remember, I told you about it?"

"Oh, yeah. *The Minister's Left Hand.* Right? Great title," I added. Alice's friend Vivian murmured her agreement. Then I planted one fist on my cocked hip. "You know, I'm writing a book, too. Maybe you ladies can tell me if you like the title."

I should have stopped then. I could see Alice's eyes begging me to, even though she didn't have a clue what I was going to say. I wasn't so sure myself. But we both knew it would be incendiary. "I'm calling it *Sleeping Under the Stars: An Exposé of the Sex Lives and Habits of Rock-and-Roll's Biggest Names.*" I gave them a mocking smile. "What do you think? The title alone should sell millions."

Their shocked silence could almost have been drawn from an exaggerated *Saturday Night Live* skit. I'd struck them all dumb, which, of course, had been my intent. Naturally, bitchy Beth Ann was the first to recover. "That's… That's disgusting. No doubt you've already done all the research."

"Beth Ann!" Alice pleaded.

"No doubt," I retorted. Let her think what she wanted. The truth was, although I'm a serial monogamist, I'd met a lot of rock-and-roll girlfriends in my time. I'd heard stories from them kinky enough to curl your hair, and perverted enough to turn your stomach. My mother would have loved it, which ought to explain why I had refused to be a part of it. I may look free and easy, but the truth is, I'm a very old-fashioned sort of girlfriend.

Not that Alice's friends would ever believe it.

"You know what?" I went on. "When *People* comes to interview me about the book, maybe I'll do the interview in front of your church. You know, the one y'all built illegally on land stolen from me."

"Enough!" Alice shouted. "I can't stand any more of this!"

That's when Beth Ann started to pray. She grabbed the hands of the two women next to her, bowed her head, and in a loud demanding voice said, "Dear Lord, almighty Father, please smite this cancer from among our midst. Send her back to the devil with a message to him that he cannot defeat Your chosen people. Save us, Lord, from the cloud of sin she carries—"

That's when Daniel clattered down the stairs. "What's going on?"

Beth Ann wasn't in the least deterred. "—and protect our children from the temptation she throws in their path."

That did it! I didn't stop to think but grabbed a vase of wildflowers and threw the water and flowers right in her face.

That shut her up. In the grim silence I set the vase down and turned to Daniel. "What's going on is that these good church ladies were damning me. They have faith in God, hope that I'll leave and charity for no one except those just like themselves. Nice church you go to, Daniel."

I turned to survey the dripping Beth Ann. "Damn, I was

sure that water would melt you into an ugly puddle on the floor. But I guess *The Wizard of Oz* was just a work of fiction."

Then I left the house. As usual, though, I had no real destination in mind. I kicked at the loose shell in the driveway and glared at the cars in the driveway. If I knew which one was Beth Ann's I'd key both sides of it.

No, you wouldn't, my conscience scolded.

Don't ruin my fantasy.

Tripod found me, with Angel fast on his heels. Funny how they'd forged a friendship. Too bad Alice and I couldn't do as well. But every time we made any progress, either Carl or Beth Ann came along to screw things up. One step forward; two steps back.

"So what?" I said out loud.

Tripod whined and his big brown eyes peered anxiously up at me.

"So what?" I repeated, fondling his ragged ears. "I didn't come here to make nice with Alice. I mean, I wouldn't mind if we could be like normal sisters. But if we can't, so what? I'm no worse off than before."

Except that I was lying to myself. Ever since Harriet's comment, I'd begun to think of Alice as not just my sister, but as Jesse/Jessie's aunt. I wanted my baby to have an aunt and a cousin to love. And to be loved by.

I was way, way down in the dumps by the time I found myself on the fence line between our place—*my place*—and Harriet's. It wasn't fair to always run to her to lick my wounds, but at the moment I had nowhere else to turn.

One day I'd make it up to her, though. One day she'd need help and I'd be there for her. For now, I was simply grateful for her open door and welcoming smile.

"Interesting look," she said when she spied my new, butchered do.

"Yeah, well." I tugged on the hair at the back of my neck, trying futilely to make it longer than two-and-a-half inches. "It turns out G.G.'s trying to find me. He's got an ad in *People* magazine. Pictures and all."

"You're joking!"

"I wish. Even worse, the *National Star* has picked up the story. God knows who else will, too."

"So your new look is a disguise?"

"Bingo. The only thing I've got going for myself is that everyone out west knows me as Red Vidrine. And since Alice is only my half sister and her maiden name wasn't Vidrine, the press may never make the connection." I paused. "Except for Joe Reeves."

"Oh, dear," Harriet said. "Maybe you'd better sit down and tell me everything."

I very seldom missed having a mother. But talking to Harriet—whining, really, sniffling into the tissues she handed me and relaxing into her plump arm around my waist—that made me miss having a mother worse than I ever had. I felt that lack inside me like a big, black void, an absence of something so vital I could hardly breathe. Almost forty years of that lack.

But Harriet was here for me now, and in desperation, I clung to her. I couldn't do this alone. I'd thought I could, but I wasn't so sure anymore. "And now those witches are over there putting a curse on me. If that's what God teaches in church, then this baby will never go to *any* church—"

I broke off at the sound of a knock. "Miss Harriet? Are you there? Have you seen Zoe?"

Damn. It was Daniel. Why was he here?

Harriet just smiled and patted my arm. "Come on in, Daniel. Zoe's here with me."

He burst in, all arms and legs and wild eyes, out of breath as if he'd run all the way here. Tripod went all wiggly with joy to see him. Harriet, of course, remained her sweet, un-flappable self. "Go in the kitchen and get yourself some lemonade, dear, while you catch your breath. And bring a lemonade for Zoe, too."

When he finally sat down opposite us he was more composed. But he still wasn't a happy camper. "You can come back, Aunt Zoe. They're all gone."

Aunt Zoe. How sweet that sounded!

"I yelled at them," he went on. "And they all left." His chin jutted out and I saw the first sign of peach fuzz there. He was growing up. "I'm never going to that church again."

"Daniel!" Harriet and I both exclaimed his name in tandem.

"This isn't about the church," I said.

"That's right," Harriet agreed. "Beth Ann Theriot has always been an unforgiving, vindictive person. She usually manages to hide it beneath a layer of piety. But I guess our Zoe is just a little more than Beth Ann can cope with."

"She acts like she's doing this to help Mom," Daniel said.

"But she's just plain mean and everybody goes along with her. Even my mom."

"No." I shook my head. "Your mom tried to stop her, Daniel. She tried." It was weird, my defending Alice, but the truth was the truth. "I don't believe Beth Ann is what your father's church is really about."

"No indeed," Harriet said. "I had many a debate with your father through the years, and I know his position well—hate the sin, love the sinner. Not to imply you're any more a sinner than the rest of us," she added to me. "But Reverend Collins would never condone praying for the destruction of anyone. He'd pray for them to change their ways, but never to cast them out. You know that's true, Daniel. Don't you?"

He blew out a breath, and his head hunched down between his shoulders. "Yeah. I guess so." He stared intently at Harriet, and his eyes reflected a world of angst and confusion. "I wish he was still here. I miss him so much. Everything's so messed up since he died."

Daniel was fatherless; I was motherless. As we sat in Harriet's warm, fussy front parlor, I felt the oddest sense of connection to him and, strangely enough, the oddest sense of well being.

Of—dare I say it?—family.

Suddenly buoyed, I smiled at them both. "You know, we're going to get through this no matter what Beth Ann and her sister witches chant in their unholy circle. I might as well tell you…" I continued to Daniel "…that I'm expecting a baby." My hand went to my stomach. "You're going to have a cousin in about five months. God willing," I added.

God willing? Where did that come from?

I guess Harriet noticed, too, because she squeezed my waist again.

"Cool," Daniel said with a grin. "I always wanted a cousin."

"All right, then," Harriet said. "We've agreed that the Beth Anns of the world can just take a flying leap. Right? They're an aggravation, but they're on the periphery of our lives, not in the center."

"Yeah," Daniel agreed. "But what about Mr. Witter? If my mom marries Carl…" He trailed off, but his morose expression said it all.

It made me feel like an absolute turd. Daniel had begged me to derail his mother's marriage to Carl and I'd halfheartedly agreed to try. But what had I done? Just the opposite.

For my own selfish reasons—justified though they might be—I was pressing instead for a hasty marriage and a hasty purchase of the house. Then I could make my hasty exit, stage left. A great plan for me. I'd have my money in hand. But poor Daniel would be stuck with Carl for a wicked stepfather.

I needed to talk to Alice, and quick. Meanwhile I needed to raise his spirits. "They're not going to get married, Daniel. We'll talk Alice out of it."

"But what if they do?"

Yeah? What if they do?

"You can come and live with me," I said without hesitation.

Holy crap! I couldn't keep one can of worms closed and now I was opening another one? "I mean, if you can't stand

living with Carl, you'll always have your aunt Zoe." Aunt
Zoe. It was sounding better and better each time it came
up. "And soon enough you'll have your cousin, Jesse/Jes-
sie."

He gave me as good a smile as he could manage. Poor
kid. It wasn't the option he wanted, but it was an option.

"Okay, then," Harriet said. "Is everyone feeling at least
a little bit better?"

We spent the rest of the morning at Harriet's, doing
chores, making lunch, generally behaving like a regular
family. It was…soothing. That's the best word for it. I felt
soothed, like a big hand was smoothing down my ruffled
fur. Like I was finding some high ground when I'd thought
I was drowning.

But that didn't mean Beth Ann the Bitch was getting
off scot-free with her evil tricks. No, indeedie. There were
ways to put a woman like her in her place, and I was just
woman enough to do it.

CHAPTER 12

On Wednesday evening I went to church.

I hadn't heard another word from Joe, or anything from anybody about G.G.'s ad or the article in the *National Star*. Maybe this invisibility thing was working.

So why was I about to flaunt my invisibility by going to Alice's church? I knew I'd be the focus of everyone else's attention.

Let's just say I had my reasons.

I dressed very carefully in a vintage, salmon-colored shirtwaist dress. No cleavage; calf-length skirt; short, cap sleeves. Very little skin showed, but that didn't make the dress any less sexy. Those post–World War II women knew what they were doing. My waist was cinched tightly by a two-inch-wide belt—good thing my growing baby-paunch was still way below the belly button—and the snug-fitting bodice defined my bosom perfectly. Mary Tyler Moore as Laura Petrie had nothing on me. I'd set my hair on hot rollers so that it was soft and bouffant. Bouncy and touchable.

I planned every detail as if I was making an entrance at the MTV Music Awards. And it worked. As I made my demure entrance to the church, just prior to the start of services, and had to stand in the center aisle searching for a seat, I could feel the eyes on me. A ripple of recognition that made its way through the place. Alice's sister, the whispers went. The one from California.

I sat down next to an older couple with a trio of children, all very well behaved. The youngest, a little girl, gave me a shy, gap-toothed smile, and my heart just melted. I was going to have a little honey like her one day soon. I could hardly wait.

But until then I had work to do.

I straightened up and surreptitiously scanned the congregation. Beth Ann was the type to sit way up front.

Sure enough, I spied her ugly mop across the aisle in the third row. And in the mysterious method that bad news travels fast, she was already peeking around trying to find me. I decided to ignore her. That's because good old Carl had come onto the pulpit along with a trio of robed ministers. Or church elders, or whatever they're called.

Like a heat-seeking missile his eyes found me, and he froze midstep. The guy walking behind him nearly mowed him down. It was kind of funny, though nobody laughed. He tried not to scowl, but I think it's his natural expression. Anyway, after scowling at me, he scowled over at someone sitting near Beth Ann.

Alice, of course, sitting off to the side with Daniel.

It was kind of like a *Three Stooges* skit, Carl trying to signal with his eyes and the not-too-subtle twitching of his head that I was here. Everyone in the congregation had to notice his sudden tic, so even those oblivious to what was going on knew something was up.

I just smiled to myself and picked up the hymnal. All during the ensuing service—sitting down, standing up, singing songs—I looked up hymns and read the lyrics. It was foreign territory for me. Even "Amazing Grace," the only hymn I knew and liked, had more verses than I would have guessed.

The truth is, all the preaching—and there was a lot of it—fell on deaf ears with me. Just when I was about to go stir-crazy and was worried I needed to get up and find a toilet, the main preacher stood and said, "Would everyone join in singing the closing hymn?"

The hair stood up on the arms when the organist started to play "Amazing Grace." I try not to believe in signs and omens, but I swear it was like God was pointing His finger at me.

So I sang. I'm a pretty good singer. Not good enough to make a living at it, but I've done some backup work. I wasn't thinking about that, though. I was just singing, following the words in the hymnal, thinking about what they actually meant and putting my all into it.

I'd never sung a hymn in church in my whole life. Even at the funerals of the several musicians I knew who'd died—mostly of drug overdoses—I'd been there mainly so I could lecture G.G. on the dangers of drug use. But I'd never really participated in the ceremony.

Today I participated.

It was so weird. For those few minutes and six verses of

"Amazing Grace" I felt like I was a part of the people around me.

Of course, I wasn't. Not really. It was just like that communal high that people get at a rock concert. That "we're all in this together" feeling that disappears the minute the traffic jam starts in the parking lot. We're all in this together, but screw you and get out of my way.

But despite my cynicism and my plan to submarine Beth Ann, I couldn't deny the strange seductive aspect to the whole church thing. It wasn't the God thing, though. If God is really God, then he's everywhere and I don't have to be in church to pray to Him. Or Her. No, the lure of church lies in the people. Even though I wanted to squash Beth Ann and her cronies, I knew there had to be some good people here. I mean, Harriet came. And Alice was, at heart, a decent person. Weak and cowardly, perhaps, without a shred of self-confidence but not truly bad. Not like Beth Ann.

When the final verse of "Amazing Grace" faded I just stood there, waiting for everyone else to filter out into the aisle. When I saw Beth Ann, I greeted her like we were best buds.

"Why, Beth Ann. I'm so glad to see you." *No lie there.* "I thought I'd follow your advice and try Alice's church."

Then I smiled at the man next to her, a bull-necked fellow with a ruddy complexion—and an obvious eye for the ladies if his examination of my bosom was any indication.

"Buddy Theriot," he said. "You must be Alice's sister from California, right?"

"Right. Zoe Vidrine." I extended my hand just to annoy Beth Ann, whose pinched expression actually looked like it hurt. He gave my hand a hearty shake and a warm, inappropriate squeeze. Now here was a way to really torture Beth Ann—if I could stomach flirting with the Neanderthal.

Before I could move on that plan, though, Harriet showed up. "Zoe. You didn't tell me you were coming to church."

Her clear gaze pinned me there. Not accusing exactly. But she knew what I was up to, like a mother with eyes in the back of her head knows when her kids are up to no good.

I tried not to look too guilty. "It was an impulse. And curiosity."

"Well, we're mighty glad you came," Bud the Neanderthal boomed out. "This congregation needs some livenin' up."

I spied Alice in the aisle against the side wall, staring anxiously at the little knot of people around me. Next to her Vivian took her arm and urged her toward the front door. Like I said, a coward.

"Zoe," Harriet said. "Could I bother you for a ride home?"

"Sure." I was in for a grilling now.

"Wonderful. Just let me go tell Vivian she needn't wait around for me," she said.

Harriet was friendly with Vivian, who was one of Alice's friends and one of Beth Ann's cohorts? I swear I felt as jealous as a junior high kid. Harriet was supposed to be *my* friend, not *theirs*.

The trouble was, Harriet was not playing that game, as she made clear on the ride home.

"What was that all about?" she demanded to know.

I shoved Jenny into third gear as we hit Highway 59. "Let's just call it research, okay? Alice and her church are enjoying the benefits of my inheritance. I just wanted to check them out."

"Humph." She lifted a handkerchief to her nose and blew.

I glanced at her. "It's true."

She folded the embroidered handkerchief into her purse. "And tweaking Beth Ann's nose had nothing to do with it?"

I couldn't help it, I laughed. "Okay, okay. I admit it. But come on, Harriet. You have to admit she deserves it."

That's when a little giggle leaked out of her. "The way Bud was eating you up with his eyes, I thought she was going to shrivel up like a prune, she was frowning so bad. But really, Zoe. At church?"

"So I'm a sinner. What else is new? So is Beth Ann."

"So are we all. Nevertheless, a church is not the place to play out your revenge schemes. I want you to promise me that you'll only go back to church if you are sincerely seeking guidance from the Lord."

Even in the dim light from the dashboard I could tell she was serious. I gave a great, exaggerated sigh. "Okay. No church for me."

"That's not what I said."

I snorted. "When I decide to go to church for real—or should I say *if*—it sure won't be to that church."

She didn't respond to that, but I knew what she was thinking. *We'll see*, was written all over her sweet, serene face. *We'll see*.

Alice avoided me the next day. All she said when she saw me around ten was, "That was low, coming to my church just to make trouble."

"What trouble? I was good as gold."

She left without answering back, just drove away. To the church, I guess. To the open arms of her venomous friends, no doubt.

I found Daniel upstairs hunched over an open textbook on his desk. He had on headphones and his body was boogying in the chair. When I knocked on the open door, he looked up with a guilty expression.

"Oh, hey. Come on in," he said, pulling off the headphones with a relieved grin.

"Thought I was your mom, didn't you?"

"Yeah." He toyed with the headphones. "She doesn't like me listening to music while I study."

"That's because she loves you and wants you to do well in school. Our mother didn't really care about school for us, let alone homework."

"But you both learned everything you need to learn, so—"

"Your mom ended up getting her GED when she was

almost twenty. I never got any kind of degree at all. Neither of us wants that for you."

He digested that for a moment. "But you became a writer, anyway. And I see all those books you read."

"I like to read. Correction, I love to read. Probably because I had nothing else to do. Luckily Oracle had this great librarian who guided my reading choices. But even he couldn't convince me to go to high school or get a GED."

He stared at me, his young face creased in serious thought. "You could still get one. It isn't too late."

That took me aback, and I laughed in surprise. "Yeah. I guess I could. But we were talking about you, not me."

"I'm studying," he protested. "Mom gave me this super long list of stuff to do—or else. And I'm doing it."

I smiled at him and a wave of warm feelings welled up in my chest. "You're a good kid, Daniel. I'm sorry it took me so long to come and meet you, but I'm glad to know you now." Then before my ridiculous emotions could embarrass me, I thumped the door with my hand. "Call me when you're ready for a break. I've got a first draft done on that article and I want to clarify a few things with you before I finalize it."

It turned out to be a nice day. He worked in his room; I worked in my study across the hall. We took a lunch break on the front porch, talking about music mostly. And I did the final edit of my article.

It was almost four o'clock when I heard the phone ring. I let Daniel get it. I had just finished my e-mail to the short-features editor at *Spin* magazine, and was attaching the article. I pressed Send just as Daniel burst in.

"Miss Harriet's sick. She wants you to come over."

I grabbed the phone from him. "What's wrong?"

"I…I can't breathe." Her voice sounded weak, a pale imitation of herself. "Short of breath."

"Okay. I'll be right there, as soon as I call 9-1-1," I said, trying not to panic.

"No." She coughed and I was afraid she wouldn't be able to stop. "9-1-1 is too slow."

Of course. We were out in the country. "I'm coming. Just hang in there, Harriet. I'll be right there."

It took maybe three minutes to get to her house, but all I could think was how many difficult breaths she struggled for during those three minutes. Thank goodness for Daniel. He practically carried Harriet to my car and sat with her in the back seat, keeping her calm while he directed me to the nearest hospital. The emergency room took her immediately. It helped that the admit nurse used to take dance lessons from Harriet, and the doctor in the E.R. knew her from church. There are *some* benefits to life in a small town.

Daniel and I were sitting in the waiting room when my cell phone rang. I hadn't been carrying it around lately, but I'd thrown it into my purse when we left the house. I checked the number. My sister. How did she know my phone number anyway?

"Hello, Alice."

"Is Daniel with you?" No hello. Just an assumption that I must be corrupting her precious child.

I thrust the phone at him. "It's for you. Your mother."

Judging from his side of the conversation she was obviously too angry at his absence to listen. At first. Once he explained about Harriet, though, and that we were both at the hospital, I heard a lot of, "That's okay, Mom," and "Yeah, I know you were worried."

"She's coming over," he said when he handed the phone back.

Wonderful. But I couldn't worry about Alice because just then the doctor came out to tell us Harriet would have to be admitted. Her chest was congested; she needed to be on oxygen and IV antibiotics, and she needed regular breathing treatments.

"Can we see her now?" I asked when he was finished.

"Sure. Exam room three."

That's when the phone rang again. I flipped it open, expecting Alice. But it wasn't Alice on the phone. It was G.G.

"Hey, babe. Finally you're taking my calls. I knew eventually you would."

I was so shocked I couldn't respond. Of all times for him to call.

He just rattled on. "Coco said you were pissed, but I knew you'd come around. So, where the hell are you, anyway?"

I hung up.

Yeah, I know. I was being as cowardly as Alice. Avoiding a situation I just didn't want to deal with. But wasn't Harriet's situation enough for one day? Did I have to deal with G.G., too?

Of course the phone immediately rang again.

"Aren't you going to get it?" Daniel asked.

"No. Yes." I flipped it open. It was G.G. This time I did all the talking. "Look, I can't chat right now. I'll call you in a couple of days, okay?"

"What the hell? Come on, Red—"

I hung up again and this time I turned off the phone. Damn it all! I didn't think he could figure out where I was from just an answered cell phone call. But who could be sure? They do stuff like that on television shows all the time.

I put that worry aside, though, when I went past the curtain into Harriet's little cubicle.

She was propped up in a sitting position, so pale and drawn that she looked almost dead. But her eyes were open and she smiled when she saw me.

"Hey there," I said, feeling more protective of her than I'd ever felt about anybody. "You scared the hell out of us, you know?" I took her cool hand in mine. "Feeling any better?"

She took a scary-sounding breath. "I'm not so scared, now that I'm here." Another noisy breath. Her eyes moved from me to Daniel and back. "Thank you so much."

"Hush. Not another word about that. Look, do you want me to crank this bed down so you can sleep?"

She shook her head. "Easier to breathe sitting up." That shook me up even more. She turned to Daniel. "Don't ever smoke. Either of you."

"I won't," he said.

"Me either," I said.

"I quit twenty-five years ago, but—" She broke off coughing, and my fear for her soared.

"Don't talk, Harriet. Just…don't. You're going to get better, you hear? Do everything the doctors say. And when you come home, I'll stay with you as long as you need me to."

That's when Alice rushed in. "I hardly think that will be necessary," she said. "The Women's Auxiliary at the church exists for just this kind of emergency." She took Harriet's other hand. "How are you?"

Harriet gave her a wan smile. "I've been better." She took a noisy breath. "But I'm so tired."

A nurse came in. "All right. Time for y'all to step out. We're taking Miss Harriet up to her room."

By the time Harriet was settled in a semiprivate room and poked and prodded by a new round of nurses and set up with a respiratory therapist, it was dusk and she was wiped out. In the interim Alice had notified the church ladies' hotline and a little group of them showed up with magazines, candy and a bed jacket.

Vivian was the one with the bed jacket, a pretty embroidered silk thing in the same shade of blue as Harriet's eyes. Harriet perked up when she saw it and even I had to give Vivian credit. It was a thoughtful gift, unlike the chocolate-covered cherries that nobody ever likes.

"Someone needs to spend the night here with her," I heard Alice say to her friends. "I can take tonight. Vivian, can you set up the next couple of nights?"

"Don't worry," I interrupted her. "I'm staying."

"You are?" Alice asked.

"That's not necessary," Harriet protested.

"I'm staying."

So I stayed and they finally left. Daniel promised to take care of Tripod; Alice said she would come by in the morning. By then it was after ten and Harriet was dozing off. I settled down in the recliner in the corner, with the TV on low.

What a day. I watched the last of the news: Jim Henderson on WWL-TV expounding on the start of the baseball season and the latest on Venus and Serena Williams.

I was half asleep when David Letterman came on with his white socks and his unbuttoned double-breasted jacket. Then I heard, "G. G. Givens. G.G. stands for Guitar God, for all you unhip people not in the know." He paused. "It obviously doesn't stand for God's Gift to women if his current troubles are any indication."

I sat straight up. Oh, no! Not Letterman, too!

But there it was, me and G.G. the butt of a joke on a late night comedy talk show. I flipped to another channel just in time to hear a different late-night host say, "…ad in *People* magazine. Wow. All I can say is this Red Vidrine must be some kind of hot chick. Most old rockers would take two twenty-year-olds over one forty-year-old."

I switched the television off. This was getting seriously out of hand. I found my phone and checked for missed calls. Coco twice since I spoke to G.G., but no G.G. Even as I stared at the phone, a call registered from G.G.

Like it was a snake, I threw the phone into my purse. Then I found a blanket and dragged it over me, right up to my chin. For tonight at least I was safe and anonymous. I'd deal with tomorrow, tomorrow.

"You and me, babe," I said to the baby growing inside me. "And you," I added, touching Harriet's hand. "We'll get through all this just fine."

At least I hoped so.

CHAPTER 13

Harriet looked much better in the morning. Considering how many nurses had come in during the night to check this, that, or the other, she couldn't have enjoyed much sleep. I know I hadn't. But she still looked better, and more important, her breathing sounded much less labored.

"Go home," she told me while the respiration therapist set her up for a breathing treatment. "Go home, Zoe, and get some clothes and toiletries for me," she added before I could protest. "Unless, of course, you're waiting to talk to Alice."

"Ha-ha. Okay, I'll go." But in the hall, who do I run into but Alice.

She stopped, and switched her purse from one shoulder to the other. "How is she?"

"Better," I answered.

"Good. I can spend tonight with her."

"No. You have Daniel to take care of. I'll stay with Harriet."

"You don't have to stay every night," she said.

"But I want to. Harriet is the closest thing I've ever had to a mother. I want to be here for her."

Her face closed in a frown. "Like you weren't here for your real mother."

I stiffened. "There's no comparing the two women. My *real* mother was never a mother to me. She contributed the egg, that's all."

"And provided you a home."

I rolled my eyes. "Let's not have this fight again."

"Why not? This whole business with you coming back here is all about the house. You might have run away from it, but you sure want it now."

"The law is the law, Alice. Mom inherited it from her grandparents, and you and I inherited it from her. I own half of Mom's estate no matter how you feel about it."

But as I strode away, leaving her in the hall, an unsettling new image had already rooted in my brain: Mom, sickly and dying, maybe even in this hospital, being nursed every step of the way by Alice.

Our mother hadn't treated me any worse than she'd treated Alice. The truth is, she never actually mistreated us. No spankings or beatings or being locked in rooms—the kind of horror stories you sometimes read about in the newspaper. No, what Caro Vidrine did was neglect us. Ignore our needs. Treat us like entertainment, or even worse, as mini-adults. She'd never given us the kind of warm, nurturing love every kid needs.

So I'd run away—or maybe I'd run toward the hope of love.

But Alice had stayed. She'd stayed, suffering through that insane, chaotic life at hippie heaven, then stayed to take care of Mom by herself after everyone else had split.

Maybe she deserved something extra because of that.

"Crap," I muttered as I started up Jenny and pulled out of the parking lot. I was *not* going to go all soft on Alice. She'd only stayed on the farm because she was too afraid to leave. Then she'd put the screws to me without a second thought, telling people I was dead. As far as I was concerned, the Mom thing was a moot point, cancelled out by all the years Alice had lived rent-free in our house.

I'd convinced myself of the absolute righteousness of my position, until I reached the house and saw Carl's car parked around back. Now what?

He was in the front parlor, bent over a pile of papers. Alice's book? When he looked up, his face set in its habitual frown, I planted a hand on my hip. "So, how're the wedding plans coming?"

His eyes narrowed. "If I thought you were really interested, I'd answer your question. But it's all about the money for you. You don't care a thing about your sister's happiness."

"*Au contraire, mon frère.*" But I didn't elaborate. The truth was, if Alice married Carl, I could bet the farm she'd be unhappy. And Daniel would be absolutely miserable. Why was she even considering it?

Why are you pushing her into it?

Shut up, I ordered my conscience, which had begun surfacing with inconvenient regularity of late. "Where's Daniel?"

"Upstairs studying."

"Geez. That's all the poor kid ever does. When does he get time off for good behavior so he can have some fun?"

"What you consider fun is not what we want for that boy."

In that one sentence he managed to tick me off twice. First was the *we*, implying he and Alice were a unit. Second was the way he'd said *that boy*, as if Daniel was an aggravation forced upon him. I know my reaction was irrational, but there it was. I wanted Carl to marry Alice and solve my problems with her and this house. But at the same time I didn't want him anywhere near my sister or my nephew.

"Whatever," was my brilliant comeback to Carl. "Whatever," and up the stairs I went.

"Don't disturb him!" Carl shouted after me.

Somehow I didn't think Daniel would consider my interruption a disturbance.

"How's Harriet doing?" he asked the minute he saw me.

"Much better. You know, in all the rush yesterday, I forgot to tell you that I sent the article in."

"You did?" He grinned, excited at the idea of being quoted in a major music magazine.

"Yeah. Anyway, I just dropped in to take a shower. Then I'm going to Harriet's to pick up a few things for her. But before I go I'll check my e-mail to see if they've read it yet and if they've accepted it."

"Awesome!" He punched the air with one fist. "Just wait till Josh sees that!"

I laughed. "You'll definitely be 'the man,' at least for a while. But first the article has to be accepted."

"Yeah. Oh," he added. "You got a phone call this morning. Maybe it was the editor?"

"A phone call on the land line?" It couldn't be my editor. The only number he had for me was my cell. And besides, he and I usually communicated through e-mail.

"Here." Daniel thrust a scrap of paper at me. "A guy named Coco."

Coco.

I stared at the little yellow square, an innocent enough looking message. But it sent a chill of foreboding through me. How had he found me here? Surely not through my thirty-second phone connection to G.G.?

"Who is he?" Daniel asked.

I realized I'd been standing there as if I was paralyzed. Inside I guess I was. But I needed to answer the kid.

"He's…someone I used to know. Not my editor."

"Must be an old boyfriend," he joked. "I mean, you don't look too happy about it."

"No. I mean, no, he's not an old boyfriend. It's business," I added because he obviously was curious. "He's a jerk, the kind of person I don't want to be around anymore."

"Oh. Well, he said to tell you to call him as soon as you get home. It sounded kind of important."

Of course it did. And of course it wasn't. "Fine," I said, turning for my room. "I'll call him as soon as I check my e-mail." But as I walked away, I crumpled the note in my fist. Coco had found me. But how?

I threw my purse on the bed, then spied yesterday's issue of the *Northshore News*. Had Joe done this? Had he called the number in that stupid ad and reported my whereabouts in return for a deal with Coco for an exclusive interview with G.G.? Or had he called *People* and made the deal with them?

Why in the hell did *anyone* care where I was?

But I knew why. G.G. was a celebrity, the first one I'd heard of who'd advertised to find his missing girlfriend. Of course the gossip rags loved it.

I snatched up the paper, shaking with fear and rage. Somebody had ratted me out and I didn't believe it was my cell phone provider. Not that fast.

That left only Mr. Joe Newspaper.

I ripped his paper in half, then threw it across the room. Unfortunately the torn pages fluttered down like so many ungainly rose petals, no solace at all for my fury.

But solace or not—fury or not—I had to deal with this new disaster. And fast.

I took the coward's way out.

I instructed Daniel not to tell anyone where I was, not even his mom, though I knew she'd figure it out fast enough. Then I packed some clothes, grabbed Tripod and hurried to Harriet's house. There I stashed Jenny in the backyard behind the potting shed, put together an overnight bag for Harriet and used her car to go back to the hospital. More than ever I needed to be invisible—how I looked, what I drove, where I lived.

Back in Harriet's room, it took me a half hour to convince Alice she could leave to get lunch in the hospital cafeteria.

"What's going on?" Harriet asked once Alice was gone. "You look all discombobulated."

"G.G.'s manager found me. He called the house and left a message with Daniel."

"Oh, dear," she said. "Did you call him back?"

"No way." I sat on the chair beside the bed. "I need to ask you something."

"Yes," she answered before I could get the question out. "You may stay at my house just as long as you like."

I knew all along that Harriet would come to my rescue. But her perceptiveness and her lack of hesitation were way beyond anything I'd ever experienced before. I could barely speak for the gigantic lump in my throat. "Thank you, Harriet. Thank you so much."

"Oh, pish. The truth is, they're more likely to let me out of this place if I have someone at home to stay with me."

That was true, but it wasn't why she'd made the offer to me, and we both knew it. By afternoon she'd had two more breathing treatments. The congestion in her lungs had vastly dissipated, and the doctor told her she could go home in the morning if she maintained that same level of improvement.

"So you don't need to spend the night here," she told me. "Go home, Zoe. You look worn out," she added when I started to protest. "Go."

I went. It was dusk and I *was* worn out. Besides, Tripod would need to go out, and both he and Harriet's cat needed to be fed.

I guess I must have been preoccupied, because when I walked through the lobby I didn't notice him. Only when I was outside heading to the parking lot did I hear him call. "Zoe. Zoe, wait up!"

Joe Reeves.

I stopped dead, then spun around. "Stop following me!"

He stopped ten feet away. "I called to you in the lobby but you didn't hear me. So I followed you out here. What's the problem?"

"I meant stop following me around. I'm not going to do an interview. I already told you that, and I haven't changed my mind. So quit with the bloodhound tactics."

He rocked back on his heels a bit. "I'm not here to interview you. Okay? I heard Harriet was in the hospital and I decided to drop by on my way home. I brought her Italian cookies," he added, lifting a small bakery bag as proof. "They're her favorite."

I rolled my eyes. "Good try, but I've already heard from your accomplice. He called me at Alice's. Now how do you suppose he tracked me down there? You're the only one who could have told him."

His face went stony. "I haven't talked to anyone about you. No one except Petey. But that was just to explain why you dumped us at the Strawberry Festival."

I drew back in horror. "You told your son about G.G.'s ad?"

"No! I told him you had an upset stomach."

A part of me really wanted to believe him. I mean *really*. But I knew better than to trust a man. Especially a newsman. "Whatever," I said in my most flippant, southern California, affected manner. Then I turned to leave.

He followed. "Who contacted you?"

I shot him a cold look. "No comment."

"Come on, Zoe. Talk to me. Maybe I can help."

"No comment," I muttered through gritted teeth.

"Damn it, woman." He grabbed my arm and spun me around to face him. I reacted just as swiftly with a wild swing to his head. But he blocked my arm. Then he caught me in a bear hug that trapped my arms at my side. I tried to wriggle free but he wouldn't let me go. "Calm down, Zoe. Just listen to me."

I glared up at him. "I *am* calm." I spat the words at him. "If I wasn't, my knee would be crushing your balls about now."

I felt him flinch and got a certain satisfaction from it. But he didn't let me go. Instead he said, "I really hope you don't do that."

"I should."

"Please don't." He stared into my eyes. "Please."

It was a ludicrous conversation considering we were locked together from our knees to our chests. To my chagrin, I started to laugh. Then he laughed, and that complicated things even more. Because it made me totally aware of his very masculine body against mine. Totally.

He must have felt that awareness, too, because he shifted a little and loosened his grasp. "If I let you go, will you promise not to run away?"

I stared up into his clear blue eyes, just inches from mine. Then I stupidly glanced down to his mouth. His lips.

Big mistake.

"Fine," I muttered. "But no interview."

He let me go like I was burning him. I know he was burning me.

It was awkward. I wrapped my arms around my waist. He bent down to retrieve the bag of cookies that had fallen to the pavement.

"I haven't talked to anybody about you being here, Zoe. No one."

"Well, someone has. G.G.'s manager—" I broke off. He did not need to know any of this. If he wasn't the culprit, fine. I was actually inclined to believe him. But I didn't need to reveal anything else to him.

"G.G.'s manager called you today? At Alice's?"

I gave a curt nod.

"That means someone else called him. Or maybe he hired a private detective to track you down."

"That would cost money," I scoffed.

He raised one eyebrow. "Considering all the free publicity he's getting, the cost of a P.I. would be chump change."

He had a point.

"Fine," I said. "You're not in cahoots with him. But I'm still not giving interviews."

He studied me a minute. "You cut your hair and dyed it. And I don't see your Jeep in the parking lot. It's obvious you're trying to hide from someone, and I'm guessing it's G.G. The question is why?"

I shook my head in despair. "Once a reporter always a reporter. Or should I say, celebrity hound?"

"I'm asking as a friend, Zoe."

That took me aback. "So we're friends now? You always go to the mat for women who dump you on your first date? You'll have to excuse me if I don't buy one word of that crap."

His jaw jutted out. "This isn't la-la land, you know. This is small-town America, where neighbors look out for neighbors. Even ones they don't know so well."

"Get out the violins. I'm about to weep. You forget that I was raised here, Joe. I know all the dirty secrets of this 'nice little town' you moved to. Which upstanding citizen and his cronies might have raped me if he'd caught me. Which 'good' people turned a blind eye to me and Alice when we were just kids and which 'good' people are still turning a blind eye to the neediest people around them."

"Wait. Somebody tried to rape you?"

I was shaking inside, but somehow I managed to say, "It was a long time ago."

"Who?" he asked. "Who was it, Zoe?"

Taking a deep breath, I drew myself up. "It doesn't matter. I got away. The point is, there's lots of material for articles right under your nose that are more important than G.G.'s stupid ad. You could do a whole series. Start with how this town ostracized people with AIDS back in the eighties, and see if anything has changed. Then you can follow up with an exposé on how truly 'Christian' the members of our several Christian churches are."

His gaze never flinched. "Why don't you write those articles for me?"

It was a preposterous suggestion. He didn't really mean it. He just wanted to shut me up.

That's what I told myself on the drive back to Harriet's house. Just another way to manipulate me and get the inside poop on G.G. and me and the whole sordid side of the rock and roll world. But I wasn't going to be anybody's freak show. Not G.G.'s; not Joe's either.

Yet around two in the morning when I couldn't sleep and couldn't find anything in Harriet's medicine chest to help me out, I sat on her porch swing, wrapped in an old quilt, and I thought about Joe's suggestion.

Not that I believed he was serious. But if I did write an exposé on this town, what would I write? I could skewer Mel Toups. No problem there. And I could heap shame on the social worker who'd visited the farm when I was seven and Alice was ten. Some social worker. The woman had ended up with a cheap source of weed, and we'd ended up still stuck with Mom.

But the truth is, Alice and I hadn't wanted to leave the farm back then. It was all we knew and better than the orphanages we envisioned being stuck in. And for all the cold, uncaring people who'd considered us those trashy hippie kids, there *had* been the exceptions. Like Harriet and her husband, Hank. And old Mr. Pinchon at the library.

"Son of a bitch," I muttered. I was not going to forgive those other cold people for ignoring a neglected kid any more than I was going to excuse my mother for her single-minded selfishness, or forget how Alice had lied about my death and tried to steal what little I did own.

I straightened on the swing. *That's* what I should write about: Alice's fraud and her church's complicity. Would Joe Reeves run that on page one?

Not a chance. But it made me feel better to think about

it. And it made me feel downright good when I found a tablet in Harriet's junk drawer and a pen by her phone and sat down at the kitchen table and started to write.

Headline: Is Lying For The Benefit Of The Lord Still Lying?

I scratched that out.

How about: When Christianity Goes Awry.

No. *Awry* was not a newspaper word.

Sex, Lies And Inheritance Fraud. That was better. Then I began to write.

I'd written hundreds of music reviews and band interviews. But I'd never done what I'd heard some writers did: opened up a vein and bled all over the page. But that's what it felt like. I started with, "I was born on Vidrine Farms, better known as Hippie Heaven back in the seventies" and, like the gush of blood from an artery, my life's story just poured out of me. I wanted it to be about Alice and how she'd claimed I was dead and sold my inheritance to her church. But it turned into this Michener-type manuscript that had to start at the Ice Age before it could progress to the present.

I spared no one. Not my mother, not my unknown father, not the Mel Toupses of the world or the pious self-styled do-gooders, like Alice.

My hand was cramping and the sun was coming up by the time I'd reached the present day. I raised my head and grimaced at the crick in my neck. I hadn't pulled an all-nighter in years. By the afternoon I'd be comatose.

But as achy and tired as I was, I felt…good. I felt clean. Cleansed.

I stared at the dozen or so pages I'd filled with my chicken scratch, which got more illegible as the pages went on. I'd never before written this much this fast.

Then again I hadn't needed to do any research. It was all me, all my history and my feelings.

But could I ever share it with anyone else?

I stacked the papers up and numbered them in the right top corner. What I'd written here wasn't for anyone to see but me. But parts of it could be a springboard for skewering certain people.

"The reference tome of my life," I said to Tripod who only thumped his tail twice, sighed and went back to sleep. I got up to make coffee. One benefit of staying up all night was that I didn't have morning sickness. So I showered, washed my hair and ate a breakfast of grits and butter. Comfort food. Then, after straightening up the place and putting clean sheets on Harriet's bed, I left for the hospital.

I was sitting at the end of the driveway, waiting to turn left when a long, black Hummer limousine went by.

I turned my head to watch it go by. A black Hummer stretch limo in Oracle, Louisiana?

It was trailed by three SUVs one of which had one of those super-duper antennas on it. What was going on?

Then a television truck went by—FOX News 8—and my blood went cold. Arctic. A limo and the news media were heading toward my house.

I tried to convince myself I was wrong. It couldn't be G.G.

But the sick feeling in my stomach said otherwise. G.G. had found me. And like the complete media prostitute he was, he'd brought the troops.

CHAPTER 14

I wanted to turn around, run back to Harriet's house and hide under her bed. I wanted to find her husband's old shotgun and confront G.G. and his piranhas with a load of buckshot. I wanted to blink and wiggle my nose and make them all disappear.

But none of those happy possibilities was going to happen. Besides, I had to pick up Harriet from the hospital. So I gunned her car and, spraying gravel, tore out of the driveway—in the opposite direction of G.G.'s entourage, thank God.

"I should have just met with him face-to-face," I muttered as I took Highway 59 at breakneck speed. If I'd cleared the air on this bust-up with G.G. first, maybe he wouldn't have got this harebrained idea to advertise for me. What did he think I was anyway, merchandise?

Then again, with a television show on the line, Coco would never have accepted my break up with G.G. The ad in *People* was a PR gimmick he would have used regardless. All I could do now was lie low until the hubbub died down.

A dump truck ahead of me forced me to slow down, and by the time I reached the hospital I was a little calmer.

It took an hour and a half to get Harriet checked out. She looked good; more important, her breathing came slow and easy.

"Thank you for coming for me, Zoe. I can't tell you how happy I am to be going home."

"You might not be," I muttered as I turned into traffic.

"I doubt that." Then sensing my mood, she peered at me. "Has something happened?"

"G.G. has arrived," I said, scowling at the road.

"Really? You spoke to him?"

"No way. I saw his limo—followed by the paparazzi— go past your house, out toward the farm." When she didn't say anything, I glanced at her. "I'm sorry I'm bringing all this disaster down on you, Harriet."

"It's not *my* disaster," she said. "And I'm not really sure it's such a disaster for you, either."

"You don't know G.G. He exudes chaos and that's the one thing I don't want for this baby. I grew up in chaos. I won't let that happen to my child."

"I understand that. But maybe if you deal with him now you can resolve things before the baby's born."

I shook my head, fighting the feeling of being betrayed. "If you knew what that life was like, you'd know that nothing can ever be resolved. G.G. needs an audience and an entourage all the time. And Coco's always sniffing out another angle. They put an advertisement out to find me, Harriet, when I made it clear he and I were done. Do you actually believe they'd think twice about using our baby for PR? I mean, look at Ozzy Osbourne's poor kids, whose personal lives were mined for entertainment value. Name one celebrity kid who grew up normal. Drew Barrymore? No. Chastity Bono? No. Sean Lennon?"

"Opie grew up okay."

I rolled my eyes. "He's the exception that proves the rule."

"Drugs and alcohol abuse are not restricted only to celebrities, Zoe. It's pervasive throughout our society."

"But it's so available in the entertainment world. I don't ever want Jesse/Jessie to see her father drunk or stoned. I don't want her going to school with spoiled-rotten celebrities' kids, or going to their houses to play or party or God knows what."

"You can't protect your child from the world, Zoe."

I gripped the steering wheel tighter. "I can try."

"Like Alice has done? Homeschooling Daniel, restricting all his activities, all his friendships? I got the distinct impression you disapproved of the way she hovers over him."

"Because he's fifteen, not five. It's time for her to cut him some slack."

"True. But children learn to make good decisions slowly, over time. Every new experience becomes another learning experience." She paused. "And then there's the question of your child needing to know his father."

"Why? I never knew mine."

She raised her white eyebrows. "Enough said."

I glared at her. "My mom was the problem in my life, Harriet. Not my absent father."

"Yes. But a sane, sober father would have helped. You can't deny that."

No, I couldn't. "The trouble is, G.G. will never be a sane or sober father."

"Maybe. Or maybe fatherhood will change him, like impending motherhood has already changed you."

I didn't know how to respond to that. I wanted to scoff, but unfortunately she had a good point. Not until we pulled into her driveway—no sight of G.G.'s little parade, thank heaven—did I say, "Maybe G.G. *can* change. But until he does, my baby's going nowhere near him. And I'm taking all bets that he *won't* change. Not even for his own child."

I hoped that would end this conversation. But as I helped her out of the car she said, "So, does this mean you'll tell him about your pregnancy?"

"No way."

"Then how can he ever get the motivation to change that you got?"

"Look, Harriet," I said, stopping at the porch steps. "My change was actually easy—get away from drunks, druggies and all other forms of human chaos. G.G.'s problems go a lot deeper. He *is* the drunk, druggie, source of all chaos. I went to a couple of Al-Anon meetings back in Palm Springs, enough to know I'm the enabler who has to set boundaries. He's the substance abuser who has to hit his bottom before he can change. According to everything I read, going straight isn't something you can do for someone else. In order to have any chance of succeeding, you have to do it for yourself. So knowing he has a kid isn't enough for him to change. He's got to want to change for himself."

"Okay. I'll go along with that. But have you considered that knowing he has a child and being denied access could make him hit bottom and finally get the help he needs?"

Another good point. Everything Harriet said made sense, and I might have been swayed if he'd been somebody else's father. But he was *my* baby's father, and I wasn't taking any chances with my child's future. Better no father than one who'd corrupt Jesse/Jessie.

As we got Harriet settled back in her house, we dropped the subject of G.G. and his future—or lack thereof—in my life. But it hung over us like a storm cloud on the horizon. Even later as she napped in her room and I tried to read the *Times-Picayune* on the front porch, it bothered me that she thought I wasn't doing the right thing for my baby.

"It's because she doesn't know how unreasonable he is," I told Tripod. He thumped his tail at me.

"And how unscrupulous Coco is," I went on. One more thump from Tripod.

"And how badly G.G. and Coco want to be back on top."

This time Tripod only sighed.

I sat there awhile, basking in the spectacle of spring sunshine. But I couldn't focus on the newspaper, and eventually I pushed off the swing and headed toward the back of the house and the woods that separated Harriet's house from mine. No harm in taking a peek at what was going on over at Vidrine Farm.

Though I stuck to the deep woods—no way was I exposing myself to view—my heart thudded loudly enough to

alert a deaf man. Tripod, who'd followed along, kept looking up at me and whining. I guess he sensed my anxiety.

When I reached the edge of the woods behind my house,
though, I saw nothing. No cars. Not even Alice's. So I circled to the left, keeping to the deep shade, until I could
see the driveway and the side of the front porch.

No limo. No television truck. That was good. But one
of those vans was parked just in front of the porch. Like it
had the right. Whatever happened to No Trespassing laws?
I pulled out my cell phone and dialed Alice's number, then
abruptly hung up. What if the jerk in the van had that spy
stuff that let them listen in on private phone conversa-
tions? The paparazzi had become very sophisticated, and I
already knew that cell phones weren't really private. Otherwise G.G. wouldn't be here.

So what could I do to keep these guys off my property?
That's when I noticed Tripod ambling toward the house.

Oh, no. "Tripod, come," I called. "Come!"

Naturally, he ignored me. To him this house was now
home, his domain, claimed from Angel. Why shouldn't he
head toward it? I watched as he made his slow, nose-down-
tail-up circuit of the yard, sniffing and marking his territory as he went.

"I'm going to kill you, you stupid mutt," I swore under
my breath. Of course, if I'd taken him to obedience classes
like I always talked about doing, I wouldn't have problems
with him listening to me.

When he spied the white van he paused, ears pricked
forward. Then he charged, baying like a lunatic. I heard a

scream and some ferocious barking. When a car door slammed, I broke out laughing.

Okay, Tripod was sometimes a pain. But he had an uncanny sense of who was friend and who was foe. Not only had he chased this foe into his van, he now stood in front of it barking like he was cursing a canine blue streak. "You cat-loving, vegetarian lapdog, you! Get the hell out of my yard!"

He wouldn't quit, even when the jerk at the wheel laid on the horn. It only made good old Tripod madder.

All the guy had to do was offer Tripod food, and he would have folded. But the jerk couldn't figure that out. Instead he got the bright idea to run Tripod down.

Run my dog down!

It was my turn to let out a string of curses that would have made an NFL linebacker blush. If I'd had a gun I would have killed the van first, and then the driver.

But I should have trusted Tripod. He'd survived one fight with a big vehicle; he wasn't about to be taken down by another. He danced just beyond the driver's side door, barking his insults as the jackass tried fruitlessly to intimidate him. But the van had a terrible turning radius, and because it sat high on jacked-up springs and was top-heavy, the fool nearly tipped the thing over. How fitting that would have been.

I cheered out loud when the van finally tore out of the yard and sped off. "You did it, Tripod! My hero!" I yelled, running up to him. Judging from his goofy grin and lolling tongue, he was pretty pleased, too. I filled his bowl of water on the back porch, then just sat there and considered my situation.

I'd have to get a No Trespassing sign. And I'd better warn Alice about what was going on.

I called the church, and of course she was there. "Here's the deal," I said. "Apparently the media has made the connection between me and Vidrine Farm. Unless you and your church want your fraudulent sale of my land plastered on every trashy newspaper in every grocery store in America, it would be wise for you to say nothing to anyone, especially the press. Muzzle your Church Ladies, too. Oh, and I'm putting a chain across the front of the driveway with a No Trespassing sign."

There was a long silence. I guess I had come on kind of strong. "Okay," she finally said. "There's probably some chain in the shed. And there's a padlock in the junk drawer in the kitchen."

I was a little surprised at how accommodating she was being. I rummaged around in the drawer. "Yes, I found it." There were two keys attached. "Where do you want me to leave the key so you can drive in today?"

After we hung up I found the chain, looped it around one side of the gate posts, then locked it to the other side and put Alice's key under a piece of board laying beside the post. I made a No Trespassing sign from a piece of cardboard and made a mental note to buy a bunch of weather-resistant ones from the hardware store in Oracle and post them all around the property.

Or would that just convince G.G. and his entourage

that I was here? Then again, if the fool in that van mentioned to G.G. or Coco the incident with the three-legged dog, they'd know it was Tripod and that I was here, too.

It had turned cloudy as I worked. Now it began to rain. Typical Louisiana weather. Sunny mornings, stormy afternoons, with a beautiful sunset by way of apology from a fickle Mother Nature. Tripod and I waited out the storm on the back porch, just enough time to make me doubt all my plans. Would G.G. find me anyway? Should I just do what Harriet said and tell him about Jesse/Jessie? Would that make him change his ways and straighten up?

I thrust a hand through my hair, and was momentarily shocked by how short it was. But that was good. It reminded me how committed I was to changing my life and protecting my baby. I would be the best parent in the world, no matter what happened and how far I had to run to avoid G.G. and his insane lifestyle.

When the rain eased to a drizzle, then finally gave up, Tripod and I started back through the woods to Harriet's. But at the edge of the property we stopped, and this time I had the foresight to grab Tripod's collar. Because there in Harriet's driveway was the same white van.

"Damn!"

He sure was one persistent son of a bitch. At least I could trust Harriet to handle him well, though I hated that she had to. Sure enough, I watched as she pointed, first this way, then that. Finally he left and she stood there waving goodbye, like he was her new best friend.

I waited five minutes to be sure he was gone. Meanwhile

the drizzle returned, and by the time I got inside, I was drenched and shivering.

"You just missed the press," Harriet said as she handed me a towel.

"That wasn't the press. That was the piranha paparazzi." I told her about Tripod's triumph at the house. "What did you tell the guy?"

"That I'd never heard of a Red Vidrine, and I'd lived here for almost thirty years. Just me and my daughter," she added.

I grinned at her. "You mean me?"

She smiled and nodded. "I figured that way if he keeps snooping around here he won't be suspicious if he spots you. So, why did you go to the house if you knew they were there?"

"I wanted to be sure, and it's a good thing I did. I called Alice and warned her to keep quiet." I explained my threat, even though I knew Harriet would disapprove.

"This isn't the kind of secret that can be kept for long," she said when I finished. "Too many folks around here know about the Vidrine Farm, and once anyone refers to Red Vidrine, the connection to Zoe Vidrine will be a snap."

"But only if they talk to someone who's lived here a long time. There aren't any Vidrines in the phone book anymore, or a listing for Vidrine Farm since my mother died. Remember, Alice was born a Blalock, and then became a Collins. I'm the only Vidrine left."

As always, we'd gravitated to the kitchen table. Harriet

handed me a hot cup of tea and slid the honey pot toward me. "I'm guessing the baby will be named Vidrine, not Givens."

"You're guessing right." I licked a spot of honey from my thumb and changed the subject. "How are you feeling?"

She gave me this tolerant, I-know-what-you're-trying-to-do look. "Don't worry, I'm not going to lecture you again, Zoe. But to answer your question, I feel fine. Just being in my house again gives me a huge lift."

"Are you due for another breathing treatment?" They'd sent us home with antibiotics, a daily inhalation medicine and a respiration therapy machine that she had to use four times a day.

She wrinkled her nose. "I guess it's time."

Together we figured it out: where to put the liquid medicine and how to assemble the inhalation mouthpiece. During the twenty-minute treatment I changed my clothes and made us a late lunch.

Later, while Harriet napped I…paced. I tried to read. I turned on the television. I even dust-mopped the living room and dining room and swept the kitchen. But nothing assuaged my restlessness.

I went out on the porch and sat on an old metal chair painted a vibrant red. It was still drizzling and the yard was so green and the flowerbeds so yellow and orange and bright that even the overcast sky couldn't completely repress them. It was spring in the Deep South, the most exuberant season of the year, though I'd forgotten that in all my time away. In California summer is the best season; in

New England it's the fall. But here it was spring, and if I'd been in a better mood I would have reveled in it.

With nothing else constructive to do, I decided to do my nails. I was sitting with my feet up on a chair, with tissue woven between my toes, letting the first coat dry when a car turned into the drive.

"Damn it!" I swore. Was that persistent jackass back?

But it wasn't that persistent jackass. It was Joe.

To tell the truth, a part of me was flattered by Joe's persistence. And I would never call him a jackass. He was probably a really nice guy who just happened to be a reporter.

I sat back down and hastily unwound the tissue from my feet. "I didn't expect to see you here," I said as he came up the steps.

"I check on my friends. It's something we do in small towns."

"You're referring to Harriet, of course."

He gave me a long, even look. "Yes."

"She's been napping," I said, squelching a stupid sense of disappointment. Even if he and I could have been friends, there was no way now. "But I'm sure she'd love to see you."

"Don't wake her."

"This is her second nap of the day. If she doesn't get up soon, she'll be awake all night."

But in her room Harriet refused to get up, though it had nothing to do with her nap. "You talk to that man, Zoe. He's a good guy with good instincts. I bet he can help you with this G.G./paparazzi mess."

"Yeah, right. Never trust the press. Use them, but don't trust them. That's Coco's theory, and judging from what I've seen—the lies and distortions and half truths they'll print—I'd have to say that Coco's right."

Harriet snorted. "Coco never met Joe Reeves." She turned onto her other side, her back to me, and pulled the chenille bedspread over her shoulder. "You talk to him. I'm too tired."

So I went back to the porch. "She's a little too tired for company right now."

He'd made himself comfortable on the porch swing with his legs splayed, and he moved the swing with just the slightest flexing of one knee.

The man flat out looked good. He had on jeans, not too tight or too baggy or torn or artificially aged. Just regular Levi's or maybe a pair of Roebucks. Did Sears still make those?

The thing is, he was such a regular, unaffected guy, supremely comfortable in his own skin. And I could just picture him bouncing a baby on one of his knees.

Don't ask me why I got that image. It wasn't just the jeans or the ordinary knit shirt that wouldn't be fazed by baby drool. Just toss it in the washer and voilà. He wasn't primped or permed; he'd probably never had a facial or a manicure. A man's man, all-American and all that crap. As far from G.G. and Dirk et al as you could find. They looked like macho men on screen. But it was a carefully cultivated image, manipulated by makeup, lighting and meticulously selected camera angles.

Joe Reeves, however, was the real thing, and my stupid, hyped-up hormones responded to him big-time.

"So…you're planning to wait here until she gets up?" I asked.

He stretched one arm across the back of the swing. "I noticed the posted sign and the chain across the driveway back at Alice's house."

I crossed my arms. "Is that going to be tomorrow's headline? Vidrine Farm Now Posted?"

"I also heard a limo was sighted near here," he said without blinking. "I'm guessing there's a connection."

I jutted out my chin and stared him down. "Only if you decide to make one."

"If that *was* your old boyfriend, G.G., in that limo, that means someone has already connected you to him. Seems to me the trick now is for you to take control of how it plays out."

"I *am* taking control. I'm avoiding the media."

"That will only stretch things out, Zoe. You know that. Why not agree to an interview, have your say and be done with it?"

I shook my head, not hiding my dismay. "Once a newshound, always a newshound."

"The interesting thing is…" he went on "…I've been thinking about why you're so adamant about not talking to G.G. or the press. And I've come up with three scenarios. A—this is all a publicity stunt, and the two of you are in cahoots." I snorted and shook my head. He went on. "B—he physically hurt you and you're afraid of him."

"I could flatten G.G. with one hand," I threw in.

"Okay. Then it must be C—you're pregnant and you don't want him to know."

CHAPTER 15

"That's…that's preposterous." Brilliant comeback, I know. But it was all I could muster.

"Considering your touchy digestive system, not to mention your volatile moods?" He shrugged.

"Did you consider any other reasons? Like, I'm moody or…or that I could be manic-depressive and those mood swings are just my version of normal?"

"Nice try, Zoe. But you forget, I've lived with a pregnant woman before."

"Which, of course, makes you an expert? What I think…" I went on when he only grinned "…is that you're looking for some angle to exploit for your story. Any angle. Of course a good reporter requires two sources before he presents anything as fact. Then again, you were a celebrity reporter once, weren't you? No corroboration needed."

"If that was true I wouldn't be here trying to get the truth straight from the horse's mouth. Why don't you sit down, Zoe?" He patted the seat next to him. "Put your feet up."

I couldn't help it, I laughed. "That's right. All pregnant women have swollen ankles, right?" I sat down in a rocker opposite him, stretched my legs out, flexed my ankles several times and crossed them. Then I smiled at him. Nothing subtle about me.

I told myself I wasn't really flirting with him. This was business flirting, and there was a distinct difference. So why was my heart thumping like a double-bass drum set?

Because I liked the stupid jerk. And though this was strictly business with him—I could tell because he took a long, exaggerated look at my ankles—for me it wasn't as clear-cut.

"No swelling," I quipped, wagging my left foot in the air. "I told you."

"You're not far enough along to be retaining fluid."

I let my foot fall to the floor. "Whatever." I'm not sure where this pointless conversation would have gone if Daniel hadn't shown up. He was on a bike, and when he spied us he speeded up, then did a wheelie and spun to a stop in front of the porch.

"Trying out for the Extreme Games?" I asked.

He grinned. "I wish. Hey, Mr. Reeves. What's up?

"Not much. I just came over to visit Harriet."

"Cool." Daniel switched his gaze back to me. "I came over to tell you that Mom—" Then he broke off and his eyes darted back to Joe.

"It's okay," I said. "Joe knows about G.G."

That fast his youthful face registered relief and then excitement. "Was that him in the limo? Did you talk to him? Man, G. G. Givens." He swept one hand through his messy hair. "This is, like, the coolest thing that ever happened around here."

Cool? Right. "I didn't see him, and I don't intend to talk to him."

"What about the reporters? Oh. That's what you're doing now, isn't it? Giving an interview."

"No, I'm not."

When his eyebrows only rose up, as if to say *then why are you sitting here talking to a reporter?* I went on. "Like he said, Joe just came over to check on Harriet."

"Oh." Daniel nodded and looked from me to Joe and back again. Then he grinned, that goofy teenaged this-has-something-to-do-with-sex grin. "Ooh."

It was all too much for me. I jumped up. "Okay. If we're done here, I have stuff to do."

Joe shook his head. "She's got a lot to learn about Southern hospitality," he said to Daniel.

"Yeah. She's, like, all business, no fun." Daniel shrugged. "Sorry, Aunt Zoe, but it's true."

"I am a lot of fun," I retorted. "I am. It's just that fun is not what I came here for."

"Like I said, all business," Daniel pointed out.

"Then what did you come here for?" Joe asked.

When I didn't answer, he turned to Daniel. "Do you know why she's here?"

"Uh…" The kid knew—at least most of it. But he also knew how to keep quiet. He shifted uncomfortably from one foot to the other, and his cheeks turned pink, but all he said was, "I'm just a kid, remember? I don't know what you grown-ups think or why you act the way you do."

I sent him a silent thank-you. "Does your mother need to talk to me?" I asked him.

"Yeah, I guess so." He put his left foot up on the pedal. "Is Pete at home?" he asked Joe.

"Not yet. I have to pick him up from his guitar lesson in a half hour. He'll be at home after that."

"I bet G.G. has tons of excellent guitar tips," Daniel said, staring hopefully at me.

A little headache was starting to throb in my temple. "All you'd get from G.G. is a really harsh reality check."

"What's so wrong with reality?" he asked.

I just shook my head. I needed to have a heart-to-heart with Daniel. But not in front of Joe. "I'll explain some other time," I said. What a cop-out.

Joe obviously thought so, too. "We'll be home around five if you want to drop by, Daniel."

The minute Daniel rode away I leaned forward, frowning at Joe. "You *want* him to drop by, don't you? So you can pump him for information about me. Using kids as sources." I made a disgusted sound. "That's low even for paparazzi."

Joe just flexed his thigh and set the swing in motion. "Relax, Zoe. Daniel always comes over after Petey's guitar lessons. Alice won't let Daniel take lessons, so he learns what he can from Petey."

My shoulders *did* relax, just a little. "Oh. Well. I guess that's nice."

"Yeah. Nice. You know, that's all I'm trying to be to you, too, Zoe. Nice. Neighborly."

"Okay, okay. I get it," I said, trying to make light of what had all the earmarks of turning into a too personal conversation. "You just want to be friends."

"Not necessarily."

So much for heading things off. That goofy, juvenile part of my brain that still wanted to believe in true love and happily ever after sat down and squashed the cynical voice in my head that was yelling, *Major bullshit straight ahead!* It was so bad I even blushed.

"Okay." I slapped the arms of my rocker and stood. "Time for me to go to work and you to go wherever it is you need to go."

To my vast and insane disappointment, he went. I acted relieved when Harriet came out of her bedroom and caught me peeking through the living room window as he drove away. I dropped the curtain, turned to her and made a wry face. "I wonder how much the *National Star* offered him for an article about G.G. and me."

"Since when does the *National Star* do real interviews?"

"Okay, then. *People*."

Harriet just smiled and shuffled to the kitchen. "I think he was here for his own reasons."

"The *Northshore News?*" I snorted as I followed her. "He already gets a salary from them. Why would he do an article about G.G. for them when he could clean up with a national outlet?"

"Because he's a legitimate journalist," she replied. "Besides, I think he's got a personal interest in this."

"And I think you think too much. How was your nap?"

She arched her eyebrows at my pointed change of subject. "It was fine." Then she smiled at me, this warm, glowing smile that seemed to radiate love, and I couldn't be annoyed with her meddling and pushing Joe at me. I'd waltzed back into her life after a twenty-three-year absence and she'd accepted me—and loved me, even—in a way my own mother hadn't been able to do. I felt an answering love well up in me, grabbing my chest, choking my throat and filling my eyes with tears of relief. Relief! Like maybe I was lovable after all.

That sounds so *Dr. Phil*, doesn't it? But it was true. Poor motherless me—and Alice, too. And maybe even my mother, who'd been raised by her depressed grandparents. Poor motherless us.

But Harriet loved me like a daughter, and she and I would love Jesse/Jessie like no other kid has ever been loved.

I threw my arms around Harriet and held on tightly.

"Oh, my," she murmured. But she hugged me back.

And later that night after an uneventful evening that was quiet and restful, I lay in my bed down the hall from Harriet's and came to some very important conclusions. First, if Harriet wouldn't move with me, I might just have to stay here with her. And second, Alice could not marry Carl. Daniel would be miserable, and he deserved better. Which meant that if Alice couldn't buy the house outright from me, I'd have to rent it to her.

Of course I hadn't even got through the G.G./PR spectacle yet. But eventually I would. It would fizzle out one

way or the other, and life would assume some sort of
normalcy. Whatever that meant.

And as for Joe Reeves. Well, this new plan of mine had
nothing to do with him. Nothing at all.

My lawyer called me in the morning.

My real estate agent called me in the afternoon.

Daniel relayed both calls to me and I called them back
at once. It turned out that the house and remaining acreage
was worth even more than I had thought. The appraiser
had also put a value on the acreage Alice had sold to the
church. The bottom line was that I had a legitimate claim
to about three-quarters of the house, while Alice probably
owned about one-fourth. I could force a sale, he assured me,
and unless she mounted a vigorous legal opposition, it
shouldn't cost me more than five thousand or so.

I told him I had to talk to my sister and I'd get back to
him.

The real estate agent told me she had two different
clients already clamoring to see the house and had I signed
the listing agreement yet?

I told her I would get back to her ASAP.

Then I called Alice. When no one picked up, I left a
message. Then I called my editor. He liked my article and
would send the copyedits in a couple of days. "What else
do you have in mind?" he asked.

Off the top of my head I pitched an article on has-been
rockers, which he liked, then one on middle-aged women
bands, which he didn't like. That was fine with me. I'd

probably do better pitching that article to MORE magazine or even AARP The Magazine.

Me, courting middle-agers!

It was kind of funny, actually. I would be forty in two more months, but it wasn't the big four-oh that was messing with my head. It was the little bambino. Motherhood had me psyched—and terrified. By comparison, getting older was a nonevent.

Though I wasn't ready to submit a proposal yet, I looked up the AARP Web site to read their submissions policy. Really, I was just killing time. I needed to talk to Alice. Finally my cell phone rang, only it wasn't Alice. "Is this Red Vidrine?" a male but high-pitched voice asked.

My heart leaped in fear. "No." I slammed the phone down.

That's right, brainiac. They're sure to believe you now.

"Who was that?" Harriet called from her bedroom.

"Wrong number."

When it rang again, I hesitated.

"Somebody with the press?" she asked.

"I don't know. He asked for Red Vidrine."

It kept on ringing. She picked up the phone. "Hello? Hello? Hello! Who is this?" She shrugged then hung up. "Whoever it was must only want to speak to you. You didn't recognize the voice?"

"No. He sounded weird, though. Like he was using this falsetto voice to disguise who he was."

"If he was disguising his voice, that would mean it's

someone whose voice you would recognize. Someone you must know."

She was right. "But who?"

"I don't know, Zoe. But whoever he is, it's obvious someone has made the connection between Red Vidrine and Zoe Vidrine. Looks like your secret is out."

"I guess so," I muttered. Then I burst out, "Why can't everyone just leave me alone?"

As if to mock me the phone again rang. I snatched it up before Harriet could. "What!"

"Zoe?"

It was Alice. "Sorry. We had a prank call. I thought you were him calling again."

"What do you mean, prank call?"

"Nothing. Don't worry about it. Look, I need to talk to you. Could you come over?"

"Actually, I was calling to say I was coming by. I'll be there in about forty-five minutes."

I've been told that I suffer from tunnel vision at times. And this was one of those times. Despite being all freaked out by the call for Red Vidrine, I was totally excited about what I was going to tell Alice. I hadn't told Harriet my plan to rent to Alice if she couldn't purchase the house herself, so I was as keyed up about her reaction as I was Alice's. They would both be thrilled, and even I was excited about it. Alice wouldn't have to marry Carl. Daniel would be so relieved and Jesse/Jessie would have a mom, a granny, an aunt and a cousin to shower him/her with love.

It was ridiculous how happy I was with this about-face of mine. Me living in Oracle. Who woulda thunk it?

But I hadn't counted on Alice's plans. That's the tunnel vision thing I was talking about.

When she arrived with Carl in tow, I groaned. "Why'd she bring him?" I muttered. I wouldn't be able to make my grand announcement with him here.

We sat down in the kitchen, me opposite Carl. What did she see in the man? I'd never once seen him smile. Harriet served iced tea then said, "Perhaps I should let you all talk."

"No, no," Alice said. "I want you to hear our good news, too."

Their good news. Uh-oh. That sounded bad. Very bad.

She smiled nervously at Carl, then at me. "It looks like we're going to be able to buy the house, Zoe."

"We're getting married," Carl interrupted her. "It's a little sooner than we'd planned, but…" He trailed off, staring at me challengingly, still not smiling. "We decided on a simple ceremony at the beginning of next month."

I heard Harriet's exclamations of surprise and congratulations. But for the life of me I couldn't dredge up anything close to that. I was getting what I'd pressed so hard for. She would have her house; I would have my money. But all I could think was that this was wrong, wrong, wrong.

"Why…why so soon?" I managed to ask.

"There's no reason to delay," she said. "Carl and I have

had a sort of understanding for some time now. But we were dithering about all sorts of details that—"

"The Church will be making a decision about the new pastor in the next ten days," Carl said. "And since you've already talked to a real estate agent, we had no choice but to act. Of course, we're assuming you'll be fair on the purchase price."

"Of course," I murmured. But all the while I was thinking I needed to get Alice alone. I needed to get her alone and tell her my new plan.

"Well," Harriet said. "This calls for a little festivity. I have a bottle of crème de menthe—homemade. How about I get out the liqueur glasses and we have a little toast?"

"Alcohol? In the afternoon?" Carl asked.

My eyes narrowed and my nostrils flared. I didn't want to toast their union, not with crème de menthe or anything else. But I sure could have used a drink. For once I totally sympathized with G.G. and his many overindulgences. Just the thought of having Carl for a brother-in-law made me want to get blind-drunk.

CHAPTER 16

"You're awfully quiet," Harriet said.

I was sitting on the top porch step. Alice and Carl had left twenty minutes earlier. He was irritated because I'd refused to set a price for the house. I'd only succeeded in putting him off by saying I wouldn't mix business with pleasure and by setting an appointment with him for tomorrow. But I fully intended to discuss things with Alice before then.

"I can't stand that guy," I muttered. "How can she even *consider* marrying him?"

"Alice is lonely. And I think she'd also afraid of living by herself."

"She has Daniel. And her church. Besides, there are lots of other men out there."

"Yes. It's too bad she and Joe can't get together," Harriet remarked.

She laughed when I frowned at her. "What's this," she asked. "Sibling rivalry? You don't want him, but she sure can't have him? They'd make a great couple. Plus Daniel and Pete would be stepbrothers."

I know she was only baiting me, but it was hard not to

bite. "If Joe was interested in Alice he would have made a move by now."

"True." She sat down in a rocker, and I heard the comforting squeak of its back and forth movement. "I should think you'd be happy Alice is marrying Carl. Everything's working out just the way you wanted."

Yeah, it was. Except that what I wanted two weeks ago I now knew was all wrong.

We watched the sun go down, a coral and pink display against an aqua sky. The whole world seemed to hush as the heavens slowly deepened to periwinkle, then violet and finally a dark, nameless shade.

Harriet went inside to bathe. I fed Tripod. Then around eight-thirty I jumped up, grabbed the car keys, and drove straight to Alice's house. Correction: my house.

Thankfully Carl's land yacht was gone. But I wasn't happy that the chain at the driveway entrance was down. I found Alice in the kitchen making a cup of tea.

"Hey," I said, tossing my purse onto the counter. "Where's Daniel?"

"Showering, I think. Do you want some tea?"

"Sure. Look," I said as I perched on a stool. "You have to keep the chain up across the driveway."

"Sorry," she said as she pulled out a mug and fidgeted with the box of tea. "Carl probably forgot to do it when he left."

"Don't marry him."

Her head shot up. "What, just because he forgot to lock that chain?"

"No. Because… He's not right for you, Alice."

"Wait a minute, Zoe. Aren't you the one—"

"Yeah, yeah, I know," I broke in. "I wanted you two to hook up and buy this house from me. But it was a bad idea, okay?" I stared intently at her. "Marrying Carl is a bad idea."

She frowned and crossed her arms over her chest. "Are you trying to renege on our deal?" Her eyes got big and round. "Is that why you wouldn't give us a price tonight?"

"No. I want to sell the house. But to *you*, not Carl."

She slid the cup of tea toward me. Hot water sloshed onto the counter, but she didn't notice. "I can't qualify for a loan on my own—as you pointed out to me just last week."

"I'll help you."

"What?"

It's not surprising that she didn't understand what was going on with me. I didn't totally understand it myself. But I knew I was right. "Look, Alice. I've been involved with guys for all the wrong reasons, and I've vowed never to go there again. I don't think you should go there either."

"Just because you don't like Carl doesn't mean he's the wrong man for me."

"I know. But the thing is, he *is* wrong for you. And you're marrying him for the wrong reasons. You can buy this house without him. You can buy it from me without the bank, and we can work out our own payment plan."

"No." She shook her head. "I can't afford the monthly payments on my own. And besides. I want to marry Carl. We've known each other for years and we share the same values."

I thought about how he'd ogled my chest that time I'd approached him in his car. I gave her a hard look. "He's small-minded, self-righteous and a bully. Are those the values you share?"

She pushed away from the counter. "I am *not* listening to this. You promised you'd sell me this house before you offered it to anyone else—and at a fair price. Was that a lie?"

"No! But—"

"Then drop it. I'm holding you to your word, Zoe. Give us a fair price and we'll buy it. Beyond that just…just stay the hell out of my business!"

I sat back in silence as she slammed out of the room. She'd cursed at me. My church lady sister had cursed at me. For a minute I just sat there, caught between frustration and amusement. Then I dumped my tea into the sink. "Fine," I muttered. "Marry the creep." Why should I care anyway? Maybe they did share the same values. After all, she was as small-minded and self-righteous as he was.

My indignation only lasted as long as my trip to the foyer. That's when I spied Daniel on his way down the stairs, the little yapper Angel in his arms. "What's up with Mom?" he asked. "Y'all have a fight or something?"

"Or something," I said. Did he know that her nebulous marriage plans had just firmed up? He didn't look upset or depressed, which I figured would be his reaction. He only looked concerned about his mother's spat with me. Although I knew it was his mother's place to tell him her "good" news, I decided, what the hell.

I shoved my hands into my jeans pockets. "I was trying to talk her out of marrying Carl."

His eyebrows drew together in a straight, dark line. "Did it work?"

I shook my head. "They're going ahead with it."

"You mean, like, it's definite now? But why?" He hit the wall with one fist. Angel barked in excitement and he put her down.

"Because she thinks that's the only way she can afford to keep this house."

"I can get a job." He hurried down the rest of the steps. "I can help and then we won't need Carl."

"I told her we could work things out, but she seems pretty set on marrying him—"

"What do you think you're doing?"

I spun around to see Alice, and she looked ready to strangle me.

"Get away from my son! You have no right filling his head with your...your garbage!"

"But, Mom—"

"Go to your room."

"But, Mom!"

"*Now*, Daniel!"

With a muffled oath he did as she said. Then she turned her fury on me. "It's bad enough you come back here and insinuate yourself into my life again. But I'll be damned unto hell before I let you infect my son with your brand of self-indulgence. Mothers make sacrifices for their children—"

"So marrying Carl is a sacrifice you're making for Daniel?

Maybe you'd better ask him if he wants that sort of sacrifice."

"He's a *child*. It's not his decision. You of all people should know that. Mother left all the decisions to us. Was that right? No. I loved her but that was still wrong of her. Now you're telling me to be like her? You need to make up your mind, Zoe. Are you going to be a good mother, which is hard and sometimes thankless work? Or are you going to end up like Mother, always taking the easy way out?"

"And marrying Carl isn't *your* easy way out? Tell me, Alice. Do you love Carl? Do you?" I repeated when she didn't answer. "Is that the kind of marriage you want Daniel to make someday? An expedient one based on similar values and beliefs and monetary benefit—let's not forget that—but no real love?"

"You mean like your relationships?" She snorted with disdain. "Fame and sex are your values and beliefs. And let's not forget their money. So don't tell me love had anything to do with it."

"At least G.G. and I liked each other. He might have his drug demons, but when he's straight he's a cool guy."

"But you never loved him. Right?"

She had me there. "That's why I left him. Loveless relationships aren't worth it. I've found that out the hard way, Alice. And I'm just trying to stop you from making the same mistake."

"Well, thanks, but no thanks," she said with a bitter smile. "I think we're done here, so why don't you go?"

When I didn't budge, she did, turning on her heel and returning to her bedroom.

I wanted so badly to have the last word with her, to leave her with some pithy remark that she'd stew over all night and come to see that I was right. But what was the point? A year or two from now when she was miserable in her marriage, Daniel would be applying for colleges as far from Carl as he could get. Then she would know I was right.

Except that my being right then didn't help anybody.

I stared around the foyer, at the bedroom door she'd closed in my face, at the parlor so magazine perfect. Maybe this house was cursed. No happiness allowed within its walls.

I turned for the door. I'd tried to help her. No one could say I hadn't. If Alice wanted to live here with Carl and make her son miserable, there was nothing I could do about it.

I walked onto the porch, enjoying its serenity but knowing it was just a pretty facade. Tomorrow I would come and get the rest of my belongings. And I would give Alice a price that was fair to both of us. Beyond that, they were on their own.

At my feet Angel barked, startling me. "Oh, no you don't," I said, scooping her up. "You're staying inside."

That's when the flashbulbs went off, a volley of them blinding me.

"What? Stop!" I held a hand up to shield my eyes, but it did no good. Paparazzi are a relentless breed of bottom-feeders.

"Get out of here before I have you arrested!"

But the flashbulbs kept popping. I turned for the front door, seeking refuge.

"Wait, Red. How's about a pose?"

"Go to hell!"

"If you don't tell us what's going on, we'll just make something up. You know how it works. So come on. Talk to us."

I slammed the door, then dug for my cell phone. But I froze before dialing 9-1-1. Even if the cops came and ushered the jerk off my property—even if they arrested him—there would be more to come. He was right. I did know how it worked: if you're in the public eye, anything goes.

And G.G. and his stupid ad had put me in the public eyes. Now I had to figure a way out.

Alice hurried to the foyer. "What's going on?"

Daniel rushed down the stairs. "It's the reporters, right?"

"Right." I turned to Alice. "Do you have a gun?"

"A gun?" She drew back in horror. "Of course not."

"Dad had a shotgun," Daniel said. "It was his father's."

"Where is it?" I asked.

We found it in the hall closet. It wasn't loaded, but a box of shells set on the top shelf. So I loaded it and turned on all the outside lights. Then I went out on the porch and proceeded to shoot the jerk's van full of buckshot. "You have five seconds to leave. Then I start shooting again!"

"Wow!" Daniel exclaimed as the idiot outside ran for his van, jumped in it and squealed out of the yard, spitting gravel like it was the Trevi Fountain.

"You could have killed him!" Alice shouted. "Give me that thing."

"At least he's gone," I muttered. "I guess now none of us will forget to lock that chain."

"We wouldn't need a chain if you weren't here," she threw back at me. "We wouldn't be in such turmoil if you'd just stayed gone!"

That's what lingered with me on my long, circuitous drive back to Harriet's house. I didn't want to go straight back in case I was followed, so I drove to Slidell, up to Bush, then came back down Highway 21. By that time there weren't too many cars on the roads, and I made it back to Harriet's with no headlights in my rearview mirror.

But the long ride gave me too much time to think. I'd come back here for good reasons, I thought. But in trying to get my life straightened out before Jesse/Jessie was born, I'd dragged Alice and Daniel into another bigger mess.

Maybe I was just a walking disaster. Maybe the problem wasn't always the other person—Dirk, G.G., Alice. My mother. Maybe it was me. Maybe no matter how hard I tried I was destined to screw up everything, including my own baby's life.

Maybe I would turn out to be an even worse parent than my own.

Back in my attic bedroom at Harriet's I cried myself to sleep. It's a stupid cliché, but that's exactly what I did. I drenched the pillow with my stupid, fruitless tears and woke up with a headache and an urgent need to vomit.

Thank goodness for Harriet. She took care of me, much

better than I deserved. Green tea and vegetable crackers got me sitting up, and a half a box of tissues finally cleared my clogged nose and sinuses.

"Come sit on the porch," she encouraged me. "The sunshine will do you good."

I shook my head, then grimaced at its renewed throbbing. "I think maybe I can hold down two Tylenol."

"Okay." She got the bottle from the bathroom. "But there's a reason for those puffy eyes and that wet pillow. And I'm wondering if there's also a reason for you avoiding the porch."

Of course I spilled it all: my visit to Alice; our screaming battle; Daniel's aversion to Carl. My total unsuitability for motherhood.

She sat beside me with an arm around my shoulder as I cried and cried and cried. "And then this stupid jerk is waiting outside with a camera, flashing it in my face."

"Oh, dear. So they've found you." The mattress creaked as she shifted position. "What are you going to do?"

I sighed. "If I can shower without throwing up…" Again I sighed. "I don't know, Harriet. I don't know anything anymore."

What I really wanted was for her to tell me what I should do. A good mother to give me good advice.

Harriet wasn't cooperating though. She just sat there giving me her unconditional love, but absolutely no advice. Then again, when had I ever followed anyone's good advice?

One last sigh. "I guess, maybe, that I ought to call G.G."

She nodded approval and waited.

"And I ought to just tell Alice a price for the house and let her and Carl figure out their own lives."

I expected her to nod approval of that, too, so I was a little surprised when a little crease formed between her eyes.

"What?" I asked. "You don't think I should?"

"No. You absolutely should give them a price for the house and then let them take it from there. I'm thinking, though, that Carl may prove to be so difficult and penny-pinching over the house that Alice just might get her fill of him before the wedding happens."

That perked me up. "So you agree they shouldn't get married?"

She sent me a wry grin. "Married, yes. Just not to each other."

"She shouldn't marry anyone," I said. "Alice needs to learn how to be self-sufficient first. That way she can pick a guy based on love, not need."

"That's very good advice," Harriet agreed. "For everyone."

I got her pointed message. "Don't worry. You don't have to preach to me. I'm all about being self-sufficient these days. No man needed."

"The only problem…" she said after a moment "…is that it can be a very lonely choice."

I suspected she was thinking about her own solitary life since her husband had died. I patted her arm. "That's why I want to be here with you. We'll have each other. And Jesse/Jessie."

She smiled. "I am so looking forward to this baby. But there *are* good men out there, Zoe. Don't close yourself off to that possibility."

Joe Reeves. His name hovered unsaid between us. But though I found him incredibly attractive—hell, I found the man as sexy as all get out—I knew there was no possibility of a lasting relationship between us.

Still, the man might have his uses.

I swung my legs around and sat on the side of the bed. "Okay. I might as well get the call to G.G. over with. Where's my cell phone?"

"Wait, Zoe. Before you call him, wash your face, comb your hair and put on some makeup. You have to be strong when you talk to him, and looking your best is the first step."

"Okay, okay." It took nearly an hour to shower, wash my hair and get me looking halfway decent. My eyes were still puffy, but the steamy shower cleared my sinuses and I was actually hungry. But first I'd call G.G.

He didn't answer.

Of course he didn't. It was still morning in California and he never woke up until at least one or so. And even if he was in Louisiana, he was probably still on California time.

So I called Coco, who never seemed to sleep.

"Hey, hey, hey," he crowed. "I knew you'd come around."

"Have G.G. call me," I said.

"Yeah, sure. But there's details you and me got to work out."

"No, there aren't. Have G.G. call me." Then I hung up. He called me right back. I ignored it. He called three times before he stopped. Then ten minutes later G.G. called. Only it turned out to be Coco on G.G.'s phone. "I'm only talking to G.G." And I hung up again.

Finally a half hour later G.G. called. "What the hell is going on with you, Red?" His voice was scratchy, his early morning growl. "Are you *trying* to torture me?"

"I want this to end, G.G. You know I'm not coming back, so why this ridiculous, embarrassing public campaign to find me? We haven't been happy together in ages. So let's just…let it go."

"But, Red." He hesitated and I thought I heard voices in the background. Why wasn't I surprised? G.G. couldn't stand to be alone. He hadn't done anything without an entourage—and I included myself in that group—for years. "But I love you," he finally said.

Not what I expected. "Love me?" I laughed. "No, you don't."

"Yes, I do," he swore. "I love you, Zoe, and I know you love me. So come home, sweetheart. Please come home."

That's when my internal alarm bells went wild. *So come home, sweetheart. Please come home.* That's not how he normally talked.

"Are you taping this conversation?" I asked. "You are!" I answered the question before he could. Taping it to release to the press? "Good grief, G.G. Have you no pride left at all?"

"Look, Zoe. Just come home for a couple of months, okay? You owe me that much. Let's ride this wave as far as it goes. Then we can split up and go our separate ways. What's a couple of months in the greater scheme of things?"

Now was the time to tell him about Jesse/Jessie. I knew Harriet wanted me to. But if we were being recorded, or if anyone was in the room with him, like Coco…

I couldn't take that chance. I didn't want our child to become a part of his PR machine, but Coco wouldn't hesitate to do so. If he couldn't have me back supporting G.G. through this next tour and on this supposed television show, then Coco would play up our split and the pregnancy to the hilt. G.G.'s failures would become my fault, while any successes would strictly be his own.

In the end I took the coward's way out. "I'll think about it, okay? I'll think about coming back. But no promises."

After I hung up, I sat there a minute. The paparazzi were circling; Coco and G.G. were salivating over all the PR; and soon enough my pregnancy would be obvious. I was trapped, unless I somehow could shift the balance of power.

I sat up straighter. Maybe it was time for me to take charge of the PR monster, instead of letting Coco and the damned paparazzi run the show. That's when I picked up the phone and called the *Northshore News*.

CHAPTER 17

At three o'clock Joe and I met in Harriet's kitchen,

Harriet approved, but I wasn't so sure I was doing the right thing. It was more like the lesser of two evils, which I've never liked. Maybe that's because I've had to do it so often: stay in my mother's insane household or hitchhike cross-country; live alone in a tiny studio apartment in a ratty neighborhood or move in with a carousing rocker and be the smiling, airhead girlfriend.

Looking back there were only two decisions I'd ever made with absolute conviction, not a shred of doubt. The first was to dump Dirk and keep Tripod. The second was to raise my baby in the calmest, most normal home I could find.

Talking to Joe now might only be the lesser of two evils, but in the long run giving a legitimate interview to a legitimate newsman might kill the story faster than trying to avoid it. And that would get me to that calm, normal home faster than any other option I had.

"Why did you change your mind about an interview?" he asked, ignoring the iced tea I'd given him. Once Harriet left the kitchen he'd become all business.

I could be all business, too. "Last night some paparazzi

low-life surprised me coming out of Alice's house. Since my location will soon become public information, I decided to beat them at their own game."

"How's that?" he asked with no expression in his voice.

I frowned. "By going to the legitimate press."

The corner of his mouth twitched in the faintest hint of a grin.

I gave him a tight smile. "You like that, don't you? Making me refer to you as the legitimate press."

He tapped his pen twice against his notepad. "I'm asking the questions here." But the corners of his eyes crinkled ever so slightly to confirm the grin.

"Okay." I smiled back at him. A real smile. "Ask away. But I did prepare a press release, if you want it." I slid the envelope across the table.

While he studied it, I studied him. He wore khaki pants today, with a teal-blue knit shirt sporting a Perlis crawfish logo. It made his eyes look bluer than blue is allowed to look. He would have fit in an L. L. Bean catalog, healthy, masculine, intelligent, but not in the least bit pretty. I could imagine him holding Petey as a baby, loving him, being there for him through good and bad.

I made myself look down at my hands knotted together on the table. It was either that or worship at his feet.

"Well written," he said. "I take it you've done press releases before."

"A few."

"You were very careful not to accuse anyone or cast G.G. in a bad light. The yellow press isn't likely to be satisfied."

"I know. But if I keep giving them the same thing, maybe they'll eventually get bored and go away."

"There isn't much here for me to write about either."

I shrugged. "I'm not that interesting."

He gave me this long steady look that maybe said otherwise. Was he still interested in me? Be still my heart.

"I notice you don't mention the pregnancy."

My stupid heart sank faster than the Titanic. His only interest here was in the story. Has-been rocker's bored ex-girlfriend was no story. Pregnant runaway girlfriend with perpetually stoned boyfriend on her trail was another thing entirely.

"That's just a theory on your part," I said. "An unsubstantiated rumor."

That's when he put down the press release and leaned forward across the table. "I'm in a quandary here, Zoe. On the one hand I'm a newsman. I follow the news, and for good or bad G. G. Givens's dogged pursuit of you is news. On the other hand, I'm a parent who happens to believe kids need a normal life, far from the gaudy lights of fame and money and all the negatives that go along with them."

"That's a lovely sentiment," I said, very cool, very non-committal. "If I ever get pregnant I'll remember it."

He let out an exasperated sound. "I'm teetering on the fence, leaning in the baby's favor. But there's a third aspect of this that I'm guessing you haven't considered."

Uh-oh.

"If G.G. is going to be a father, he deserves to know. He deserves to know his child and be a part of his or her life."

"Two things," I snapped right back. "One, I'm not pregnant." *Sorry, little one, but this is for your safety.* "And two, G.G. wouldn't care."

"Yes, he would."

I glared at him. "No. He wouldn't."

"He'll care," Joe went on. "And he might turn over a new leaf and become a better man if he knew he had a child to answer to."

I laughed out loud, an ugly sound of derision. "Like my mother? Like your wife?" When his brow lowered I pressed the point. "She's an actress, right, who picked her career over her family?"

"She and I disagree on a lot of things," he stated. "But all in all she's a good mother. She loves Pete and he loves her."

"But you have custody. Either she gave him to you or you fought her and won. I'm thinking it's the latter, right?"

It took him several long seconds to nod.

"Do you think if G.G. had a baby—with anyone…" I clarified "…that he couldn't afford to fight for custody if he wanted to and win? And even if he didn't, even if he only had visitation rights, don't you think ten or twelve years from now he couldn't tempt that child with money and all the surface glitz his kind of life revels in? No child of mine is going to—"

Oh, crap! That practically sounded like an admission.

I took a deep breath and tried to look like I wasn't as worked up as I was. "I guess it's a good thing he and I never had a baby together."

He shook his head in obvious amusement. "Yeah. I guess

it is. But if you did have a child together and somehow managed to keep it a secret, eventually that baby would want to know who her father was." He paused a beat. "Wouldn't you?"

Like a knife in my heart his words sliced into my deepest hurt. Was it deliberate? Did he somehow know that I had no clue about my own father? Or was it just a fluke? Had he accidentally touched on the one thought I'd denied myself access to? I'd been pregnant for maybe seventeen weeks and known about it for six or so. Yet not once had I allowed myself to compare what I was doing for Jesse/Jessie to my own childhood.

Who was my father? I didn't know and never would.

Sorrow, rage and a world of pain snarled my insides, but somehow I held it together. I crossed my arms. "My, my, you've been a busy boy, haven't you? Googling me, I bet. Researching my childhood as well as my adult years."

"I'm a reporter. It's what I do."

"And now you think you know me and how to push my buttons."

His eyebrows lifted. "Which button was that?"

My eyes narrowed. "Nice try. Look," I went on, trying to get this interview back on track. "You have the press release. Do you have any questions?"

"I have a lot of questions about you, Zoe. But I'm guessing you won't answer most of them. So here's the deal. Whatever I find on the Web I'm treating as public information. That includes your mother and Vidrine Farm."

"Fine." It wasn't fine, but thanks to that paparazzi jerk

it would all come out anyway. "But I hope you'll consider Alice's feelings about this, even if you don't consider mine."

"The public record paints a pretty miserable picture of your childhood, yours and hers. It's interesting how differently your lives have turned out."

"You think?" I said, trying to be blasé and sarcastic all at the same time.

Again he tapped his pen against his notepad. "That's actually an interesting angle for an article."

I clenched my teeth. "Leave Alice out of this."

He leaned back at my vehemence. "I don't think that's possible. Your lives are too intertwined "

"Maybe so. But you don't need to go probing her sore spots, exposing personal things that aren't anyone else's business."

"You made them other people's business when you came back here with the press on your trail."

"I didn't plan that."

He didn't respond, and all of a sudden it hit me. He thought I *had* planned it. "I didn't plan any of this," I swore.

He remained noncommittal. "Whether you did or didn't isn't the issue. You came here, your boyfriend put that ad in *People*, and the media frenzy began. Those are the facts. And the fact that you want to control this interview seems like the next obvious step."

"I'm not trying to control it!" But of course I was, and we both knew it. "Fine." I threw my hands up in the air. "Write what you want. That's what you reporters do anyway. You rant and rave about freedom of the press, but you don't give a damn how accurate you are." I pushed up from the table. "I believe we're done."

"One question," he said, ignoring my fit of temper. "What are your plans after all this dies down?"

I glared at him. "I'm going to take lesbian lessons. Men have been such a disappointment."

That's when he smiled and his eyes lost that cool, assessing look. "That would disappoint an awful lot of men, Zoe." *Especially me*.

He didn't say it, but he sure implied it.

After he left I just sat there more confused than ever. Why was I letting him unnerve me this way? "Forget him," I muttered. And that's just what I tried to do for the next two days. I lay low at Harriet's house, mostly eating and reading and watching the occasional soap opera. I stayed inside, but Daniel came by every day with junk food and news. Too much junk food, not enough news.

There had been no more limo sightings, and Mr. Paparazzi had apparently got what he wanted, or else had left for better photos from more important celebrities.

"So what's up with your mom?" I asked him one afternoon while Harriet was on the phone with an old friend from her USO days.

"She and Carl are all busy trying to get a loan from the bank."

We'd negotiated a price that took into account her sliver of remaining ownership in the house. I thought it was very fair. Carl had acted like I was stealing money from his sock drawer. It had taken Alice a while to calm him down and negotiate a final price. Even then he wanted me to finance it, not the bank.

Like I would tie even one penny of my money to Carl. Besides, if his credit history was that bad, why was Alice marrying him? It couldn't be for love.

"They set a date to get married," Daniel muttered. "Like just before the act of sale." He plopped down on Harriet's couch. "Can't you stop them?"

"How?"

"I don't know."

That's when Harriet hurried in. "My friend Sam in North Dakota says the latest issue of the *National Star* is out, and there's a big spread about G. G. Givens and his missing girlfriend."

Oh, damn. "Did you tell him about me?"

"No, no. He's a big fan of G.G.'s guitar work, and when he saw the reference to this part of Louisiana, he called me. Anyway, he says there's a picture of you looking surprised. Probably the one on Alice's porch."

"Did they tell where I was?"

"They only mentioned a farm north of New Orleans. He read the article to me and it mainly quotes G.G. and his undying love for you—and all the songs on his new CD dedicated to you."

I rolled my eyes. "Don't believe it, Harriet. This is all about maximizing press exposure."

"Do you want me to go pick up a copy of it at the Walgreens?" Daniel asked.

"Would you?" I said. "And can you get a copy of the *Northshore News*, too? Doesn't it come out today?"

"Tomorrow," Harriet said. "Are you expecting Joe's article then?"

I shrugged. "I don't know."

I don't know. That simple statement encompassed every aspect of my life. I didn't know what to do about G.G., about Joe, about Alice and Carl. I just wanted to curl up in a hole, go to sleep and wake up when this whole mess was over.

But no such luck. Right after Daniel pedaled away, Alice showed up, the *National Star* in hand. "You should be ashamed of yourself!" she shouted, shaking the paper in my face.

"What did I do? I've done everything I can to avoid those people. Is it my fault they're so tenacious?"

She wasn't buying that. "I've spent twenty years undoing the reputation of that house. Twenty years of hard work and…and doing everything I could to make people see that I was nothing like—"

She broke off, but I knew what she meant. "Like Mother? Oh, Alice. Everyone knows you're nothing like her."

"You said I was." Her voice and face were that of a hurt little girl.

"Only in the way you drift around, looking for someone to take care of you."

She shook her head. "I don't care what you think, Zoe. All I care is that you've dragged me and my house back into the muck." She thrust the paper at me. "Look at this. My house on the front page of a trashy paper like this."

My jaw stiffened. Self-avowed Christian that she was, she cared more about that house than about her only sister. "Maybe now you'll listen to me when I say keep the chain up on the driveway."

"Zoe," Harriet said in a warning tone.

"Okay, okay," I said with a sigh. "Thanks for bringing the article over, Alice. Was there anything else?"

She just glared at me and turned as if to go. Then with a sigh of her own, she sank down on Harriet's sofa. "I came to invite you to the wedding."

Whoa. That came out of the blue. "You want me, who's dead set against you marrying Carl, to be there?"

Wearily she nodded her head. "But only if you can be there to support us. Marriage is hard enough, Zoe, without having your family opposed to it."

She meant me *and* Daniel.

I sat next to her and took her hand. It was awkward for me, but overall okay. "The problem is that Daniel will know I'm faking it. And even if I *did* support you, he's old enough to make up his own mind about people. He's growing up, Alice. In two years he'll be going away to college. Maybe you should put off the marriage until then?"

Her eyes hardened and she pulled her hand from beneath mine. "No. Daniel needs a good, moral father image. Whether or not you and he recognize it, Carl is a good, God-fearing man. He may be strict, but eventually Daniel will see that it's for the best."

She stood and hiked her purse strap onto her shoulder. "So, should I put you on the guest list or not?"

Not. That's what I wanted to say. But I couldn't. In her own brittle way, Alice was reaching out to me and I needed to be there for her. And then, who's to say the marriage would last? Once she got sick of him, she could always divorce him. After all, I told myself, it was only the Catholics who didn't allow divorces. And Alice wasn't Catholic.

"I'll be there," I said. "And I'll be an angel. I promise."

"Okay." She nodded. "Okay. Harriet is my witness that you'll behave."

After she left I felt absolutely drained. Trying to save Alice from marrying the wrong man was the first time in my life I'd tried to be a good sister. But it had backfired.

Then Daniel returned on his bike and things got worse.

"What did Mom want?" he asked before spying the crumpled *National Star.* "Oh. I guess she was pretty mad."

"She'll get over it," I said. "Sit down, Daniel. We need to talk."

He sat silent for maybe thirty seconds of my explanation before he burst out. "Then I'll run away!" He leaped to his feet. "I don't want him for a stepfather! I don't even like it when he *visits* us. How'm I supposed to stand having him *live* with us?"

"Calm down, Daniel," Harriet ordered. "I admit none of us understands the attraction, but your mother obviously cares for Carl."

"No, she doesn't. She's just afraid to be alone. Just like Zoe said."

I cringed. Me and my big mouth. "I should never have

said that," I told him. "I don't know Alice well enough to know what's going on in her head."

"Well, I do. Look," he said. "Did you mean it before when you told me I could always come and live with you?"

"Yes," I said after the briefest pause. "But no talk about running away. I mean it, Daniel. We'll work this out with you and your mom."

Not that I expected Alice to willingly agree to let Daniel live with me. But somehow I would work it out with her. After all, I'd been the one to set this ball into motion. It was up to me now to work things out before the ball flattened everything in its path.

CHAPTER 18

Each day turned out worse than the last. I say that
because after Alice's announcement, and Daniel's threat,
my only hope was that Carl and Alice's loan application
would be denied, which might make Carl think twice
about marrying her, since he seemed to want the minister's
job and house more than he wanted the minister's wife.

No such luck. Alice called the next afternoon with the
proud news that the loan had been approved, and that she
had been hired to run the small office of a local contractor
and member of their church whose secretary had quit to
stay home now that her second baby was due.

"That's wonderful," I said, which was only half a lie. I
was thrilled that she'd be working at a real job now, earning
her own money and dependent on no one. But she'd still
be married to Carl.

"The closing is set for two weeks from tomorrow," she said.
"So we're planning the wedding for a week from Saturday."

"Okay," I said. No way could I say *great* or *fine* or even
cool. "How's Daniel taking it?"

She hesitated a moment before saying, "He'll come
around."

Which meant "not well."

I wanted to tell her of Daniel's threat to run away, but I didn't want to alienate him by ratting him out. It was a ticklish situation to be in.

I rubbed my slightly rounded stomach after Alice and I hung up. "I guess kids are harder than I thought," I murmured to Jesse/Jessie. "But that doesn't mean *you* ever have to be this difficult."

Since I was already in the doldrums, I decided to call Joe and see how his tell-all article was progressing. It hadn't come out in the last issue, and I was on pins and needles about it.

"He's on the phone," the woman who answered at the newspaper office said.

"Would you have him call Zoe, please?"

"Does he have your number—wait. Did you say Zoe? Zoe Vidrine?"

"Yes," I cautiously answered.

"Oh. Well, then. Hold on, will you?"

What was going on?

Thirty-seconds later that deep, touch-me-in-this-primordial-way voice of his came on the line. "Funny you should call."

I shivered, partly in a visceral reaction, partly because this definitely didn't sound good. "Funny why?"

"I just had a visit from an old friend of yours."

I swallowed hard but refused to bite. So he went on. "His name is Coco—"

Oh, no!

"—and he was pumping me for information about your whereabouts."

"Why…why would he come to you for information about me?"

"He saw the sign outside the office and figured we'd be plugged in to the community."

"And you believed that?"

"No. He was probably looking to maximize press coverage and figured a small-town hick like me would fall all over himself trying to help a big celebrity like G. G. Givens."

I hesitated to ask. "So, did you help him?"

"I told him I was busy today finalizing the next edition, but I could give him some information in a couple of days. Don't worry," he added as my heart sank like the proverbial lead weight. "All I plan to do is hand him a copy of our Sunday edition."

"Oh." That answered that. "So the article about the farm and the hippie commune and how Alice and I were raised is coming out then."

"Yeah. Would you like an early copy of it?"

"No." I was dying to read it, but no way would I tell him that. "It can't tell me anything I don't already know."

He digested that a moment. "I'm hoping you'll like it, Zoe. I tried to be fair to everyone involved."

"Fair? Right. Let me ask you this," I went on, my anger building. Or was it disappointing sense of betrayal? "How about I do an article on your private life, your paparazzi days?"

"I was never in that group."

"And about your divorce," I went on, not missing a beat. "And why you moved to Oracle. Maybe throw in something about how your ruined marriage has affected your poor kid. I guarantee there are just as many people in this area who want to know your dirty secrets as want to know mine. For the most part people don't like the press. I mean, they want to see themselves in the paper, but they're afraid they might be misrepresented. Those two things, acknowledgment and truth, war within them. So they'd love to get the dirt on someone with that kind of power over them. Even someone they've accepted into their community. Like you!"

"Are you angling for a job here?"

His calm in the face of my rampaging emotions drove me a little crazy. "I have much bigger markets in mind," I bit out, trying hard to sound superior but failing.

"Hmm. Shopping that book of yours around, I guess."

"Book? What book?" I responded.

"I believe the title is *Sleeping Under the Stars*."

I gasped. Alice had told him about that? "That was a joke! I'm not writing any such thing!"

"A joke?"

"Yes, a joke. Alice was acting so high-and-mighty..." *And I just had to take her down a peg, rain on her parade, just like Carl had. Had she really believed me?* "Look, I have to go. Thanks for nothing."

"Wait, Zoe."

"No. Goodbye, Joe."

I hung up. Then I called Alice at home. I had to straighten things out with her. Plus, I didn't want to sit here alone, thinking about Joe Reeves and what he must think of me.

"Hi, Daniel. This is Zoe. Is your mom home?"

"This is Carl, not Daniel."

Ugh. "Oh. Hello, Carl. Is Alice there?"

"No. She's at the church."

"Okay, I'll call her there."

"Wait. There's something I need to talk to you about."

He wanted to talk to me? My radar went on alert. "About what?"

"I'm thinking you should lower the price of the house."

Was he crazy? "The price stands as it is."

"Are you sure?"

There was something extra sleazy in his already sleazy tone, and it made me wary. "What are you getting at?"

"I hear that trashy magazine you're in this week pays real good for information."

Son of a bitch! I scrambled around trying to think, to buy time. "You do know they pay better for pictures than just information," I said. "I've dealt with that industry before. If you call them they'll just string you along while they track down your phone number. Then they'll send a photographer down to secretly follow you around. They'll find me without you, and you'll end up with no money—and no house, I might add. I'll kill the deal, Carl. So forget about trying to blackmail me."

"You can't kill the deal," he sneered. "We have a signed contract and you can't back out of it."

He had a point, and I hated him even more for it. What a lowlife! Did Alice know what he was up to? Then I remembered how he'd ogled my chest that day, and I knew what I had to do. There was one sure way to get Alice to dump this sleaze ball.

"Why are you doing this, Carl?" I asked in a deliberately shaky voice. "I thought we had a deal. Alice told me you got the financing for the house, so why are you being so mean?"

"Yeah, we got the financing. But we have to pay a premium interest. That means a higher note and it's just too much."

"Wait. You two have bad credit and can't get a lower interest rate, so you want *me* to eat the difference?"

"That house is half Alice's no matter what you say!"

"No, it's not. But now that you mention money, I could use more than I'm getting from this sale."

"No way!"

"Hold on, Mr. Green Jeans." *Time to bait the hook.* "I have an idea that could get both of us some extra money."

I heard this greedy silence, then, "What kind of idea?"

"Like I said, they pay better for photos. So maybe you should take some pictures of me. We'll sell them, split the money, and I'll skip town before they get published. That way we both win."

"Wait a minute. You want to share money with me? Why don't you just send the photos in yourself and cut me out?"

"Don't think that hasn't occurred to me. But Alice *is* my sister. It's bad enough I've embarrassed her. The least I can do is provide her with some extra cash. But you can't tell her about our deal," I added. "It's got to be strictly between you and me. Swear to God, Carl. You won't tell Alice we're the source of the pictures."

Would he take the bait?

I added one more inducement. "Besides, if she ever finds out the source of the money, she'd probably reject it on principle."

It worked because, greedy hypocrite that he was, he took less than five seconds to say, "That sounds…good."

Just talking on the phone with Carl was creeping me out. The thought of stringing him along face-to-face almost made me gag. "You know what? It's probably not safe to discuss this on the phone. Some paparazzi use eavesdropping equipment to find people. Can you meet me at that grotto behind the church in two hours? You know, that grief center in the woods. I'll bring the camera."

My camera was the key to my hastily developed plot. After we hung up I dug out the old thirty-five millimeter. I found a roll of film, exposed it to the light, then rewound it and loaded it into the camera. That was my insurance: let him *think* he was taking real pictures of me when all he'd really get was blank negatives.

After we hung up, I set out in search of Alice, because my thrown-together plan required that she be there, too. But as I drove, my mind spun. The answers to a lot of question were beginning to fall into place. Like how Coco had got Alice's phone number and who had called Harriet's house asking for Red Vidrine in that fake voice. It had to be Carl. So much for being God-fearing. All he wanted were his thirty pieces of silver. How could Alice not see him for what he was?

Alice's car was at the church, but instead of her I found her friend Vivian.

"Alice went with Beth Ann to visit several of our shut-ins," Vivian told me. "Is it about the closing for the house? Because if you want I can reach her on Beth Ann's cell phone."

I wrinkled my nose. "No, don't do that. Any idea when they'll be back?" Already my plan was falling apart.

"No later than three," Vivian said. "Beth Ann has to pick up a carpool of kids at the Global Wildlife Center."

"Beth Ann has children?" My face must have reflected my horror at such a thought.

To my surprise Vivian made a similar face. "Thank goodness, no. Then again, I've often thought her frustration with her childlessness might be why she's so…bitter. And rigid."

I stared in surprise at Vivian so long that her cheeks turned pink and she ducked her head. "I shouldn't have said that," she murmured. "It was unkind."

"No, no. Actually, it explains a lot." And Vivian's comments revealed a lot about herself, too. She'd always seemed more accepting of me than the others. Maybe if I'd met Alice's friends under different circumstances we might not have been so at odds.

No. Beth Ann and I would have been at odds no matter what. She was rigid and controlling and downright mean.

But Vivian and even Alice's other friends were probably okay when Beth Ann wasn't bullying them around. Too bad Carl couldn't marry Beth Ann. Now there was a match made in hell.

"You know," I said to Vivian, giving her a genuine smile. "Despite how it may appear, I really do want the best for Alice."

She gave me a wary smile. "I'm glad to hear that. Alice has a really good soul. That business with her selling part of your land—she didn't do it out of greediness, you know. It was to help the church. And it has helped."

"I know." The surprise was that I really *did* understand. My sister might be an annoying blend of self-effacement and self-righteousness, but she wasn't greedy for her own sake.

Unlike Carl.

Since Vivian was being so pleasant, I decided to go for broke. "What do you think of her marrying Carl?"

She picked up several papers on her desk and began to tap them into a nice, neat pile. "She seems happy about it."

Aha! "That was awfully noncommittal," I said. "It's enough to make me think you're no more convinced he's the right guy for her than I am."

She looked up at me, no attempt at pretense on her face. "I just want the best for her."

I sat down opposite her. "Believe it or not, so do I. And I don't think Carl is it."

"Have you ever mentioned that to her?"

"Like she would listen to me. But yes, I tried to talk to her about him—and failed. How about you?"

She shrugged and tilted her head to one side. "I haven't directly criticized Carl. After all, he's a good, churchgoing man. But…I advised her to go slow, to think about it and not be in such a hurry to be married again. But this business about losing her home, well, that pretty much panicked her."

And that's all my fault.

I don't like feeling guilty, but there was no evading my part in the bad decision Alice was making. "She doesn't have to marry him to keep the house," I said in my own defense. "I told her we could work out the money stuff between her and me."

This time Vivian's smile was wider. "That was really good of you, Zoe."

I sat back in the chair. "Thanks. Unfortunately it didn't change her mind. She seems determined to marry him."

Vivian grimaced. "Maybe we're wrong and she's right. Maybe they *are* a good match."

The phone rang and while she answered it, I considered how unexpected this conversation was. Vivian and I were pretty much on the same page. *Face it, Zoe. Not everyone in this church is awful.*

In fact, most of the people were probably decent folk. Maybe they were a little too leery about people who were different from themselves because they'd built this very insular community, all white, mostly blue-collar, rural and suburban families. They might not be very approachable en masse, but separately they were okay. Except for Beth Ann. And Carl.

"—and you'll never guess who's here," I heard Vivian say. She smiled at me. "Your sister."

She handed the phone to me. "Hey, Alice. Where are you?" I asked.

"I stopped to visit a church member who's homebound. What are you doing at the church?"

"Looking for you." I turned away from Vivian and lowered my voice. "I was wondering, could we get together today? Just you and me to talk over a couple of things."

She paused a few seconds. "Don't you think we've pretty much talked everything out already? Because I don't want to listen to you bad-mouth Carl."

"I won't bad-mouth him," I promised. "How about you meet me in that grotto behind the church at about two-thirty. Okay?"

"You mean at Lester's cypress cathedral? I don't want any more of those awful photographers following you to the church."

"No one followed me. Look, Alice, it won't take long. Besides, your car's already here. You'll be here anyway."

She obviously didn't want to meet with me, but she agreed. When I handed the phone back to Vivian, she gave me a questioning look, but I just smiled. "Thanks. I really enjoyed our talk.

"Yes. Me, too. Maybe you'll come back to church services one day. *With* Alice."

I chuckled. "As opposed to coming on my own and shocking her and everyone else as before?"

"Church is supposed to be about faith in God."

I thought about Jesse/Jessie and how I'd never wanted to get pregnant, and yet now was *so* happy to be carrying this baby. And how I'd come here to take the money and run, yet now was contemplating staying with Harriet and making a home here.

Maybe God *did* work in mysterious ways. And maybe it *was* time for me to explore the idea of faith in a higher power.

I looked at Vivian and saw all the goodness shining in her eyes. "If I ever do come back to this church, I promise it will be for the right reasons, okay?"

"Okay," she said with a satisfied nod. "Okay."

I felt good as I left the church office, as if I'd made a first step toward making a new friend. It felt…right.

Then I stepped outside, saw the path to the grief/meditation spot the church had built in memory of their late pastor, and that good feeling fled.

I was about to wreck my sister's engagement and in the process probably throw this church into utter turmoil. It was for a good cause and I hoped one day she'd see that. But it was a pretty safe bet that no one at the Simmons Creek Victory Church would ever let me inside its hallowed walls again.

CHAPTER 19

I parked Harriet's car at her house, then walked through the woods to my house—Alice's house, too. I halted in the shelter of the trees and just stared at it. If you discounted all the emotional baggage hovering around the place, it was actually lovely. Magnolia trees framed the back view; the St. Augustine lawn was thick and green; and the colorful annuals I'd added to Alice's all-white flowerbeds gave a cheerful lift to the house's otherwise serene appearance.

It helped that Carl's Oldsmobile wasn't there.

My sister had done a wonderful job on the place. She'd turned an ugly, depressing old house into a real home, a safe haven. Certainly I could never have done it. I would have bulldozed it, but Alice had more finesse than me. And more vision.

But I wasn't a complete waste of time. Sometimes that bulldozer mentality of mine was the only way to go. Like today. I was going to mow down Carl and his selfish designs on my sister, her house and her connections to her church. I was going to save her and Daniel, come hell or high water.

My stomach grumbled. I was hungry, as usual these days.

I unbuttoned my jeans and took a breath of relief. These were my fat jeans, a pair I hadn't worn in years, and they were getting too tight. I rubbed my stomach. "Pretty soon there'll be no hiding you," I said to the sweet little heart beating in my womb.

That's when the most amazing thing happened. A flutter, just this little fluttery movement that might have been my stomach gurgling. Only it wasn't.

"Is that you, Jesse/Jessie?" I whispered. I felt another little flutter. A kick? A turning over? A response to my voice?

It was my baby!

I can't explain the intense joy that filled me, that lifted me up like a helium balloon in the Macy's Thanksgiving Day Parade. One little flutter, and I understood once and for all what real, never-say-die love was all about.

This was my child! My reason for being.

To sweeten things even more, I suddenly felt connected to every other woman in the universe who'd ever experienced this moment, this life announcing its presence in no uncertain terms.

I'm not the weepy sort. But once my tears started, they just wouldn't stop. My family was beginning: me and Jesse/Jessie—and Harriet and Daniel and Alice, if she ever got over being mad at me.

But like all good things, this most perfect moment of my life had to end. Beyond the corner of the house I saw a car pull into the driveway. A limousine.

My heart plummeted. That could mean only one thing: G.G.

"Not yet," I protested. "Not yet!"

I'd have to deal with him eventually. But not today!

Of course, that same paparazzi jerk's van trailed the limousine. Too bad Tripod wasn't here to eat the idiot. Then again, my dear mutt would probably be overjoyed to see G.G. and maybe even Coco. After all, they were notorious for slipping him all kinds of treats a dog should never eat.

Sticking to the trees, I edged around for a view of the front of the house. Daniel stood at the top of the steps with Angel in his arms, barring the way for Coco. Then G.G. got out of the limousine. The damned photographer had his camera out, snapping pictures like this was the meeting between Reagan and Gorbachev.

Poor Daniel was obviously caught in the middle. He knew no one should be on the property. That's why I'd posted it. But this was Guitar God Givens, who was on the top five list of every aspiring rock and roller's list of heroes.

I watched as Daniel shook his head, then backed up as G.G. mounted the steps. Angel was yapping a warning for all she was worth, but it didn't work. When G.G. and Daniel shook hands, the camera flashing like a hazard light on the highway, I knew Daniel was too starstruck to be counted on to chase G.G. away. Even Angel succumbed when G.G. scratched her behind the ears. He'd always been better with animals than with people. Probably because a dog's expectations were so low. Food, water, occasional affection.

Of course the photographer loved every bit of it.

Damn G.G. and his publicity-seeking soul! He was

putting on the full-court press. First Joe. Now Daniel. It was just a matter of time before he found me.

All I needed, though, was one more hour. Then I could deal with him. Just not yet!

I whipped out my cell phone and called the house. "Answer it. Answer it," I chanted as I watched Daniel dithering on the porch. Finally he went inside.

"Keep your voice low," I ordered him when he answered. "Don't let G.G. know it's me on the phone."

"Aunt Zoe?" His young voice cracked in excitement. "How did you know?"

"I'm in the woods behind the house. But don't let him know that. Keep him busy as long as you can, just don't tell him anything about me. And whatever you do, don't call your mother for the next couple of hours."

"Why?"

"Daniel, please!"

"Okay, okay," he said. "But you gotta know, Zoe, he told me he really misses you."

Right. "I'm going to call him right now. But don't let him know I called you. Okay?"

"Okay."

For once G.G. answered his own phone. "Zoe! Whoa. What a coincidence," he said. "You'll never guess where I am."

"And you'll never guess where I am. I decided to come home. To Palm Springs," I lied. I figured it was worth one last try to get him away from here. "I decided you were right. We do need to talk."

"You're in Palm Springs? No way. Damn it all! I'm out here in Podunk or wherever it is your sister lives."

"You're pestering my sister?"

"Hey, I'm just trying to find you. Are you at the house?"

"I'm at the airport. In Dallas," I ad-libbed. "I have a two-hour layover."

I watched as he turned and stomped to the limo. "Damn it all! Do you know how much time I've wasted traipsing around after you?"

"That's your own fault. I told you not to."

He slammed into the back of the limo like the big sulking baby he was. The reception immediately got worse.

I switched the phone to my other ear. "Look, you're breaking up. I'll see you when you get back, okay?"

"You're messing up my life, Zoe! You're costing me a lot of money—"

I hung up, turned off the ringer and shoved the phone into my pocket. Then I held my breath and just waited. Sure enough, the limousine did a sharp turn and in a cloud of dust took off. Daniel came down the steps and stood there gaping after it. G.G. hadn't even bothered to give the kid an autograph. Selfish jerk.

But at least he was gone.

The white van took a little longer to go. What was he waiting for? He and Daniel stared at each other from across the yard. Then Daniel put Angel down, and like a white streak she charged the photographer. I guess he'd had enough of dogs chasing him, because he jumped in his van and nearly rolled it in his haste to leave. Angel chased him all the way down the drive, then trotted back like a conquering Amazon.

You know, I was beginning to really like that dog.

I heaved a huge sigh of relief. Another disaster averted. If only my plans for Carl went as well.

With a half hour still to go before our tryst, I returned to Harriet's and changed clothes. Lately I'd been dressing down and not wearing any makeup at all. But Carl might need some coaxing, so I fluffed up my hair with light styling wax and some spray-on shine. I did my eyes in a sultry evening look with charcoal eyeliner and long, long lashes, and I used Deep Pouty Pink to emphasize my lips.

It was no problem finding a tight blouse. These days they were all tight. To a red V-neck sleeveless shell with decorative black piping I added a short, black swirly skirt and ankle-strap heels. Then I studied myself in the bathroom mirror.

Red wasn't usually my best color, but with my hair so dark and messy, and kohl-rimmed eyes, I looked like a young Joan Collins, ready to seduce the very next man who happened by. Lucky fella.

As I left the bathroom with my heels clicking on the hardwood floor, Harriet woke up. "Where are you off to?" she asked, giving me a suspicious once-over.

"I'm going to see a man about a house," I replied in a tone I hoped sounded breezy.

She shook her head in dismay. "You look ready to devour whoever he is. What's going on?"

"I'm making things right. Okay? First with Alice, then

with G.G. I'll explain everything once I get back." Then I left through the back door, heading for the woods and the path past Alice's house and on to the church.

I'd forgotten about the heels, though. They sank into the ground, forcing me to walk on my tiptoes the whole way. It took twice as long, I was sweating and my calves were killing me when I finally reached the grotto. Some hot chick I was. I was also as nervous as a fifteen-year-old on her first date.

What if he didn't come?

What if he came to take the photos but didn't bite on the sexy poses I planned to strike?

What if Alice came too early? Or too late? Or forgave him his trespasses?

I thrust my hands through my hair and tried to take a couple of calming breaths. "You're making yourself crazy," I muttered to myself. "Just…just cool it." So I sat on one of the benches and gazed over the peaceful marshy scene.

A white egret stood across the way, framed by a glorious display of wild purple irises. Postcard pretty, it was almost too perfect to be real—until the bird's long graceful neck darted out, and it speared some unseen morsel.

As silent ripples faded away from the egret, I looked up at the sky. The bright green of new cypress needles emphasized the crisp blue of the heavens, and some sweet, musty medley of flowers and dampness and spring completed the picture.

It was beautiful here, an undisturbed landscape. No wonder Alice and her church members had honored their beloved pastor with this place of quiet meditation.

I bent over to see his name on the bench's frame. "You know he's not right for her or for Daniel, don't you?" I murmured to the brother-in-law I'd never met.

A breeze quickened beneath the cypress shade. If I believed in such things I would believe it was him answering me. Then I slid my fingers once more across his name. I *did* believe in such things. The oddest shiver rippled up my spine. Odd, but not at all scary. I believed the Reverend Lester Collins *was* here and he wanted the best for his family.

I sat back and tilted my head to stare straight up through the cypress branches to the sky. If I believed he was here, then why not go the whole way, follow this trail to its logical conclusion? If the good Reverend's spirit was here, so was God's. In fact, maybe my being here was no accident at all. Maybe I was supposed to get pregnant and come here and reunite with Alice so I could save her from Carl.

The old me would have laughed at such a notion and said it was getting mighty deep in here. But I didn't feel like laughing.

Maybe there was an even larger plan, that I would be saved from my dead-end life by interceding in Alice's and Daniel's. And then there was Harriet and the mothering she so freely offered. And Joe—

I shook my head. I didn't know *what* was up with Joe Reeves.

I blinked up at the blindingly blue sky. "I don't know what You have in mind, God. But I think…I think maybe I'm going along for the ride."

It felt good saying that out loud. Believing it. Accepting it. I'd thought I was so free the day I headed east, away from California and G.G. and the chaos of that life. But running wasn't the same as being free. Besides, I wasn't free. I had family now and responsibilities. And I wanted them.

The old Janis Joplin lyrics insinuated themselves into my head, about freedom being just another word for nothing left to lose. That wasn't the kind of freedom I wanted. Because it turned out that I had a lot to lose, more now than at any other time of my life.

"So you're here."

I jerked as the intrusive grate of Carl's voice brought me crashing back to the moment. So much for serenity.

I looked over at him, keeping my every movement slow and languid. I had a part to play and I had to keep control of the situation. "Of course I'm here, Carl. I brought the camera, and I've been thinking about poses," I went on, unfurling my tall self from Lester's bench. "I could do a few prim ones. You know, earnest expression—Rocker's Girl Goes Mayberry. That sort of thing. But they'll pay a lot better for suggestive poses."

His icky gaze ran over me, and I actually shuddered in revulsion. *That's not the way to maintain control, Zoe!*

I set the camera on the bench, then put one foot on the seat, revealing my legs almost up to my crotch. "I know you're a man of the church," I went on. "So you might find poses like this hard to deal with." Then I leaned forward over my raised knee and braced my arm on it so that my breasts were thrust forward. "But I promise you, this is the kind of stuff they want."

His eyes had gone almost black, like they were dilated all the way. And it wasn't just because the cypress cathedral was so shady. The man had lust in his heart.

"Being a man of God doesn't mean I'm repulsed by an attractive woman," he muttered.

No shit, Sherlock. But I feigned surprise. "Why, Carl, and here I thought you didn't like me."

He scowled. "Satan tempted Eve and sent her to tempt Adam."

Oh, yeah, that "women are the downfall of men" theory. Ignoring his remark, I picked up the camera. "Do you know how to operate a thirty-five-millimeter camera?"

He smelled faintly of mold when I got close to him. Like sweaty sneakers. "Here's the film advance switch. Look through here and focus by turning the lens."

"I know," he said, snatching the camera from me.

"Hey! Be careful with that. Do you know how to adjust the shutter speed and f-stop?"

"How old is this camera anyway?"

I gave him a brittle smile. This was not proceeding exactly as I'd hoped. "It's a classic. Let me set it for the lighting, then all you have to do is focus and shoot."

I set the shutter speed at one-thirtieth. Then I aimed it at him and rotated the aperture setting. The lens I'd brought had a zoom component, enough to make him look a lot closer than he was. And enough to make the direction of his nasty little eyes obvious. He was ogling my chest big-time. Maybe this *was* going as I planned.

"Okay," I said, bringing it to him and leaning closer than

necessary. "You see this zoom thingie? You can get really creative with it, cheese it up a little, if you know what I mean?"

Then I returned to the bench, and shrugged one shoulder of my sweater down to reveal part of my black and red trimmed scrap of a bra. "I'll pretend to protest you being here." I held one widespread hand up between us. "Now you focus so you get my eyes and lips and my left breast and shoulder. Tell me if I need to move my hand or shift around on the bench."

He didn't say a thing, just sighted through the camera and started clicking. And sweating. I struck a couple of other poses, but it got creepier by the minute. I hadn't done any camera work in a long time. And never in front of a guy who was obviously aroused.

I swallowed my revulsion as best I could. "Why, Carl." I glanced suggestively at his crotch. "I didn't think you had it in you."

He let the camera fall from his face. His eyes were hot and he was breathing hard. My plan was working but I was hating every minute of it. "Turn around," he ordered in a hoarse voice.

I did as he asked. "Like I'm running away?"

"Bend over."

Bend over? Did he have some secret porno fetish? "I didn't sign on for cheesecake," I told him.

"God made women to serve men."

I wasn't exactly following his logic, but I was willing to play along. To a point. "How about this instead?" I put one knee on the bench, grabbed the back with both hands, and looked over my shoulder at him as if I was trying to get away from him, which, incidentally, I couldn't *wait* to do.

"Lift up your skirt."

"That's not the kind of pictures we're taking," I said.

"Why not? You said they paid better for the sexy ones."

"But not posed ones." *Idiot.* "They want to catch their subjects in sexy, compromising photos. Like this." I turned and lay back on the bench. I rested one arm over my eyes, with the other trailing the ground. With my back arched, my breasts were thrust high.

I heard the camera clicking. Thank goodness I'd exposed the film. "You know, this would be a great make-out spot, so quiet and private. Except, of course, for the good Reverend's name on the bench."

"The good Reverend," Carl spat out. "Once I marry Alice and take over this church, Lester Collins can go to hell."

Where did that come from? Too bad Alice wasn't here to hear that. "Didn't you like him?"

"Shut up and take off your blouse."

What? I jerked my arm away to find him with his pants unzipped and his hand inside, rubbing up and down. Besides being violently repulsed, I was also panicked. He was going way too fast with this whole thing.

"Now, Carl," I said, swinging around to sit up. "What do you think you're doing?"

"Nothing you don't want," he said in this rough, breathless voice. "I know why you brought me here, and it wasn't just to take pictures."

He was right about that, but wrong about my true motives. I rose to my feet, debating whether to run or try and placate him. "I thought you wanted the money from the pictures. You know, to help buy the house."

"I got enough pictures. Hurry up now. I'm ready to go."

"Ready to go? You don't expect me to—" I broke off. I desperately needed to buy time.

"Don't act so coy," he snapped. "We both know you're not too particular who you open your legs to."

Oh, my God, I wanted to kill the son of a bitch! But he was digging his own grave, just like I wanted. So I somehow swallowed my fury. "But you're my sister's fiancé. I could never—"

"She'll never know." He advanced on me, walking awkwardly because of his you-know-what.

I backed away. "I might tell her."

He laughed, this creepy, crazy laugh, and that's when I knew he was seriously unhinged. "Do you really think Alice would believe your word over mine? She wants to marry me. You're nothing more than an embarrassment to her."

How I wanted to curse the little creep to hell and back! But there was too much truth in his words. I *was* an embarrassment to Alice, a reminder of everything she'd worked so hard to rise above. And even though I was trying to save her from a terrible marriage, the fact was, this would be one more gigantic embarrassment to her.

I'd known that from the beginning, but I'd figured it would be worth it. And eventually she would forgive me. Now Carl's confidence shook mine.

"Fine," I said, straightening to my full height. "Let's get it over with then. You'll have to take off your pants though. You look like a damned hobbled horse."

"Hung like one, too," he said.

Yuck!

It was amazing how fast he shed his pants. "Get over here," he ordered me.

No way. No way. No way.

Then a twig snapped off to my side and my hopes soared. Alice?

No such luck. I instinctively cringed away from the clicks of a camera on automatic—the favorite tool of the professional celebrity chaser. I covered my face and ran, leaving Carl to his own fate.

Unfortunately I ran straight into Alice.

"What's going on?" she asked, craning to see past me.

"Just run," I told her, grabbing her arm and propelling her away. "I'll explain later."

Then Carl started to curse a blue streak, and she stopped. "Carl?" She shook off my grasp. "What's wrong?" Then she saw his skinny, naked, white legs—all three of them—and her eyes got huge.

The photographer had started to laugh. And it *was* kind of funny. But when Alice turned back to me, her eyes accusing me not Carl, it wasn't funny at all. Her lips moved, but for a few awful moments no sound came out. Then, "How could you? How could you do this to me? Don't you have enough men?" She started to cry. "Did you have to steal mine?"

CHAPTER 20

From there it only got worse.

While Alice hovered over Carl, who was babbling about Eve and the serpent and my being the daughter of Satan, the photographer couldn't stop laughing—or shooting pictures. Then two men and a woman came charging over from the church office. One of them yelled, "We heard someone screaming and called 9-1-1. Who's hurt?"

9-1-1?

In short order Vivian and two more women huffed up, followed by a police car and a fire truck. By then, of course, the vermin photographer had disappeared into the woods and was probably halfway to the nearest photo lab.

That left me as the only villain on the scene.

"Is this the camera?" the cop asked Carl.

His eyes got big. "No. Not that one. Give it to me."

"Actually, that's mine," I said from my tense perch on Lester's bench. I had developed this perverse attachment to Lester as my only ally here.

"It's mine!" Carl demanded, glaring at me.

That's when I realized that he thought it was full of pictures of me that only *he* could have taken. What had been an asset for him before, had suddenly become a liability. He wanted the camera so he could expose the film and destroy any proof of his greed.

Of course there were no photos, but he didn't know that. No reason not to torture him, though. "That camera is mine," I insisted. "If you look on the bottom you'll see a small rose decal with the initials R.V. written on it."

"R.V.," the cop said. "Aren't you Zoe Vidrine?"

"I see my reputation precedes me. Yes, I'm Zoe. But I also go by Red. Red Vidrine."

He glanced at the bottom, then nodded. "R.V. But I might need this for evidence."

"Evidence for what? Is this a crime scene?"

Alice turned hard eyes on me. "Only if betrayal and hatefulness are crimes."

She despised me, and I guess I deserved it. But I had to defend myself. "Carl's the one who betrayed you, Alice."

Right then Joe showed up. I wanted to disappear into the ground when his eyes—every bit as hard as Alice's—fixed on me. "What's on the film?" he asked.

I was not in the mood for explaining myself, so I said, "How'd you get here so fast?"

"The police dispatchers routinely give me a heads-up when a 9-1-1 call comes in. When I heard it was from the church, I came over. What's going on here, Zoe?"

I glared at him. "Why don't you direct your questions to good old Carl? Why don't you ask him what's going on and why he wants my camera so bad?"

"Don't listen to her!" Carl cried out from the comfort of Alice's embrace. "She's a Jezebel, the daughter of Satan!"

Joe didn't spare him a glance. "This was no accident, you meeting him here. Was it?"

Everyone was listening. Here was my big chance to explain myself, to make them see that my intentions were good: to save Alice from a big mistake.

But my back was up and I was mad. Why should I have to explain myself to them? And why should I try to save Alice when she was so ready to make me the bad guy in this? God-fearing, church-going Carl couldn't possibly be in the wrong. Not in her eyes.

I lifted my chin a notch. "He's absolutely right," I said. "Carl and I arranged to meet here—"

"She lured me!" he cried.

"Right. I lured you here. That's why I told my sister to meet me here, too."

All eyes swung to Alice.

"Is that true?" Joe asked her.

I stood up before she could answer. "As far as I can see, there's been no crime committed here. Am I right?" I asked the bemused cop.

"I don't see one," he admitted. "Unless one of you is pressing charges against the other."

"Good," I said, giving Carl a smug smile. "Then I'll take my camera and go."

"What about that other man with the camera?" Carl protested. "She tricked me to come here, then had him waiting in the woods."

"What man?" Joe asked before the cop could.

"He's a paparazzi jerk who's been hounding me," I said. "Ask Alice. She saw him." I glanced at her, daring her to lie. Then I held my camera toward Carl. "The pictures that guy took are a lot more interesting than these. Aren't they, Carl?"

That shut him up. And it put a question mark on Alice's face. Before she could speak up, however, he put an arm around her, forging them into this united front. "You can't back out on the house sale." He sneered the words at me. "We have a legally binding agreement."

That didn't warrant an answer. Instead I stared at Alice. "You know I was not trying to steal your boyfriend."

She knew. At the same time, though, someone had to be blamed for messing up her neat image of a perfect little family, and I was the best candidate.

"No," she said. "You didn't want him for yourself. You just didn't want me to be happy."

"That's not true!"

"Of course it is! You saw my beautiful house and had to have that. Then you saw me with Carl and had to ruin that. And why? Because you can't make your own relationships work." She shook her head in disgust. "God help that baby of yours."

Maybe everyone gasped when she revealed my close-guarded secret. Maybe they started to whisper and point. I don't know. I was too overwhelmed by a feeling of being naked in front of them all. Especially Joe.

"She's pregnant?" Carl made a tsk-tsking sound that turned me blind with fury. How dare *he* judge *me!*

Then someone put a hand on my arm—Vivian of all people—and I started to breathe again. "I'll take you home," she said.

I shook my head. "That's not necessary."

"I want to."

"No." I pulled away. A part of me was grateful for her quiet support. But I was angry, too. And I didn't need her pity.

"I'll take her," Joe said.

"I'll take myself!" I snapped.

That's when a new commotion started up back at the church. Cars screeching; a phenomenal audio system pulsing out a G. G. Givens song. Until the car door slammed closed.

Crap, crap, crap! I stared at the figures across the field. G.G. was here. Of all times! Now I would have to deal with him like I should have before I left California.

But that didn't mean I had to do it in front of all these people.

I pointed toward the church. "I think you should know that the heavy metal devil is pounding on your front door. Literally."

Every head swiveled that way. The cop even clapped his hand onto the butt of his holstered gun, as if a horned beast was rushing them. I rolled my eyes.

That's when Joe said, "Was this all part of the plan, Zoe? The big PR gimmick? Runaway pregnant bride?"

It's funny how one person's bad opinion of you can so absolutely destroy you. Alice's betrayal was awful enough. Joe's was the final blow. "Go screw yourself," I muttered.

"And then go chase after G.G. I'm sure he'll do any kind of interview you want. And don't worry about checking your facts. If Dan Rather didn't do it, why should you?"

Then I took off, walking as fast as I could, which wasn't fast at all because of my stupid shoes.

My plan had backfired.

Actually, it had worked perfectly, with Mr. Paparazzi being the icing on the cake. Except that Alice had still sided with Carl.

How could she?

Because women are stupid when it comes to men. Especially lonely women who are desperate to belong somewhere with someone. Wasn't I that same stupid woman? Hadn't I contorted myself to fit with whatever man I was with? Hadn't Alice?

I brushed away an unwanted tear before it could fall. The one thing I had to say for Mom. She'd done whatever she wanted to. People had contorted themselves to be with her. That's how Alice and I had learned to do it, from trying so hard and in so many ways to get her attention. And love.

It hadn't worked for us then. It wasn't working any better for us now.

I tripped on an uneven spot and caught myself on a tree, scraping my thumb. It started to bleed, and that's when I started to cry. "Stupid tree!" I tore off my shoes and flung them at its solid trunk. "Stupid shoes!"

"Stupid idiot," I muttered when I started barefoot along the path strewn with prickly cypress needles.

By the time I crossed behind my house where Tripod and Angel lay content on the back porch oblivious to my misery, and crossed onto Harriet's property, I was a blotchy, snotty mess with stupid, bloody thumbprints on my stupid skirt and blouse.

I paused when I spied Harriet sitting on a garden bench in the sunshine with her cat on her lap. It was just like the first time I saw her twenty-five years ago, and again three weeks ago. She looked so calm and serene, so out of place in the insanity of my life. How had I ever thought I could just move in here and share in this peace and serenity?

It was so obvious that sort of contentment wasn't meant for the likes of me. But I wanted it so badly. Not just for me, though God knew I needed it. Mainly I wanted it for Jesse/Jessie.

I stood at the edge of Harriet's garden and watched her reading and gently stroking her old cat.

Please, God. Help me do things right for once in my life.

I guess I've prayed before in one fashion or another. But never have I prayed with such…I don't know exactly what to call it. Sincerity? Desperation?

Humility.

Please, God. Show me what I'm supposed to do for this child of mine. And for me.

I didn't hear any answer, any great pronouncement from above. Not that I expected it to come in that way. But as I wiped my face and tried to pull myself together, Harriet looked up at me and smiled.

I smiled back. But my heart began to beat faster, and the

oddest sensation ran through me. Was Harriet the answer to my prayer? She'd been right in front of my nose, and I already appreciated her. But was there more to it?

Suddenly it all seemed so clear. She'd offered me her unencumbered love all along, but also her simple logic— which I'd fought to ignore. Maybe that was part of the answer I sought. And maybe this town and the people in it were, too. Especially Alice and Daniel.

I started toward Harriet.

"Land sakes," she said when she saw me shoeless and disheveled. "What on earth?"

I sat down at her feet and promptly poured out the whole sordid tale. How I lured Carl to betray his true nature for Alice to see. How Vivian and Joe and the police and then G.G. all showed up. "When I left everyone was rushing to defend their church from G.G. Even Joe. It was hilarious, actually. Like G.G. gives a flip about them or their church."

I stared down at a ladybug crawling along the hem of my skirt. "I guess I'd better call him."

"Joe?" Harriet asked.

"No." I looked up at her. "G.G. I have to call him and tell everything and try to figure out some way to let him see his child but not ruin her life."

"I'm here to help," she said.

"I know," I whispered as new tears welled in my eyes. Tears of gratitude this time. "That's what's so amazing about you."

"Oh, pish," she said, patting my hand. "You help me, I help you. That's what family does," she added with this beautiful motherly glow in her soft, blue eyes. A grandmotherly glow.

I wiped my eyes and laughed.

"That's better," she said. "Now go wash your face and we'll call G.G."

In the bathroom, however, I decided to call Joe first. "This is a test," I said when he answered.

"A test?"

"Yes. To see what kind of journalist you really are. I'm offering you first chance at an interview that includes me and G.G."

I heard this long silence, then, "So this *was* a PR gimmick."

The disappointment in his voice was restrained, but it was still there, and it pierced my heart like a vicious barb. "I can't speak for G.G. But as for me, none of it was ever about PR. I left him because I knew his lifestyle was too toxic for a child to grow up in." When he didn't respond, I went on. "Anyway, do you want the gig or not?"

"Sure. Why not? But you ought to know that there are some interesting developments going on over here."

"Over here? Where? Are you still at the church?"

"Yep."

"Did they hurt G.G.?" I pictured farmers with pitchforks killing the devil at the church steps.

He chuckled. "Officer Landry looked ready to arrest him, until I reminded him that G.G. hadn't broken any laws. Not even trespassing laws."

"Give him time. So, where is he now?"

"Closeted in the Sunday school classroom with Alice and Vivian."

"What?"

"You shouldn't have run off so fast, Zoe. You missed all the fireworks."

The fireworks? "That's what I do," I muttered. "I cut and run. But not anymore."

"No?"

All of a sudden the conversation seemed much more personal, like we weren't talking about G.G. and me, but instead, Joe and me. It made me nervous. "Just as you guessed, I am pregnant. G.G.'s baby," I added, because he *was* a newsman and he would have to ask. Only I didn't want him to ask me that question because I didn't want him to think that I was the type to spread it around. "That's why I left him," I went on. "To make a quiet, good home for my child."

"I can understand that."

I hoped so. "So, as soon as I reach G.G. and set a date and time for the interview, I'll call you."

"Why don't you just come to the church right now? Everybody else is here."

Oh boy, did I *not* want to do that. But I knew I should. So I got up, put on some lipstick and a clean outfit. Then I got in Jenny Jeep and drove to the church.

When I saw how many cars were in the parking lot, I nearly drove on by. Had everyone with a cell phone called everyone they knew? Even as I hesitated on the highway with the blinker on, a blue Chevy Astro van full of teenagers turned into the lot.

Good grief!

Gritting my teeth, I turned in, too. Mr. White-Van-

Paparazzi had returned, probably trailing G.G. When he saw me he grinned smugly, lifted his camera, and started snapping. I wanted to flip him off, but I didn't. First of all, he would love a picture of that. Second, I needed to be the bigger person. I had to start setting a good example for the sake of Jesse/Jessie. So I just stood tall and walked confidently to the church annex. I ignored Carl, who slammed out of the building. One of Alice's Church Ladies called out to him, but he ignored her as he hurried away. I lifted my chin just a little higher as I strode past Beth Ann and tried hard not to hiss.

I was here to finish this mess with G.G. If these people wanted to live vicariously through our semicelebrity brouhaha, I ought to feel sorry for them. How boring must their lives be?

Joe opened the annex door for me, and I tensed at the sight of him. He didn't look angry, but was that good or bad? If it was professional detachment, then that connection between us that I'd imagined while we were on the phone was just that: my imagination.

"They're in here," he said, heading toward a door decorated with children's little multicolored handprints. "Don't look so grim," he added. "Nothing's ever as bad as it seems."

I hesitated at the door and looked directly at him. "Do you really believe that?"

Slowly he nodded. "Yeah, Zoe. I do. Life has a way of working itself out, just not necessarily like we expect."

"Tell that to Carl. He sure didn't look too happy."

He only gestured with his head. "Go on in."

I tried to read his eyes. Was this going to be good or bad? But he wasn't revealing anything. That's when I realized that I was approaching this all wrong. As usual. I was basing my reaction to what might be happening on how others felt about it. I'd always thought I was so tough because I could deal with anything life threw at me. But that was only being reactionary. Somebody threw a curveball at me; I ducked. That was my own hard-shell version of exactly what I accused Alice of. I reacted and ducked; she went with the flow. The fact remained that we both drifted according to the stream we were in.

Bailing out of my old lifestyle could be seen as running away, just like when I left home at seventeen. But this time, for the first time in my life I'd been running toward something. Granted, it was a nebulous something: a better life for my child and me. But I didn't need to feel guilty about that. I wouldn't.

So I marched into the Sunday school room with my head high and my determination in place. They wouldn't bulldoze me or beat me down no matter what went down.

But inside the room my confidence wavered. I should have laughed, because everyone was sitting in little kid chairs, with their knees higher than their behinds. They looked like a group of chastised children. But all I could see was Alice, my sister whose love I desperately wanted to deserve. She looked at me with eyes puffy from crying. I'd done that to her.

Vivian was the only one standing, and she promptly told me to, "Sit down, please."

I did, at Alice's table, not G.G.'s and Coco's.

"Red," G.G. said when he realized this short-haired brunette was me.

"Shush," Vivian ordered in this take-no-prisoners, Sunday school teacher's voice.

"Now," she began, standing before us with her hands clasped loosely at her waist. "It's long past time we settle this matter. You're late, Zoe. And Carl refuses to participate. But I don't really think we need him here, do we?"

Alice shook her head.

Heartened, I turned to my sister. "Listen, Alice."

"You'll have your chance to speak," Vivian interrupted me. "For now, could you please just listen?"

I was desperate to straighten things out with Alice. But somehow I trusted Vivian to run this show.

"All right then," she said. "I believe it might be best if we follow some sort of chronological order here. Zoe, why don't you begin by explaining to Mr. Givens why you left him."

"Yeah," Coco said. "Why'd you run off and screw everything up?"

"Mr. Coco," Vivian said with raised eyebrows. "One more word and you'll be asked to leave. I've only allowed you to stay because Mr. Givens requested it."

Naturally. "You know what?" I said. "G.G. may want him here, but I don't. This is between you and me, G.G."

"What about *her?*" Coco pointed at Alice.

"She's family. And *she's* the mediator," I added before he could object to Vivian's presence, too.

Coco glared at me. "I go where G.G. goes. We're a team, right?" He looked at G.G. for confirmation.

G.G. shook his head and gave a great, put-upon sigh. "Dude, if it will get this over with faster, just go."

I'd like to have thought that G.G. was being a grown-up for once. But he had this sulky, I-don't-want-to-be-here expression on his lined face. Obviously this public relations, wild-goose chase Coco had orchestrated was wearing on G.G.'s nerves. I noticed also that he didn't look in the least like a man dying for love over his runaway girlfriend.

"Okay," I said once Coco stormed out of the room. "Here goes." I leaned forward. "Last month I discovered that I was pregnant."

That got G.G.'s attention. "You're pregnant? Like, you mean, you're gonna have a baby?"

"That's right. You are going to be a daddy."

"But…" His eyebrows pulled together in a frown. "I don't get it. Why'd you leave?"

"Why? Because I don't want my baby raised around all the drugs and alcohol and partying and craziness in your life. Children need calm and security and consistency."

"A baby," G.G. said. I watched as his shock gave way to delight. "Hey. I can get him a little kid-sized guitar."

"Why?" I asked, trying hard not to get mad. "Why would you do that?"

"Why? Because he's G. G. Givens's kid, and that's what I do. Play guitar better than anybody else."

When I waited, he went on. "Don't you see how cool it would be? G.G. and G.G., Jr., together on tour."

I shook my head. "No, that would not be cool. By the time this baby is old enough to go on tour, you'll be sixty-six."

He drew back in horror. "No way!"

"Yes, G.G. This kid is having a normal childhood if it kills me. No touring until he's eighteen and decides on his own that he wants to tour with you. By then you'll be sixty-six. Or dead if you don't change your ways. Here's the thing," I went on. "This child is going to live in a normal household in a normal town, and go to school with normal, everyday kids. No celebrity parents. No limos picking her up and dropping her off."

"Her? It's a girl?"

In exasperation I sat back in my little chair. He wasn't really listening to me. But then, what did I expect?

That's when Vivian broke in. "Zoe is moving here, Mr. Givens, and she's raising her baby in Oracle. Am I right, Zoe?"

She smiled so warmly at me that I had to smile right back. "Yes. You're absolutely right."

She turned that smile of hers on G.G. "That means the two of you will have to come to some sort of agreement on support and visitation. Things like that."

"I don't need his money," I said. "Or want it."

"That's all fine and good," she said. "You don't have to take it. In that case he can put it aside in a trust fund for when your child is ready to go to college or something like that."

"But he can't go on tour with me?" G.G. asked. He was

having a hard time with that concept. Probably because of all his fried brain cells.

I stared straight at him. "I don't want your money, G.G. And furthermore, you're not getting visitation rights until you've been sober at least a year."

Vivian held up her hands. "You two can work out those details later. It's enough that we've established why Zoe came here. The next question is for you, Mr. Givens. Why did you take out that advertisement in *People* magazine?"

He looked at her as if she was stupid. "To find her, of course."

"Yes. But why?"

"Because…because Coco said we needed her."

"For that television show?" I asked, trying to squelch my sarcasm.

"Well, yeah. I mean… Yeah."

"Did Zoe know about the ad in *People* before she left?" Vivian asked. I held my breath. G.G. had never been a liar. That's why he needed Coco around. I prayed that he would stick to his m.o. because, even though Joe wasn't here, I wanted the truth to get back to him. I wanted him to know that I was never a part of their scheme.

"No," G.G. said. "Coco figured that out after she left." He grinned at me. "You gotta admit, Babe, it was a good idea. I'm gonna be on Letterman next week."

"That's good, G.G. I'm happy for you." And I was. His career and his fans were more important to him than anything else. At least now that was on the upswing.

"Okay," Vivian said. "Now for you, Alice."

We all turned to face my sister, who sat hunched over in her pint-sized chair.

"Your life has been turned upside down lately," Vivian began in this kind, nurturing tone. "But that's not entirely Zoe's fault, is it?"

Alice hesitated, and her eyes cut to me and held. "No. Not entirely."

We all waited for her to continue. Even G.G. "I love my house," she finally said. "It means the world to me. I redid everything—everything—myself. I turned it from a...a hellhole, into the perfect place for a minister's family to live. After Lester died—" She broke off and took a shaky breath. "After that the house became even more important to me. I guess I didn't want things to change."

She lowered her face into her hands and began to cry. G.G. looked upset, like he wanted to comfort her. But with a shake of her head, Vivian stopped him.

When Alice finally looked up, she seemed more composed. "It's been awful since Lester died," she went on. "I've been so lonely. And Carl... Well, he seemed like the next best thing. I knew I didn't love him like I should." She looked over at me. "You're right that I shouldn't marry a man I don't love."

I grabbed her hand. "Someone will come along who you can love. Someday he will."

She nodded. "I hope so." She paused then said, "I know why you told me to meet you in the woods behind the church. Not to steal Carl from me, like I said. You wanted me to see what he was really like, didn't you? And I guess I'm glad you did. But why did you have to choose that place? I loved the cypress cathedral. It was Lester's special spot. Only now you've ruined it for me."

I felt horrible. Why *had* I done that? Then I remembered sitting on Lester's bench, asking the spirit of a man I'd never met to help me.

Could he have led me there?

I shook my head in amazement. "You might not believe this, Alice. I hardly believe it myself. But I think Lester guided me there."

"What?" Her eyes got huge. "My Lester?"

I nodded. "I felt his presence so strongly. It was weird. I don't know. Maybe he was trying to protect you from a bad marriage, and I was the only way he could do it."

That started her crying again, only this time it was good crying. She reached out for me and we hugged and I started to cry, too. This was my sister, my *only* sister, and I loved her more than I ever could have guessed.

"Who's Lester?" I heard G.G. ask.

"Alice's deceased husband," Vivian answered.

"Well, damn," G.G. exclaimed. "This is pretty cool. Kinda like that TV show about that chick who talks to ghosts. I really like that show." His brow creased as he studied me with new intensity. "So, are you like that, Red? A ghost whisperer?"

It was such a ridiculous question I started to laugh. And once I started, I couldn't stop. Alice started to laugh, too, and then Vivian and G.G. That's when the door opened and Joe stuck his head inside. "I take it everything is going to be fine?"

His eyes locked with mine, and that's when I knew for sure. "Yes. Things are going to be fine."

I smiled at him, putting everything I had into it. *Things are going to be better than fine.*

And his answering smile echoed back. *Better than fine.*

EPILOGUE

Just to satisfy the curious, Jesse/Jessie showed up on October second and officially became Jessica Leslie Vidrine. Leslie in honor of Lester, whom I've become very attached to.

Alice coached me through my eight-hour labor, and the next day Joe drove us home to Harriet's house and the beautiful little nursery Daniel and Pete had painted in shades of green and yellow.

G.G. was on tour at the time in Europe—a very successful tour, as it happily turned out. But he sent a monstrous arrangement of purple irises, white calla lilies and green wood fern to me and baby Jessie that lasted for almost ten days. By then I was settled into my role of sleep-deprived nursing mother. But I wouldn't have had it any other way.

"Gumbo's almost ready," Harriet said the day after Halloween. It was All Saint's Day, which I remembered from my childhood. Many things from my childhood were starting to take on new meaning. Happy, positive meanings.

And speaking of positive, want to hear what happened to Carl? Carl left the Simmons Creek Victory Church in disgrace over the pants-off incident. A very nice fellow from Pearl River became the new pastor, and even Beth

Ann improved her attitude under his guidance. It didn't hurt that her influence over her Church Ladies group waned significantly with Alice and Vivian's defection.

Alice loved her new job—and her new hairdo and her new niece. She and I had worked out a very lenient purchase plan for the house, and though she had to pinch pennies she wouldn't have to much longer. One of the Christian publishing houses had bought her book. It would be out right before Easter. Added to that, she'd agreed to let Daniel finish his last two years at Covington High, where Pete went.

As for Joe…

First he became my boss, paying me for one feature article a month that explored some overlooked aspect of life on the fast-growing north shore. Racism among the upwardly mobile; the suburban drug culture; the nature of bullies, which had humiliated one Mel Toups.

Of course the first article was about Hippie Heaven and the woman who'd been at its center.

I can't say I'll ever get over the chaotic childhood our mother forced on us. But writing it all down helped me to understand it a little better and also to understand that it was up to me to make peace with my past. It's the only way to build a truly peaceful future.

Which brings me to the present, to my beautiful redheaded baby girl and the man who wants to be her father. Joe and I finally managed a good first date—and many more, I'm happy to report. But more important than the dates was that he was always around, being a good friend to me with no demands.

Then a week after Jessie was born, he proposed to me, diamond ring and all. And we hadn't even slept together!

I, of course, started crying and said yes. I've got two more weeks to go before I'm officially cleared by my doctor to have sex. But I'm thinking of making Joe wait a couple more weeks until the wedding night. We're getting married on Thanksgiving Day. Appropriate, I think. And we're holding the ceremony in Lester's cypress cathedral.

I love that place. Alice and I often go there together. And Joe and I go there all the time with Jessie.

"Gumbo sounds great," I belatedly replied to Harriet. "When is Joe arriving?"

"I'm here," he said, coming in the front door, all six feet hunka hunka of him. "Hey, gorgeous." He bent over to kiss me—or so I thought until he planted one on Jessie's fuzzy head.

She wriggled and cooed. I felt like doing the same whenever he was around.

"Hey," he said. "She smiled at me."

"She's only four weeks old," I said. "One of my books says they don't smile until six weeks."

"That's a smile," Joe swore. "Look." He tickled her tummy, and sure enough Jessie's eyes opened wider and she showed her little pink gums in a toothless smile.

"I love you," I said, and it came out as natural as a breath.

Joe looked up at me, our faces only inches apart. "You talking to me?"

I had to compress my lips together to stop from crying.

Gosh, I'd become such a sentimental weepy sort! "Yes," I whispered. "I love you and her and…everything."

"Me, too," he said and bent closer to give me the kiss I wanted.

"Okay. Enough of that," Harriet said. "Call the boys, will you, Joe?"

As we sat down to a dinner of gumbo, cornbread and pecan pie—Harriet, Joe, Pete, Daniel and me with Jessie on my lap—I could not have been happier. It only made it better that Alice wasn't here because she was out on a date with her boss's younger brother, a man Daniel actually liked.

Beneath the table, Joe caught my hand in his and winked at me. That's when I knew I couldn't wait for our wedding night.

As if reading my mind, he silently mouthed, "Two weeks."

I felt a blush coming on and ducked my head. Then I glanced sidelong at him. "Two weeks," I mouthed back.

And after that, a lifetime.

True Confessions
of the
Stratford Park PTA

by Nancy Robards Thompson

The journey of four women through midlife;
man trouble; and their children's middle
school hormones—as they find their place
in this world...

HARLEQUIN®
Next™

Available October 2006
TheNextNovel.com

HN62

There's a first time for everything...

Aging rock-and-roller Zoe learned this
the hard way...at thirty-nine, she was pregnant!

Leaving behind the temptations of L.A.,
she returns home to Louisiana to live with
her sister. Despite their differences, they come
to terms with their shared past and find that
when the chips are down there is no better
person to lean on than your sister.

Leaving L.A.

by

Rexanne Becnel

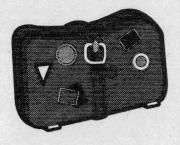

HN57

Available September 2006
TheNextNovel.com

A stunning novel of love and renewal…

Everyone knows sisters like the Sams girls—three women trying their best to be good daughters, mothers and wives. Then in one cataclysmic moment everything changes… and the sisters have to uncover every shrouded secret and risk lifetime bonds to ensure the survival of all they love.

Graceland

by Lynne Hugo

Available October 2006
TheNextNovel.com

HN63

HARLEQUIN®
Next™

REQUEST YOUR FREE BOOKS!

2 FREE NOVELS TO INTRODUCE YOU TO OUR BRAND-NEW LINE!

There's the life you planned. And there's what comes next.

Just like a blue moon, friendship is a beautiful thing

Hoping to rekindle a sense of purpose, Lola resurrects a childhood dream and buys a blue beach house. When she drags three of her fun-loving, margarita-sipping friends out for some gossip and good times, they discover the missing spark in their relationships.

Once in a Blue Moon

by Lenora Worth

Available October 2006
TheNextNovel.com

HN64